Read it to Belker

"I'LL FIX UP OUR BEDROLLS," SAID LONGARM . . .

Rebecca said in a small, uncertain voice, "Marshal Long? If I ask a favor of you, would you do something for me?"

"Why, sure. Anything I can."

"Maybe this is your whiskey talking, but I don't think I could sleep, if I tried to sleep alone tonight. Would you mind very much if I shared your bed with you?"

Longarm stared speechless. Then he spoke. "My bedroll's ready whenever you are . . ."

TABOR EVANS

LONGARM

AT
ROBBER'S ROOST

A JOVE BOOK

Jove books are published by Jove Publications, Inc.,
200 Madison Avenue, New York, NY 10016

Chapter 1

Even though Longarm had seen no signs of it through the morning, he'd ridden through the day's dangerous dawning hours with his senses tuned to the possibility of trouble. When he'd arrived at the Denver & Rio Grande depot in Montrose, he had been met by a red-faced lance corporal who had delivered to him the cavalry remount horse and pack mule requested by Marshal Vail through army channels. The corporal had alerted Longarm by mentioning that there were still a number of Ute war parties ranging the area.

"We got a bunch of 'em corralled in a pen inside the stockade," he'd said, "but there's a lot more still roaming around looking for trouble to get into."

"Any big parties loose that you know of?" Longarm had asked as he pulled his saddle cinch tight under the belly of the rawboned roan the man had brought up from the Cantonment on the Uncompahgre, a dozen miles to the south.

"None as I know about." The cavalryman had surveyed Longarm's tall, broad frame, and looked at the well-cared-for Winchester that leaned against the bed-roll waiting to be put on the horse. "But you look like you ought to be able to handle the bunches we've run into. Five or six is a big one. Mostly there's not more'n three or four."

Longarm had nodded. "I'll keep an eye out."

There had been no sign of movement anywhere he'd looked, and as the sun climbed higher and the tall pines and thick juniper brush of the Rocky Mountains' western foothills gave way to sparse blue sage, grass, and stunted piñon, he'd begun to relax. The vegetation

5

grew thinner as the land dipped into the wide valley of the Dolores River, and he'd thought there wasn't enough cover to hide a bunch of Utes sizable enough to be dangerous.

His first warning was the thud of a throwing-club hitting the ground between the hind feet of the horse and the forefeet of the plodding mule. The cavalry-trained roan didn't react to the noise, but the whizzing of the short club past the mule's nose spooked the pack animal. The mule snorted and jerked its head. Longarm kneed the roan into a turn, dragging the mule with it. As his horse wheeled, he drew his Winchester from its saddle scabbard.

A meager stand of piñon, which had been completely motionless when he'd ridden past it a few moments earlier, was shaking now. Longarm's eyes searched the gnarled, twisted trunks of the low-standing trees, trying to determine whether there were legs mixed with the slender trunks of the piñons. One of the brown trunks moved in a manner no tree trunk could. Longarm snapshotted above it. His slug cut through the branches, but he'd sighted on the wrong side. A bronzed body dashed out of the covering tangle. Keeping the clump of trees between himself and Longarm, the Indian zigzagged toward the next piñon stand. Longarm's rifle muzzle followed the Ute's course long enough for him to be certain of his sighting, then the gun spoke and the Indian dropped.

An arrow sailed out of the trees beyond the fallen Ute, but dropped short. Longarm sighted by instinct into the trees, his target the spot where the arrow had started its flight. The Winchester's sharp crack was followed by a thrashing in the tangle of low branches. Longarm could not tell how accurate his aim had been. He toed the roan ahead, but the pack mule slowed his progress. There were no more arrows, and the ground-hugging branches that drooped from the low trees did not move.

Longarm slid his rifle back into its boot, and drew his Colt as he reined in and swung out of the saddle. He could see nothing in the tangled deadfall that lay

6

matted around the trees' roots, hiding the ground. He picked his way into the copse, the dry limbs cracking under the soles of his stovepipe cavalry boots. A few steps took him to the center of the stand of trees, and revealed the sprawled body of a second Indian, his bow still clutched in one hand. Longarm saw that the slug from the rifle had torn out the man's throat. He grunted and was about to turn away when the deadfall beyond the Indian's corpse began to shake and crackle.

Longarm stopped in his tracks, his Colt poised. He never had cared much for blind shooting, and he didn't intend now to fire at a target he hadn't yet identified as unfriendly or dangerous. He stepped to one side of the line on which he'd been advancing. A glint of golden hair caught his eyes through a small gap in the tree limbs. He moved still farther to one side, and now he could see the white forehead and wide, appealing blue eyes of the woman who lay bound and gagged in the copse beyond the body of the dead Ute.

Holstering his Colt, Longarm took out his jackknife and cut away the leather strap that gagged her and the thongs that held her hands and feet immobilized.

"You all right, ma'am?" he asked.

"Yes. At least I think so." She looked at him, fear still distorting her face. "I don't know who you are, but you certainly can't be any worse than those Indians." Her voice rasped out of her dry throat.

"You don't have anything to worry about," he assured her. "My name's Long, and I'm a deputy United States marshal out of Denver." He took out his wallet and unfolded it to show his badge.

"Oh, thank God!" she breathed. "There's so much deviltry—" She glanced at the body of the dead Ute, and another tremor shook her. Then the tight rein she'd been holding on her emotions gave way, and she began sobbing.

Longarm let the girl cry until the deeps sobs no longer shook her body. Then he suggested, "Maybe you better tell me what-all happened. It won't be any easier if you try to put it off."

"I suppose." The girl took a deep breath. She raised

7

her head, and the first thing that caught her eye was the contorted body of the dead Ute, with the blood congealing black on his bullet-torn throat. She shuddered and said, "Can't we get away from—" She indicated the corpse.

"Sure we can." Longarm took her arm and led her to where the horse and pack mule stood waiting. "Maybe you'll feel better if you take a drink of water." He took the canteen from the pommel of his saddle and held it while she drank. Then, when she'd managed to swallow a few sips, he moistened a corner of his bandanna and wiped her dirt-streaked face. "You feel like telling me who you are and where you're from?"

"My name's Rebecca Forest. And I've been living in Nucia, teaching school."

"Nucia," Longarm frowned. "Can't say I recall anyplace by that name, here on the western slope."

"I don't wonder." Rebecca's speech was still halting, her throat still dry and rasping. "It's a new town, just getting built up."

Longarm interrupted her. "You need something more than water to get you settled down." He took out the nearly full bottle of Maryland rye that he'd wrapped in his extra pair of socks before putting into the saddlebag, pulled the cork, and offered it to Rebecca. "Here. You take a little swallow of this. It'll ease your throat and make you feel better."

She swallowed a mouthful of the whiskey, gulped and gasped, and her eyes began watering. Through an occasional cough, she said, "I'm not used to drinking anything this strong. It—it burns my mouth."

"Here, have another swallow of water."

During the few moments needed for the water to overcome the bite of the whiskey, Longarm studied Rebecca Forest's face. He judged her to be in her late twenties, perhaps even a year or so into the thirties. She didn't have the indrawn lips and harsh frown lines on her brow that he'd seen other schoolmarms acquire early in life, though. Her lips were full, under a slightly uptilted nose. Her face was round, giving her a girlish

8

appearance at first glance, though a second look showed the beginning wrinkles at the corners of her eyes. She wore a long traveling cloak that fell straight from her shoulders, giving him no hint as to whether she was slim or plump. Her eyes were blue, watering now, but the moisture was beginning to clear away, and they were fixed on him questioningly.

Longarm said, "Don't try to hurry. When you feel like telling me about things, I'm ready to listen."

"You were right a minute ago," she said with a nod. "It won't be any easier if I wait. The Utes jumped the wagon yesterday morning just after we'd left Nucia."

"Now, just a minute," he broke in. "First off, who's *we*?"

"Oh. There was Mr. Kelleher and his wife and me. Mr. Kelleher is—was—the head of the school committee. They were taking me to Grand Junction, to catch my train."

"You were getting ready to leave?"

"Yes. I'd stayed on until the new teacher got there, to go over things about the school and the students with her."

"You better tell me where this Nucia place is."

"It's a new town, as I said. It's northeast of the Dolores River. The nearest old town to it is Nuravan, if you know where that is."

Longarm nodded. "I've seen the name on a map, is about all." He delved into his memory for details of the army ordnance map he'd studied before leaving Denver. The map, he knew, was already out of date. Since the Denver & Rio Grande had begun pushing its rails to the west three years ago, cutting through the notch between the Sawatch and Sangre de Cristo Mountains, to loop along beside the Gunnison River, a whole new area of potentially rich farmland had been opened in Colorado. Settlers had been pouring into the Gunnison valley, and on the western slope of the Rockies there were more new towns than a man could count on the fingers of both hands.

He said—a question rather than a statement— "It'd be about thirty miles from here, the way I reckon."

9

"I'm not very good at distances," Rebecca replied. "Not in this mountain country. But I think that's about right."

Longarm guided her back to the subject she was so obviously finding difficult to discuss. "Now, then. You and those other folks, the Kellehers, you were heading from Nucia towards Grand Junction when that party of Utes set on you?"

She nodded reluctantly and went on, "There were five of them. Mr. Kelleher only had time to fire one shot before he was killed. Then Mrs. Kelleher picked up his rifle, but they shot her too. Three of the Utes had guns, you see."

"How'd you happen to be left alive?"

"I did what Mr. Kelleher told me, got down in the wagon bed." Another shudder shook her. "I imagine I'd be dead too, if I hadn't."

Longarm frowned. "What about those other three Utes? The ones that had rifles? You think they're close around here yet?"

Rebecca shook her head. "I don't think so. They went off late in the afternoon yesterday, headed back west. The ones who had me came on this way, eastward."

"And I guess you wouldn't know if the other three figured to come back and join up with the two that had you?"

"No. My goodness, Marshal Long, they talked in their own language. I didn't understand anything they said."

"They hurt you at all?"

Rebecca looked at him searchingly. "You're asking if they—if they raped me, or anything?" She shook her head. "No. They weren't very gentle when they tied me up, but they didn't harm me. They grabbed me and sort of dragged me when they saw you coming, after they left their horses in a little draw, over there." She pointed.

"You got off light," Longarm told her. He looked at the sun. "I guess if we set off right now, I can get you back to Nucia a little bit after sunset."

10

Indians' trail pouches. Except for one item, they were remarkably alike in contents. There were parched corn and venison jerky in both, a few spare steel arrowheads, and some coins that might have totaled a dollar, if all had been counted.

There were tightly wrapped deerskin packets, wound around with hard, dry sinew, in each pouch; Longarm recognized these as the Indians' individual medicine bags. The only article not duplicated in both pouches was the scalp he found in one of them. Longarm fingered it carefully as he inspected it. The scalp was fresh, though it had started to dry and curl around the edges. It had obviously come from a child. The skin was soft and white, the hair fine-textured and reddish gold. He shook his head, his jaw tensing grimly, before returning the grisly trophy to the pouch. Then he started for the place pointed out by Rebecca as the spot where the Utes had hid their horses.

He found them in a narrow draw cut by erosion or some long-dry creek. They were mustangs, wiry and still half wild. Longarm approached them cautiously. The Utes weren't as skilled with horses as the Comanches, and he knew that half-broken Indian mustangs had unpredictable tempers. He took his time in walking slowly up to the animals, speaking in soft tones, making no sudden moves. The horses bridled and reared when they heard the strange voice and caught his unfamiliar scent. It took him a good halfhour to gentle them down to the point where he felt safe in untying the braided leather tethers that had held them in place.

When the mustangs finally decided to follow him, Longarm led them to the bodies. Neither pony had a saddle, just a doubled leather pad bound by a braided horsehair surcingle above a small, coarsely woven blanket. There were braided-leather lariats on both animals, though. Longarm lifted the bodies one at a time, and draped one corpse over the back of each mustang. He used the lariats to secure them. It was obvious that Rebecca wouldn't be able to manage either of the half-broken animals. He left the laden ponies tethered to one of the pinyon trees, and went back to where she sat waiting.

"I guess you know how to ride a horse?" he asked. "At least a little bit?"

"Very little, I'm afraid, Marshal. I'm not really a good rider."

"How'd the Utes carry you when they took you away?"

"One of them tied me to himself, and I rode on the horse's rump." Rebecca managed a pale smile. "If I hadn't been tied on, I know there were times when I'd have fallen off."

"If that's the way of it, I won't even try to get you on one of those half-broken Indian mustangs," Longarm told her. "I'll give you a choice. You ride in the saddle in front of me, which might turn out to be a little bit crowded, or I'll fix up some kind of pad for you to ride the mule."

"But the mule's loaded," she pointed out.

"I can shift that packsaddle to one of the Ute ponies and put both bodies on the other one."

"If you don't object, Marshal Long, I'd feel a lot safer riding in front of you on your horse. He looks like he's gentle enough."

"Maybe not gentle, the way you mean, but he's a cavalry-trained animal. Got a good steady gait. All right, then, come along." As they started toward the pinyons, Longarm added as an afterthought, "I guess I better tell you to keep hold of your stomach, at least until you get used to seeing those two bodies dangling over their nags' backs."

Rebecca said nothing in reply to this, but he could almost see the effort she was making to steel herself as she walked beside him around the piñon trees to the spot where the Indian ponies waited, tossing their heads against the restraint of their tethers. She kept her eyes elsewhere as much as possible while Longarm hitched the mustangs together and then tied them to a lead-rope behind the mule. He swung into the saddle and extended his hand to Rebecca. She had a bit of difficulty getting settled, until Longarm's patient directions got her right foot securely fixed between his booted leg and the stirrup-leathers. Once she was firmly in place, it was fairly easy for him to show her how to swing her left calf over the roan's withers and hook her knee around the saddle horn, as though she were riding sidesaddle.

"We'll travel slow," he told her as they started, to make her feel more secure. "It ain't all that bad a grade up over the pass, and once we're past that, it's easy going to Grand Junction. Mostly level, even if we will be riding across slanted ground a lot of the time. We'll get there all right, if we just mosey along and take our time."

"I'm sure I'll be all right," she responded, "just as soon as I get used to this strange position. But—just for a little way, while we're starting out—would you mind putting your arm around me and holding me on?"

"If you'd like for me to."

Longarm embraced Rebecca's waist with one arm, holding her to him. Using his free arm and hand with the reins, he started the little procession on its way. After a backward glance to make sure the Ute mustangs were going to let themselves be led without fussing or balking, Longarm reached automatically for a cheroot. He had the cigar in his hand when he realized that there was no way for him to smoke it, with the girl's face so close. Resigning himself to a smokeless ride, he tucked the thin cigar back into his vest pocket.

Rebecca held her body stiffly at first, but, bit by bit, he felt her tension ebbing away as the horse kept to a smooth, even gait up the dim, zigzagging trail that led to Columbine Pass. The muscles of her stomach and sides, which had been so taut under his forearm, began to relax. Soon she settled her weight fully back against Longarm's hips, instead of trying to lean forward each time the roan pulled itself forward over a hump in the uneven ground. Once she'd begun to feel secure, both of them found the going easier. Rebecca soon learned to shift her torso to follow Longarm's movements in the saddle, as he leaned to compensate for the slants in the terrain.

15

Steadily they climbed, and more and more of the cone of Spruce Mountain became visible. At the top of the pass, the tip of the mountain's peak was only slightly above the level of their eyes, and beyond the mountain they could see the shifting colors of a countless number of buttes and thin, rocky pinnacles as they changed in the ebbing sunlight. By the time the sun had entered the last hour of its evening plunge, a strange sort of intimacy had woven itself around the pair, though they'd done very little talking. Rebecca seemed to be thinking of something she found troublesome. From time to time she would shake her head; and on her face, which Longarm could see in half-profile, a small frown would form.

As the shadows lengthened, he began looking for a sheltered spot with water near at hand, where they could camp for the night. Not until the ragged edge of the western horizon had begun to bite into the rim of the reddening sun did he see anything suitable. Then he spotted the glint of running water a quarter-mile ahead, a small creek dancing downslope to add its waters to the green flow of the Gunnison. Near the creek, pines clustered beyond a rock outcrop. Around the stream itself, a wide belt of lush green promised ample forage for the animals.

Longarm pointed to the trees. "We'll go over there and set up camp while there's still enough light to see by."

"Good," she said. "I was wondering when we'd stop. I think I'm beginning to get very tired."

Longarm was a veteran of too many overnight camps to waste any time setting up this one. He hobbled the mule and the roan, tethered the mustangs, and within ten minutes after they'd halted, he had the packsaddle lashings off and the tarpaulin pulled aside.

"If you'd like to do something," he told Rebecca, "you can get out a skillet and find the bacon and spuds while I get a fire going."

He walked into the cluster of pines and dragged out dry branches to the spot where a tongue of rock crept out into the grass that covered the ground on the

16

stream bank. He broke twigs with his fingers, limbs with his bootheel, and kindled the fire with the same match he used to light the first cheroot he'd been able to enjoy since the beginning of their ride.

Rebecca came up. In one hand she carried the skillet, filled with raw potatoes, and in the other a slab of bacon. "I'd peel the potatoes, but I don't have a knife. And I can't slice the bacon, either."

"Don't need to peel the spuds," Longarm said. "Just rub 'em good in this wet grass, or dip 'em in the creek, if you'd rather. I'll slice up the bacon while you're doing that."

He cut thick slices of bacon, and when Rebecca came back from the creek with the dripping potatoes, he sliced them, peel and all. As soon as the bacon started to sizzle, he laid the potato slices in the bubbling fat. Rebecca watched Longarm's matter-of-fact camp cooking with a question in her eyes, but when they folded their legs under them and sat beside the fire to eat, she found the potatoes' skin crisp and slightly salty, an added fillip to the blandness of the potatoes. Longarm turned the skillet bottom-up on the rock beside the fire when they'd finished.

"I didn't say anything about coffee," he told her. "We'll have some in the morning. Right now, I think the best way to top off supper's with another drink."

He stood up and went to his saddlebags, which he'd hung on a low limb jutting from the nearest pine tree when he'd unsaddled the roan. He drew out the bottle of Maryland rye and unwrapped it.

"That drink you had back where I found you was medicine," he told Rebecca as he brought the bottle to the fire and offered it to her. "This one's to enjoy and to loosen up your nerves so you'll drop off to sleep easy."

She hesitated. "I'm not sure . . ." she began. Then, with a smile, she took the bottle. "I guess you know what's best."

"I ain't forcing it on you," Longarm said.

"I know that, Marshal. But I don't think I'll need any lullabyes to get me to sleep tognight."

17

"While you're sipping, I'll fix up our bedrolls," Longarm told her. He unrolled his blankets from the slicker that had been wrapped around them, spread the slicker for a groundcloth, and folded one of the blankets lengthwise on top of it. Then he moved a short distance away and started to spread the second blanket.

Rebecca said in a small, uncertain voice, "Marshal Long? If I ask a favor of you, would you do something for me?"

"Why, sure. Anything I can."

"Maybe this is your whiskey talking, but I don't think I could sleep for being afraid, if I tried to sleep alone tonight. Would you mind very much if I shared your bed with you?"

Chapter 2

Rebecca's request left Longarm speechless for a moment. It was the last thing he'd expected to hear from her, and he wasn't quite sure he understood what she expected.

She saw his hesitation and said quickly, "I don't expect to do anything but sleep, if that's what's bothering you, Marshal. I just—well, I guess I'm just afraid, that's all. Even knowing you'd be right close by wouldn't set my mind at ease enough for me to sleep." She was still holding the bottle of whiskey. She took a second fast swallow, gulping as the rye trickled down her throat.

Longarm said carefully, "Well, if you're sure that's what you want . . ."

"I'm sure."

"Then I'll oblige you, of course." He turned back to the blankets and re-spread them, unfolded this time, one atop the other. "I guess the bed's ready, whenever you are. I'll have my nightcap, then have a look-see at the animals before we settle in for the night." He took out a cheroot and lighted it from a burning twig that he picked from the edge of the fire.

Wordlessly, but watching his face closely, Rebecca handed Longarm the whiskey. He drank, then set the bottle beside the fire, where it would be handy when he woke up in the morning. Then he nodded to Rebecca and went to check the horses. He knew they'd be all right, but thought this was a good way to let Rebecca find a bush and relieve herself before going to bed with the embarrassment of his presence.

Longarm took his time inspecting the animals. He

19

hadn't yet relieved the pack mule of its saddle, so he took it off, standing the wooden X-frame far enough from the tethered beasts so none of them would kick it over during the night. The bodies of the Utes on their mustangs had stiffened in rigor mortis during the afternoon, and were as unyielding as boards. Getting them off the ponies and reloading them in the morning would be an impossible job. Longarm shrugged and left the dead Utes where they were. Before going back to the fire, he stepped to one side of the animals and emptied his own bladder for the night.

Rebecca was undressing when Longarm got back to the fire. She'd hung her heavy cloak on the limb that held Longarm's saddlebags, and was stepping out of her dress. It slid down around her feet in a heap, leaving her standing in a white chemise that looked pink in the light of the dying fire. She stepped out of the dress quickly and hung it over the cloak, then scampered back to slide between the blankets. Longarm stood by the fire, taking another drink while he finished his cheroot. He was conscious that Rebecca's eyes were on him all the time.

After a final puff of fragrant tobacco smoke, Longarm flipped the butt of the cigar into the coals. The fire no longer blazed, but the moon was coming up behind the pines that sheltered the campsite. The trees cut off the moon's direct rays, throwing the bed and its surroundings into a deep shadow, made deeper by comparison with the brightness that glowed on the area outside the trees.

Longarm stepped over to the blankets and arranged his gear for the night—boots under the bottom blanket for a pillow, coat and vest folded neatly on the ground at his head beside the bedding, his Colt on top of the heap, his hat laid over the pistol to protect it from dewfall or a sudden shower. He slid between the blankets, carefully avoiding brushing against Rebecca. She lay quiet, and he thought he could feel her body stiffen as he pulled the top blanket up over his shoulders.

20

"You resting comfortable enough?" he asked, before the silence between them grew too heavy.

"I'm fine," she replied. "The grass is softer than a lot of mattresses I've slept on since I've been out here in the West."

"I'd about as soon sleep on the ground as in a bed."

"In your work, you just about have to sleep wherever you can find a place, don't you? And enough time?"

"Oh, it ain't all that bad. A man gets used to it."

"You said you're heading west. How far west?" she asked.

"Over into Utah Territory, down along the Green River a ways."

"That doesn't mean much to me. I've never been there."

"From what you said a minute ago, I got the idea you'd traveled in the West some."

"Not all that much. I was in Kansas awhile, and up in Wyoming Territory, in Cheyenne. But I haven't stayed anyplace very long."

There was something in Rebecca's tone that warned Longarm not to pursue the line of questioning he'd started. He asked, "Where do you call home?"

"Indiana. A little town called Bloomington. It's all farming country, where I come from. But settled, not like here. There aren't a lot of wild Indians shooting people—" Rebecca stopped short and began to quiver again.

"Now just take it easy," Longarm said.

"I—I can't help it, Marshal! When I think about the Kellehers, alive and laughing one minute, and then bloody and dead the next, I just—" Rebecca stopped suddenly. "I just feel like I've got to prove to myself that I'm still alive!" She rolled on her side and her hands clutched Longarm's biceps. "Do you understand that, Marshal? I need to know I'm still alive, after coming so close to being killed yesterday . . ."

"Sure. I understand what's eating at you." Longarm was telling her the truth. He'd seen many people unaccustomed to violence, both men and women, experience the shock of a close brush with death. Often

21

they'd go about their routines in a normal fashion, doing everday chores as though nothing at all had happened, then suddenly realize how narrow their escape had been and lapse into a delayed shock. Many of them reacted as Rebecca was reacting now. They suddenly felt a driving need to prove to themselves that they were still alive, to let themselves go in a reaffirmation of their very existence.

She said, "Help me prove I'm alive, then!" Her lips were suddenly on Longarm's, working ravenously as though she wanted to take his entire face into her mouth. She pushed her tongue between his teeth and pulled herself even closer to him. Her hands were at Longarm's chest now, unbuttoning his shirt, seeking the feeling of live flesh.

Longarm responded as any man would. He turned to face her, and his hands sought Rebecca's breasts. They were full and firm, and she arched her back as he caressed them through her thin chemise. One of her hands moved to his crotch and began to grope frantically up and down his thighs. She felt his beginning erection through the cloth of his breeches and, in her eagerness, tried to straddle him, to rub against him. Longarm helped her by opening his fly. She found what she was seeking, and grasped the stiffening flesh.

They were getting entangled now in the blanket that covered them. Longarm whipped it aside and pulled Rebecca's flowing chemise up around her waist. She released him long enough to let him pull the garment over her head, then pressed her bare breasts to his face, rubbing them across the stiff hairs of his mustache, groaning as the bristles of his day-old beard rasped back and forth across her nipples.

Rebecca's hand returned to Longarm's erection, stiff now and ready. She rose to her knees, her legs spread wide on either side of Longarm's narrow hips, and positioned herself quickly, brought him to her, then dropped in a single wild plunge that took him sliding into her hot depths.

"Oh yes, yes, yes!" she cried. "Now I know I'm a

woman and alive! You're big and hard and it hurts me, but it's a wonderful hurt!"

Longarm was still recovering from his surprise at the speed with which Rebecca had moved to take him into her. He sat up, moving carefully, and half-lifted her until he could turn sideways and lay her down facing him without breaking their connection. She sighed with the ebbing of the pain she'd given herself with the sudden penetration.

"Ah, that's even better. Now I'm full of you without hurting."

Longarm began to rock their bodies slowly. He was not thrusting, but sliding back and forth, still deeply inside Rebecca, moving with a slow rhythm that satisfied her need to be filled without causing her pain.

Rebecca sought his lips for a deep tongue-twining kiss. Her fingers played gently along his ribs and shoulders, caressing his muscles as they flexed and relaxed with his movements.

"You're so very strong," she whispered. "As strong as you are long and big. Oh yes, Marshal, you make me feel very much a woman and very much alive."

"Good. I'm glad you're happy," Longarm told her, his voice soft and level. He was far from being as aroused as she, but he reminded himself that he hadn't had the same experience that had stimulated her emotions so greatly.

"Oh, I am," she replied. "Happier every minute. I'm feeling—I'm feeling—" She gasped as her body began jerking spasmodically. Suddenly she began sobbing. "I didn't want to let go! Not so soon! I wanted to wait for you!"

"It's all right," Longarm assured her. "I'm not in a hurry. We'll just lay quiet for a while. We've got the whole night ahead."

Rebecca's sobs stopped. In the reflected moonglow, Longarm saw her smile at him. She said, "Yes. We have, haven't we? But can you stay hard long enough?"

"Oh, I'll be with you for a while," he promised. "You don't need to worry."

"I won't, as long as I can feel you in me as deep

23

and big as you are now." Rebecca twisted her hips a bit to show her appreciation.

Longarm responded with a series of fast, hard lunges that caused her to gasp and throw her arms around him in a tight embrace.

"Go on!" she urged. "Do that again!"

He repeated the staccato thrusts, and Rebecca squirmed with pleasure as he sank into her time after time. Her response aroused Longarm. He rolled to place himself above Rebecca, and she brought her legs up high around his waist.

"Now!" she panted. "Now go ahead! As deep and fast as you can!"

Though Rebecca had allowed him little time to rest after her quick climax, Longarm was ready to satisfy her again. He drove into her with long, measured strokes, feeling himself building faster than usual, responding to Rebecca's pleased gasps.

Her eyes were rolled upward now, her head arched against the blanket as she strained to hold herself back. He held to his steady motion while she squirmed in ecstasy, her small, high sobs cutting the still night air. She reached her pinnacle and wanted to relax, but Longarm was driving now. He was building faster, but was not yet ready. Rebecca's cries of pleasure took on a tinge of pain, but her body took control as Longarm continued to thrust into her. After a moment of languor, her shuddering sobs began again and continued while Longarm maintained his relentless, pounding pace until he felt her final spasm and released his own control, letting himself down on Rebecca's still-shivering form.

After a long while, Rebecca released a sigh of deep satisfaction. "You're more man than I've ever met before. Almost too much."

"And you're a lot of woman, Rebecca." Longarm lifted himself off her and stretched out beside her on the rumpled, wrinkled blanket.

"You didn't take me for such an abandoned woman when you first saw me, did you?" she chuckled.

"I got to admit, you fooled me. I put you down for

24

a nice, quiet schoolmarm, scared to death of what had happened."

"Oh, I was scared, all right. I was terrified. I'm just now getting over it, thanks to you." Rebecca sighed. "It's too bad I didn't get captured by the Utes before." Then she added, "But I'd only want to have that happen if I knew you'd be along to take care of me. And I am an abandoned woman, you know. That's why I had to leave Nucia."

"Hmph," Longarm grunted. "I guess folks have got a way of being narrow-minded where schoolteachers are concerned."

"Oh, it wasn't anything I did while I was there. I made the mistake of letting it be known I'd been divorced."

"You mean they turned you out of your job when they found out about it?"

"That's exactly what I mean, Marshal."

"You hadn't done anything while you were there to give them cause to fire you?"

"No." Rebecca hesitated. "Well, I won't lie to you. I did a little bit of carrying on. But I was discreet about it. Nobody knew I'd been seeing Robert. Then I got a letter from the lawyer my ex-husband hired when I left him, and my snoopy landlady opened it. She claimed she thought it was addressed to her, but my name was on the envelope. And she spread the word all over Nucia."

"And the school committee fired you, just like that?"

"Without notice or a letter of recommendation. The only one of the school committee who spoke up for me was Mr. Kelleher. So I guess I'm to blame for him and Mrs. Kelleher getting killed."

"No, you weren't to blame. The Utes were. And they paid for it. At least, those two over on the mustangs did."

"I'll try to convince myself of that. I suppose I will, after a while."

A thought occurred to Longarm. "Look here, Rebecca, if you got let out of your job the way you did, what're you going to do for money?"

"I don't have to worry about that. There wasn't anyplace in Nucia to spend anything on, except to pay my board. I've saved most of my year's salary, over two hundred dollars. I've got it in double eagles, sewed in the hem of my cloak over there."

"So you don't have to worry for a while, then?"

"No. I just bought a train ticket as far as Denver. I thought I'd see if I can find a job there. It's a big enough town so my wicked past might not be found out." She frowned. "Didn't you say you work out of Denver?"

"Out of the marshal's office there, sure."

"Maybe I'll see you, then, when you get back from wherever you're going."

"It wouldn't surprise me a bit. Of course, I don't know how long I'll be gone."

"I'll be there for a while. I guess I can ask where you work without it embarrassing you? To find out when you'll be back, I mean?"

"It won't embarrass me one bit. Only don't look for me to get back too soon. A month or two, maybe."

"Where is it you're going in Utah Territory?"

"About to the middle of it. And wherever else I have to, until my case is closed." Longarm propped himself up on one elbow and looked down at Rebecca. "But this ain't a time to talk, you know. There's a lot of the night still left." He bent over to nuzzle her plump breasts. "No use in wasting it, as far as I can see."

"No." Rebecca's hand came up to grasp and fondle him. "If you're ready, I am."

Later, when Rebecca had fallen into an exhausted but happy sleep, Longarm lay awake staring at the declining moon through the tops of the pine trees and thinking about the circumstances that had brought him and Rebecca together.

Billy Vail had called him into the office and waved him to a seat in the red morocco-covered chair that stood at the end of the heavyset chief marshal's paper-littered desk.

"You'll be going to Utah Territory as soon as my clerk gets the paperwork done," Vail had announced.

"Oh, not again, Billy!" Longarm had protested. "Listen, I had enough of them Saints over there to do me for a long time to come. Ain't there somebody else you can put on this job?"

"There probably is, but I want you to handle it. You've been there before, so you know what it's like."

"That's what I'm complaining about, Billy," Longarm countered. "I damn near didn't get back from the last case I had over there around Deseret. For all I know, those Angels are still looking to nail my hide to the wall."

"You won't have to worry about the Avenging Angels. You'll be down in the southeast corner of the territory this time," Vail told him with a casual wave of his pudgy pink hand.

"What's going on down there?"

Vail reached into his desk drawer and pulled out a map of the Utah Territory. He spread it on his desk. Longarm stood up and bent over the desk to follow the chief marshal's finger as it jabbed at a spot on the map.

"This is Fort Cameron," Vail said.

"It sure don't look like it's in the southeast part to me," Longarm objected. "More like right spang in the damn middle of it."

"It is," Vail agreed equably. "But that's not where your case is. You see, the Mormons never have colonized the southeast part of Utah Territory. They started to, once, but Brigham Young changed his mind and sent the colonists down into Arizona Territory instead. So the army's been handling the policing in that area—sort of an unwritten agreement between the army and the Saints.

"Well? If it's under army jurisdiction, why in hell do I have to go there? Ain't the army big enough to handle their job without running to us for help?" Longarm demanded.

27

Vail nodded. "I'd say they are, except that the army's decided to close down Fort Cameron."

"Well, let 'em!" Longarm shot back. "It's their fort, so it's their privilege to shut it down if they've a mind to."

"You'd better wait until I finish," Vail warned him. "The boys with the big brass balls back in Washington, in the War Department and Justice, have worked out a deal. As soon as Fort Cameron's closed, we're going to be given jurisdiction over that southeastern corner of Utah."

"Jesus God, Billy!" Longarm exclaimed. "Ain't we got enough territory to worry about now? Why in the billy-blue-hell do we need part of Utah tacked on to what we got?"

"Because Washington's decided that's the way it's going to be," Vail snapped. "And as far as this office is concerned, that's the end of the argument."

Experience had taught Longarm that there was a point beyond which it wasn't wise to argue with his chief. He said more calmly, "Well, if I'm going to go, I guess I better find out what kind of job the army's decided it don't want to handle."

Vail slid a finger eastward across the map. "This is the Sevier River. It wanders on south nearly to the Arizona Territory line. What lies east of it is going to be our problem as soon as Fort Cameron closes."

"When's that going to be?" Longarm asked.

Vail shook his bald head and shrugged. "Nobody seems to know, except that it'll be pretty soon. And on up here to the north—" the chief marshal moved his finger again— "you come to where the Muddy River and Starvation Creek join up to make the Dirty Devil River."

"I bet it is, too," Longarm snorted. "I've seen those things they call rivers over in Utah Territory. They're mostly dry wash with a puddle here and there. Rivers, my ass!"

"Shut up and listen!" Vail told him. "Now. Our territory stops on a line drawn east from the head of the Dirty Devil to just above the place where the

28

Green and the Colorado come together, and on over to the Colorado state line. You got that clear? Everything north of that line is Mormon country."

"Don't worry. I ain't going to get into their part. Not if I know about it," Longarm assured Vail.

"All right." Vail's finger moved south on the map and stopped at one of the half-dozen dots in the big rectangular area that indicated a town or settlement. "This is Hanksville. That's where you're going."

Longarm nodded. "All right, I know *where*. Now, suppose you tell me *why*."

"To pick up a trail the army lost six months ago."

"Six months! Hell's bells, Billy! That's as bad as six years. What were they trailing, and how'd they lose it?"

The chief marshal sat down, leaned back, and rubbed a hand across his shiny dome. "They were trailing two wagonloads of Springfield rifles, and I don't know how they lost the trail. It just stopped dead at this Hanksville place. Now that the fort's being closed, the job's been handed to us. I want it cleaned up right now, without waiting for us to get official jurisdiction."

"How'd they come to lose two wagonloads of rifles, anyhow?"

"They'd hired civilian teamsters to haul the guns from the railroad at Ogden. The escort got ahead of the wagons on a steep cutback going over a pass, and the wagons just disappeared. They brought in scouts and traced the wagons as far east as Hanksville."

Longarm acknowledged Vail's explanation with an abstracted nod. He'd been studying the map while the chief marshal talked. He said, "That Hanksville place is a million miles from nowhere. It looks to me like it'll take some doing just to get there. The U.P. line at Ogden's a mite more than two hundred miles north. The Denver & Rio Grande's pushing iron west, but they still ain't got past Grand Junction."

"They haven't passed a law against riding a horse," Vail said tartly, arching one black bushy eyebrow.

"All right, Billy, don't get your balls in an uproar.

29

I'll take the D&RG to Grand Junction and rent a livery stable horse there."

"No. Justice keeps prodding me about spending too much money renting livery stock. You'll get a remount from the army."

"You mean at Fort Cameron? Hell, it's as far to there from the U.P. as it is from Grand Junction to Hanksville."

Vail measured the map distance with a practiced eye. "I think you're right," he conceded. "Well, go north to Fort Collins—" He stopped, shook his head. "Damn it, I keep forgetting, the army closed Collins quite a while back. Looks like you'll have to go south for your horse, to Fort Lewis."

"Hell, Billy, that's almost to the New Mexico line. I'd be going further out of my way than if I went to Ogden." Longarm traced the distances with a finger. "You know, the way it looks to me, there ain't no way for me to get there from here."

"Wait a minute," Vail said suddenly. "I just thought of something." He pawed through the papers on his desk until he found what he was looking for. "Here. There's a new cavalry post just a little ways south of Montrose, near Colona. It's just been activated to put down the Utes who're giving the new settlers along the railroad a bad time. There'll be a remount station there."

Longarm looked at the spot Vail indicated. "I can ride the rails to Montrose, all right, but how do I get to the post? You sure don't expect me to go ten or twelve miles shank's mare."

"Don't worry. I'll go through army channels and have a trooper meet you at the depot in Montrose with a horse."

"And a pack mule too," Longarm said. "I'll have to tote grub and feed for the animals. There's no place for me to get a meal, and no graze across that bare stretch west of Grand Junction."

"That's settled, then," Vail said. "Now there's one thing more I want you to take care of, as long as you're going to be there anyhow."

"You mean trying to find a shipment of rifles that's been gone six months ain't enough of a job?"

"This other thing goes with the missing rifles. While the army was nosing around Hanksville trying to get a line on the guns, they got the idea that there's crooked work going on in the courthouse there. The sheriff's office, mainly."

"What sort of crooked work?" Longarm asked.

"About what you'd expect. Outlaws getting turned loose for lack of evidence at their trials, no trials at all for a lot of them. Signs of rustling. Hell, you know what to look for."

"And you want me to take care of that—in my spare time?"

"You might find out that the two are connected," Vail told him.

"Wouldn't surprise me." The deputy marshal sighed resignedly. "All right, Billy. When do you want me to go?"

"Right now. Get your gear together and start out. I don't want Washington riding my ass about it."

Watching the fading moon through the pines, recalling the reason why he was where he was, Longarm wondered what he'd be running into ahead. Whatever it was, it probably wouldn't be as pleasant as his encounter with the woman sleeping beside him. At the moment, he didn't really care. He snuggled closer to Rebecca's soft, warm body, and drifted off to sleep.

31

Chapter 3

"Well, there it is," Longarm said to Rebecca. They'd just rounded a bend in the trail above the river, and the first scattered houses of Grand Junction had come into sight, glowing in the bright midmorning sunshine.

"Yes. And I hate to see it. I haven't had enough of you, Longarm. I don't know which I enjoyed most, the first time, when I learned how much of a man you are, or the last two times, when you proved it to me."

"I don't guess there's much we can do to move the town away. You'll be fine, though. You might have to wait a half-day, or even a day, for a train out to Denver, but you sure won't have to worry about any more Utes carrying you off."

"You're sure you don't have time to wait until my train leaves?" she asked. "There'll be a hotel in town where we could stay until I've got to go."

"Now you know better. We already talked out that idea."

It had been Rebecca's suggestion, only half-serious when she'd first mentioned the possibility as they lay awake during the day's dawning hours. She'd awakened Longarm with her urgent caresses, and they'd spent the time before sunup in another pulsing, pounding, and mutually satisfying embrace. She'd brought the idea up again during the short time it took them to cover the remaining distance to the town, and Longarm's reply had been the same each time. Now he repeated it again.

"You know I can't stop. Not that I wouldn't enjoy pleasuring you a lot more. But I'm running late now, and all we'd be doing is putting things off a few hours.

32

No, Rebecca. Soon as I turn those dead Utes over to the sheriff and make sure you're going to get away all right, I'd best be riding on."

"But we'll have plenty of time to be together in Denver, when you get back there."

"Sure. Whenever that is."

"Make it soon, will you, Longarm?"

"That's one thing you don't need to ask me to do, Rebecca. I don't relish staying over in Utah Territory any more than I like the idea of going there in the first place. The sooner I can wind up my case, the better I'm going to like it."

And that's even truer now than it was this morning at Grand Junction, Longarm told himself later in the day, recalling the goodbyes he and Rebecca had exchanged.

It had been a hard ride since he'd crossed the Colorado just west of Grand Junction and started following the river toward the border between Colorado and Utah Territory. The river hadn't seemed able to make up its mind which direction it wanted to take. It had led him west from the town, then, judging by the position of the sun, had looped to the northeast. Late in the afternoon, the stream had changed course again. Longarm took out his ordnance map and smoked a cheroot while he studied it. As far as he could trust the map, the shifting of the stream to flow southward through a wide, rocky canyon took place just about on the border between the territories. Folding the map and stuffing it in his coat pocket, he toed the roan into motion again.

If you ain't in Utah Territory now, old son, he told himself, *another half-hour or so of riding and you damn sure will be.*

There was no marker to indicate the spot where Colorado ended and Utah began. There was nothing but the same soft brown limestone on both sides of the Colorado River, the sides of the riverbed cut in horizontal strata where the river's changing depth through the centuries had scored the rock along its surface, and marked the level at which the river had flowed from time to time. There was nothing green within five miles of the trail Longarm followed along the shelving wall of the river canyon. Only beside the banks of the stream was there an occasional patch of vegetation, in pockets where the water had left grains of dirt in some small level spot when its flow diminished.

From the time the sun dropped low enough to shine under Longarm's wide hatbrim and into his eyes, he'd been squinting into the harsh light, following the advice given him by the sheriff at Grand Junction, to make sure he stayed with the main trail.

"You got a hundred miles to go to get to the Green River, after you turn away from the Colorado," the sheriff had said, his manner that of one lawman trying to be helpful to another. "There's only one place you can get across the Green for a hundred miles north or south. You sure don't want to miss it."

"I don't aim to," Longarm said. "I got an army ordnance map that ought to keep me going right, though."

"Army ordnance, shit!" the sheriff snorted. "Maps made up by a bunch of pink-cheeked shavetails just out of the Point, who never seen the country! I guess they're better than nothing, but don't risk your life on one of 'em."

"You got any suggestions, then?"

"Just don't let that main trail get out of your sight. There's a bunch of forks off of it, and a man's got to look two or three times, or he'll be fooled into taking one."

"What'd happen if I did? Those off-trails lead some-place, don't they?"

"One or two might. Most of 'em just peter out. You get off one of 'em, chances are you'll wind up in the middle of nowhere. All you'll be by the time somebody else passes that way is a stack of coyote-chewed bones."

Longarm frowned. "There's bound to be some kind of landmark showing where the main trail cuts away from the Colorado."

"There is. A little bunch of five or six shacks across the river from the side the trail's on. They'll be the last

34

houses of any kind you'll see before you get to the Green, and that's a good hundred miles due west."

"Thanks. I'll keep a real close watch."

For the better part of an hour, Longarm had been keeping the close watch he'd promised, but all he'd seen on the opposite bank of the river were a small herd of antelope and a rectangular cairn of stones, obviously the grave of some traveler whose travels had ended forever on the stone banks of the treacherous Colorado. There hadn't even been any of the rattlesnakes and big centipedes that the sheriff had also warned him about.

Dusk began gathering as the sun dipped out of sight below some distant mountains—perhaps the range that lay beyond the Green River, Longarm thought. He debated pushing on as the air cooled, but decided he'd better not. The trail was hard enough to follow in full daylight. At night it would be too easy for him to miss one of its twists and wander off in the wrong direction.

Play it safe, old son, Longarm told himself. *You don't need to be in all that much of a hurry to get where you're heading. The case ain't going to run away. It'll still be waiting for you when you get there.*

Just before darkness was complete, he found a slant where the river could be reached. With the horse and mule watered and fed, Longarm made a dark camp and, after eating sparingly of jerky and parched corn, took a nightcap of Maryland rye and wrapped himself in his blanket.

An hour after sunup the following morning, he reached the cluster of houses that marked the beginning of the trail's slant to the west. The houses on the other side of the stream looked deserted, but his sharp eyes had spotted figures moving around them when they first came into view. It was pretty apparent that whoever lived in the dwellings wanted no truck with passing strangers, and chose to discourage chance visitors by staying invisible.

Something you might keep tucked away in the back of your mind, old son, he mused as he searched out the trail's new direction. *If a fellow did a little stirring up over there, he just might find a few faces that'd match some wanted fliers. But that's for later. Best get on right now to this Hanksville place, wherever in hell it might be, up ahead.*

Slowly the day dragged on through noon and into the afternoon. The ground turned rough after the trail shifted its direction. The horse and mule were climbing almost constantly, over a series of humps that led to progressively higher ground, and frequent rest stops were necessary. It was late afternoon when the ascent ended on the crest of the humped ridge, revealing a second series of humps descending into a narrow but grassy valley below. A sparkling, narrow strip of blue water showed in the bottom of the valley, and beside the little stream, just off the trail, stood a split-log house. A trickle of almost invisible smoke rose lazily from its chimney.

Longarm sat on the ridge while he lighted and smoked most of a cheroot, studying the valley. There were a few cattle scattered up and down its narrow length, not enough to be called a herd, but the number a rancher just beginning his spread might have. There was a big corral beyond the house, however, a pole enclosure big enough to hold five times as many steers as Longarm could see on the valley floor. Now only a half-dozen were penned in the enclosure.

Longarm shook his head. He'd seen the pattern before in cattle country: a small ranch with a corral far bigger than was needed to take care of the herd visible around it. Sometimes it was brought about by accident, a rancher acquiring a new place and beginning with a small herd, using an old corral. More often, however, the pattern indicated a rustler's stopover. He decided he'd reserve judgment, though, and started the roan down the humps toward the valley floor.

Going down proved to be slower work than climbing up. On its west side the ridge was steeper, the humps narrower. The horse and the more sure-footed mule picked their way carefully, and needed to be rested often. The afternoon was well along before Longarm got to the floor of the valley and turned off the trail in the direction of the little cabin. He'd barely turned the roan onto the path leading to the house when three people came out, two men and a woman. One of the men, tall but slight of build, was much younger than the other. There was something familiar in his walk, but Longarm was unable to place him. The younger man left the others and came forward while Longarm was still a score of yards from the cabin door.

He called, "Glad to see a new face, stranger. Light and visit a while. We saw you coming down the ridge, and—" He stopped as a frown formed on his face. "Wait a minute! I know you!"

"I got a feeling I've seen you someplace before, too," Longarm said, pulling up beside the man.

"Hell!" the man exclaimed. "You're a federal marshal. Your name's Long, but they call you Longarm."

Longarm looked closely at the man. "Sure. It comes back to me now. You're—let's see—"

"Jim Peters. And you arrested me up north about three years ago. Up in the Powder River country."

Longarm nodded. "I was up there, then, all right. That was a real rustler's picnic."

He studied Peters's face. Vaguely, he remembered a fresh-skinned young cowhand with sandy hair and freckles, for whom he'd felt a bit sorry at the time. If this was the same man, Longarm thought, he'd put on a lot more age than three years ought to allow for. This Jim Peters was rawboned and weather-tanned, and instead of the somewhat ingenuous look that Longarm remembered, he wore the expression of a man who'd taken more than a few knocks. Still, he decided, it had to be the same man. Nobody in his right mind would claim arrest as a past association unless it was true.

Peters said, "I'm the fellow you caught out on open range with a running iron in his saddlebag."

"I recall it now. There'd been a herd drove off that range three or four days before, and I was trying to pick up a trail."

"Well, you got on mine, I guess. And took me in."

"Now you know I had to do that. You had the running iron on you."

"Sure I did. An old one I'd picked up at a dead fire twenty miles away. Hell, I was so green, then, I didn't know it was against the law even to be carrying one. I sure hadn't used it, anybody could see that. It had rust all over it."

"So it did. And I told the judge that, if you remember, when I was testifying."

"It didn't make any difference. He gave me eighteen months. I served twelve." Peters tried to keep his voice matter-of-fact, but Longarm detected a note of bitterness in his carefully flat tone.

"You got to remember, Peters, the way the law read, just having that running iron was illegal."

"Even if I hadn't known it before, I damn sure found it out, didn't I?"

Longarm said, "Well now, maybe you just better forget that welcome you gave me. I'll ride on——"

"No," Peters interrupted. "I won't back down, Marshal. I guess you're still a federal government man, aren't you?"

"Oh, I haven't changed jobs. I'll show you my badge, if you're curious."

"That makes no difference. I invited you to stop, and I won't go back on that. I—I don't hold a grudge against you. I can see you only did what your job called for."

"It sure wasn't personal, if that's what you're getting at. And I didn't pass that eighteen-month sentence on you; the judge did that."

"Sure. Like I said, I don't carry a grudge. Come on. I asked you to stop for coffee. Let's go drink a cup."

"As long as you're sure." Longarm dismounted. Leading the roan and the mule, he walked beside Peters to where the others were waiting.

Peters said, "This is my wife Coretta, and my foreman, Clem Bailey. This is Marshal Long. He's the federal man who took me in that time I got arrested up north."

"Oh my!" Mrs. Peters exclaimed. "The one you——"

Peters interrupted her. "I've already told the marshal that I don't hold a grudge against him, Coretta. Let's go inside and have some of that coffee you just made."

Longarm studied Peters's wife and Clem Bailey. Coretta was young, probably about her husband's age, in her middle twenties. She was a wispy woman, frail-looking, with thin light hair pulled back from a center part into a tight bun, which added several years to the age she looked. Her features were regular and unremarkable. Bailey was burly, set low to the ground. His long brown hair showed strands of gray, and his face was creased with hours of facing sun, rain, wind, and snow in the saddle. His hands were big, with battered, swollen fingers.

There was a moment of bustling as they sat down around the pine-board table that occupied much of the cabin's space. After they'd gotten seated, with coffee cups filled, Longarm asked Peters, "You been here long?"

"Not very. Only about eight months. Took a while to save up enough to get me started. If you looked down from the ridge, I guess you saw I haven't been able to buy or trade for much stock yet."

"I noticed."

"You missed seeing a lot of the critters, I'd bet," Bailey volunteered. "They're strung out all up and down the creekbed."

"That figures. I know steers scatter around pretty much, in country like this."

"Oh, there'll be a good bunch when we round 'em up," Bailey went on. "Jim's going to make a good spread out of this place."

"You think you'll ever get enough to fill up all that corral you got behind the house?" Longarm asked.

"I didn't build the corral," Peters said. "It came with the place." Then he added, "Clem's right, though. I'll make a good spread here. That's why I'm trying to keep him on. The way things are now, there's too much work for me to handle by myself, and not quite enough to keep us both busy."

"I had the place figured for a one-man spread,"

39

Longarm said. "I guess you'll be selling off a few head this year, too? Just to keep going?"

"I might," Peters replied. "Haven't really made up my mind yet."

"Where would you drive to, though, to sell a herd?" Longarm asked with a frown. "I don't know this country well, but I can't recollect any places close around where you could ship a herd to market."

Bailey broke in again, "There's a few places. I don't guess Jim'd try to drive the few head we could spare, though. Easiest thing to do would be to put ours in with a herd going from one of the other ranches."

"Quite a few spreads in these valleys, are there?" Longarm asked the foreman casually.

"None close enough to matter."

"Not enough water or grass?" Longarm pressed.

"There's enough for us," Peters said. "That's all I'm interested in."

Longarm turned to Coretta. "Must be sort of lonesome for you, Mrs. Peters, way off here by yourself."

She said, "Oh, we have—" She stopped short and, after a pause, finished somewhat lamely, "We have enough to do so that we don't miss not having company."

"I see. Who is your nearest neighbor, by the way?"

Before she could reply, Peters cut in, "You know, Marshal, I haven't been here long enough, and been too busy, to get acquainted. I really can't remember which spread's the closest to us."

"Any of them right along the trail west?" Longarm persisted. "I'd sort of like to know what landmarks to look for."

It was Bailey who answered. "There's not any spreads right on the trail. All of 'em are like Jim's place here, tucked away in one of the valleys or a canyon."

"What you need is a railroad to cut across here, I guess," Longarm remarked after an awkward pause. "Pull things together and bring in a lot more ranchers."

"Jim says he doesn't want—" Coretta began.

Bailey cut her off quickly. "What Coretta's saying

40

is that Jim figures we can hang on until the railroad gets here."

"Well, that'll be a while," Longarm said, ignoring the interruption. "There's too much rough country between here and Grand Junction for the D&RG to push iron across it very fast. I'd say three years, anyhow."

"Why, that doesn't worry—" Coretta began again.

This time it was Peters who broke in. He asked Longarm, "Did you come over to Utah Territory looking for somebody, Marshal?"

"You might say I got a sort of open ticket," Longarm answered. He saw from their questioning looks that they expected him to explain, but he said nothing more.

Coretta broke the awkward pause. "Can you stay the night with us, Marshal? I guess there'd be room in Clem's lean-to, around back."

"Now I thank you kindly for the invitation, Mrs. Peters," Longarm said. "But there's still a lot of daylight left. I better keep on making tracks while I can see the trail." He noticed that neither of the men seconded her invitation. Nor did they invite him to have a second cup of coffee when he stood up. He said, "I better be hunching along. Thanks for the coffee."

"Any time," Peters said shortly. "But I don't expect you'll be close enough to drop in again, unless maybe on your way back?"

"Hard to tell." Longarm started for the door. "You know how it was up in Wyoming, and it'll be the same here. I just go wherever my job takes me."

Back in the saddle and on the trail again, Longarm began sifting the impressions he'd carried away from the encounter. The setup at Peters's ranch didn't ring true. The small herd and the oversized corral; the haste that both Peters and Bailey showed in picking up Coretta's words before she could say too much; the very characters of Peters and Bailey; all pointed to the ranch's actual use as a stopover for rustled herds.

It don't make sense, though, Longarm mused. *Unless there's some spreads around here with herds big enough*

41

*to draw rustlers. And so far, I ain't seen enough graze
or water for there to be anything but little shirttail
outfits. Got to be another answer to it, old son. And
you better steer clear of letting it get in the way of
what you were sent here to do. Billy Vail would boil
over sure, if you was to get sidetracked from your
main job.*

Unanswered questions always nagged at Longarm,
and this one stayed with him as he rode on toward the
Green River. It continued to gnaw at him as the dusk
deepened, and left his mind only when he began looking for a suitable spot to bed down for the night. The
rough, arid country offered few possibilities. Longarm
finally settled for a semi-sheltered rock overhang a few
yards off the trail, where there were no sudden drop-
offs that could lure a hobbled horse or mule to de-
struction during the night. It was another fireless camp,
and Longarm made short work of giving the animals
a grain ration from nosebags, and crawling into his
bedroll.

At some point during the night's dark hours, he
snapped awake. His bladder was uncomfortably full,
and he thought this was why he'd awakened. For a
moment he lay quietly, looking at the wan quarter-
moon that spread a pallid light over the stark landscape,
creating dark shadows at the bases of the boulders
and rock outcrops that were its only features. Longarm
slid out of his blankets just as the muzzle blast of a
distant rifle streaked red and the slug plucked at his
empty bedroll in the split-second before the sound of
the shot cracked open the still night air.

His finely tuned instincts took command instantly.
He dropped flat and rolled into the darkness below
the overhang. His rifle lay by the gunshot bedroll.
Hugging the ground, he stretched out and grasped its
muzzle, and snaked the Winchester to him. All the
while, his eyes were searching the area where he'd
seen the muzzle blast.

Nothing moved. The unrelieved blackness of the
shadows that puddled under the shelving stone ledges
through which the trail ran, and at the bases of the

42

huge, free-standing boulders that bordered it, offered total concealment for the unknown sniper.

In the near-distance past the trail, a horse whinnied. Longarm strained both ears and eyes, but could not pinpoint the animal's location. A rock dislodged by a carefully placed foot thumped dully as it bounded down a shelf beyond the trail.

Longarm risked stepping from beneath the rock overhang in order to get a wider view of the terrain. The quarter-moon gave too little light for him to make out anything except the contrast between brightness and shadow. There was no sign of motion in any of the shadows.

Stepping carefully, the rough ground stabbing at his bare feet, Longarm circled the overhang and belly-crawled to the top of the ledge that formed the jutting shelf. The height increased the area that was visible to him, and he now saw a flicker of movement on the other side of the trail. It was little more than a blur of gray-toned shadow in a world of unrelieved blackness and ghostly blue-green moonglow.

Flattening himself on the rock ledge, Longarm watched the moving blur. It zigzagged slowly in his direction, and now and then he heard the grating of ironshod hooves on the hard ground. Slowly the blur took form. It became a rider, letting his horse pick a careful way toward the trail. The rider's face was hidden in the black shadow of his hatbrim, but the barrel of the rifle he carried gleamed clearly in the dismal light.

Longarm pushed himself back as far as possible on the ledge, and kept his head down. He lay motionless, watching the man on horseback. The rider stopped when the horse reached the trail. He lowered his head, craning his neck to peer under the overhang. He brought up his rifle and let off a shot into Longarm's abandoned bedroll.

This was all Longarm needed. He'd kept the rider in his sights ever since the man's outline became distinct. His finger was ready on the trigger. He squeezed off a shot. The rider flew backward in his saddle, stiffened momentarily, then flopped to the ground. His rifle fell with a clatter on the rocky soil.

The fallen man lay motionless. Longarm stood up and picked his way to the overhang. He pushed his feet into his boots, strapped on his gunbelt, put his Winchester down, and made his way to the trail.

When the horse heard Longarm coming, it tossed its head and whinnied. Longarm muttered a few soothing sounds in a low voice, and the animal stood quietly again. The rider had fallen facedown. Longarm's eyes were well adjusted to the half-light now. He took the dead rider's shoulder and turned the body over. He didn't need to strike a match to know that he'd never before set eyes on the face of his would-be assassin.

Chapter 4

After he'd dragged his attacker's body off the trail and tethered the man's horse with his own animals, Long-arm folded his legs under him and sat in his blankets while he lighted a cheroot. The half-emptied bottle of Maryland rye sat beside the bedroll, and he uncorked it and took a satisfying swallow between puffs on the cigar. He groped in his vest pocket and dragged out his Ingersoll watch. The derringer clipped to the other end of the gold-washed watch chain dangled idly while he snapped the case open and read the time by the glow of his cheroot.

It was four o'clock. Dawn would begin to show in another hour or less. There was time for a little think-ing before he took up the trail again.

Old son, there's just three things possible here, he told himself. *Maybe that fellow followed you from Grand Junction, or maybe he spotted you coming to-ward him on the trail, or maybe he was holed up back at the Peters ranch and was sent out after you. What you got to do is try to figure out which of those three things it was and then make up your mind what you're going to do about it.*

There's an outside chance he could have trailed be-hind you since you left Colorado Territory, but that just ain't likely. If he'd been somebody you helped send up, or got crossways of, that might be different. But a man you never clapped eyes on before wouldn't have any reason at all to follow you this far or wait this long. Anyhow, you'd have been sure to catch on, if there'd been somebody skulking along behind.

All right. Say he spotted you coming toward him,

and figured he'd just cut you down and take your horse and saddle and guns and the mule and whatever's on it and any cash you might be carrying. There are plenty of outlaws roaming around who'll kill for that little bit of loot and never bat an eye over doing it. And maybe that's the way this happened. I've seen men killed for a lot less than I'm packing, and figure I'll see it again.

What's most likely is that this fellow was hid out back at Peters's place. And after I left, Peters and Bailey got to talking it over and sent him after me. Or maybe it was Peters himself who put this jasper on me. I don't figure it makes sense for a man to give up a grudge as easy as he said he did. But that place has got a bad smell. I sniffed it even before I found out who it belonged to. So that's the way it probably come about. That Bailey fellow looks like a real hardcase who wouldn't bat an eye at getting rid of somebody who might cause trouble for him. And I know about Jim Peters being sent up, there in Wyoming. Might even be that he decided to stay on the wrong side of the law, once he got himself a record. Maybe he made some connection in the pen that set him up down here.

Longarm lit a second cheroot and took a thoughtful sip of rye while he turned over possibilities and watched the thin line of gray on the eastern horizon grow and turn slowly to pink. He couldn't afford to discard the possibility that the effort to kill him was the result of a chance encounter with a footloose badman, but he favored the more likely one that the assassination effort had originated at the Peters ranch.

But when push comes to shove, he reminded himself, there ain't one damn thing I can do to prove it. If I load this fellow on his horse and take him back there, all they got to do is say they never seen him before, don't know him from Adam's off-ox. And I got no way to prove they did, no way to bring things to a show-down.

Even if I could bring a showdown, it might not be smart right now. I got my assignment to finish up first. Maybe if there's time later, I can tend to Peters and

46

Bailey. Let them set and stew and wonder what happened to their man. If they're the ones that sent him, that is.

Having reached his decision, Longarm relaxed. He chewed a piece of jerky for breakfast, washed it down with sips of stale water from his canteen, followed it with a final sip of rye, and rolled up his bedding and tied the roll behind his saddle. Then he dragged the body of the unsuccessful assassin off the trail and into a gully. He searched the man's pockets before covering the body with stones, but found nothing except a few tattered greenbacks and a pouch of cigarette makings. He put the dead man's rifle back in its saddle scabbard and, after checking to see that no blood had spattered the saddle, added the horse to his string. At the first ranch house he encountered, he'd see if anyone recognized it, and leave it in custody of the rancher.

There were no ranch houses that he could see from the trail as he rode on to Green River. At least, he thought, Bailey wasn't lying about that. The morning was still young when he reached the crossing at Green River. Even from a distance, he could see the untidy clumps of houses clustered on both sides of the ford. There were two or three times more than would have qualified the place as a settlement. In that sparsely populated area of Utah Territory, any group of more than ten houses automatically became a town, and even the smallest towns in cattle country had a livery stable. The stable became Longarm's first stop.

"I got a riderless horse here that I picked up on the trail coming in," he told the proprietor quite truthfully. "Figured maybe you can tell me who it belongs to."

"Hmph," the liveryman grunted after stepping out and looking at the animal. "That's Pete Todd's animal, or I'm a monkey's uncle." He looked narrowly at Longarm. "Where'd you say you found it?"

"I didn't say, but it was about twenty miles to the east."

"Funny." The liveryman scratched his chin. "Pete was through here about three days ago, heading in that

47

direction. I can't figure what might've happened to him."

"Now that's something I can't tell you," Longarm replied, still sticking to the letter of the truth. "Be all right if I leave it here, in case he shows up and claims it?"

"Well . . ." the liveryman chewed and spat a stream of tobacco juice. "Well, I guess it'd be all right."

"This Pete Todd fellow," Longarm asked. "Does he work for a ranch hereabouts, or something like that?"

"I don't rightly know where Pete works, mister. Here and there, I'd reckon. I see him four, five times a year, mostly when he's passing through."

"Passing through from where to where?"

"Couldn't say. I don't ask a man about his personal business." There was a rebuke in the liveryman's voice.

"Well, it ain't like I care," Longarm replied. "I was just wondering, same as you. If you'll keep the nag until Todd shows up, I guess we'd both be obliged."

"Sure. You're more than welcome. You want me to tell Pete who brung the critter in, if he asks me?"

"Why, he wouldn't know me, any more than I'd know him," Longarm replied. Then, indicating the town that straddled the riverbank, he asked, "Is there a place here where I can buy a meal? Been so long since I had a regular meal, my belly thinks my throat's been cut."

"Try that house two doors from the saloon, the one set back from the street a ways," the liveryman advised him. "Miz Lummis sets a breakfast and a supper table for whoever's looking for grub, besides her regulars. She'd be able to wrassle up something for you, I guess."

"Thank you, kindly." Longarm touched his hat. "I'll be moving on, then."

An hour later, with a belated but welcome hot breakfast under his belt, and his head crammed by Mrs. Lummis with more information than he'd really asked for about the settlers at Green River and the road to

Hanksville, Longarm started out on the last hundred miles that remained between him and his destination.

Noon was near and the sky was cloudless. The trail was well defined, but rough and winding. It curved around towering buttes, dipped into shallow valleys in gentle curves, and zigzagged on cutbacks along the precipitous walls of deep-cut canyons. He was riding a hundred miles, Longarm thought as the afternoon wore on, in order to cover fifty miles or so as the crow flies.

Darkness came earlier than usual, and sunset found him still on the trail. The sun dropped quickly behind a great plateau to the west; the plateau was topped by a strangely rounded peak, a dome or knoblike formation. Longarm was beginning to wish that he'd stopped at the river he'd crossed an hour earlier when he saw a shallow canyon ahead. He'd ridden to its edge and looked down into a valley that was almost green, watered by a threadlike stream that trickled over a rocky bed. Now there was only enough daylight left for him to pick his way down the valley slope and make still another fireless camp beside the stream.

As best he could figure, Hanksville was still nearly thirty miles ahead of him when he started out the next morning. In that broken, rugged country, thirty miles was a full day's ride. He set his jaw and moved along, letting the roan set the pace, but keeping it moving steadily ahead. Full darkness was less than an hour away, and Longarm's canteen as well as his bottle of Maryland rye were both almost empty when he saw the town taking shape on the far side of a shallow, lazily rolling stream. The road led to the streambank, and the wheel ruts and hoofprints showed him that the river was fordable. He crossed into Hanksville.

It was not the kind of Western frontier town to which Longarm had grown accustomed. In this lumber-poor area, stone was the preferred building material—thin, flat, sand-colored stones stacked like irregular plates, with river clay used as mortar. Every house, every store on the main street looked like a fortress. There was little glass in evidence. Most of the buildings lacked even simple framing on their windows, which had been left simply as open holes in the foot-thick walls. A few had narrow wooden window frames to which cheesecloth had been tacked to serve as screens. He noticed only a handful of buildings with metal or wooden shutters. The street was an inch thick with dust where wagon wheels and hooves had ground the hard soil to loose powder.

Longarm couldn't tell, after a glance along the slightly irregular main street, whether the town was getting ready to go to bed or just waking up after a hot day. There were a few pedestrians walking close to the buildings, a few horses at the hitch rails in front of stores, a solitary buggy rolling away from him, a pair of riders approaching. On the building that bore a faded sign proclaiming tersely "Saloon," there were no swinging doors. In fact there was no door at all. Longarm reined in, tied his animals to the hitch rail, and went inside.

No lamps had yet been lighted, and the interior of the saloon was dim. As Longarm's eyes adjusted to the change from the still-bright sunlight of the street, he saw that there were only three customers and the barkeep in the place. One of the customers was asleep in a chair tilted against the back wall. The barkeep was at the end of the plain pine bar, talking to a patron. The third customer was standing at the center of the bar, drinking beer from a bottle.

There were no draft-beer taps visible behind the bar; and only a few bottles, most of them unlabeled, stood on the mirrorless backbar. The sight of the beer drinker made Longarm suddenly aware of his own parched, dusty throat. When the barkeep came up, he said, without waiting for the man to ask for his order, "If your beer's good and cold, a glass of it'd go down mighty good right now."

"No draft beer," the man said. "I can open you a bottle, if you want one."

"Bottle or glass, it's all the same to me, as long as it's cold."

"Cool." The barkeep turned away. He took the wooden top off a water-filled barrel and plunged an arm into it up to the elbow. He found what he'd been fishing for in the barrel, and brought out a dripping bottle of beer.

Longarm put money on the counter and said, "Have one with me."

"Don't drink. But if you feel like treating, I'll take a sody." The barkeep dipped into the barrel again and felt around for a moment, finally pulling out a bottle of dark liquid. "Sarsaparilla. Good for what ails a man." He snapped the caps off the bottles with an expert thumb, and shoved the beer across to Longarm. Then he raised the pop bottle and said, "Here's to you."

Longarm tasted the beer. It was almost cold, compared to the tepid water he'd been sipping from his canteen. The barkeep had drained his sarsaparilla in a series of gurgling gulps. He put the bottle down and appraised Longarm with small beady blue eyes set in lashless lids under sparse, almost invisible blond brows.

"Looks like you been traveling a ways," he observed.

"A ways," Longarm confirmed with a nod. "Be glad to stop awhile and sleep in a bed for a change. Which brings to mind that I'll be needing a place to stay. You got a hotel here in town?"

"Not now. Used to be one, but it closed down. Mrs. Holcomb up the street rents rooms, though."

"I'll look her up. How about a restaurant? I'm going to be ready for supper pretty soon now."

"Catty-corner across the road, open till a little bit after dark." The barkeep dropped his voice and said, "If I was you, I'd eat at Mrs. Holcomb's. The food's better. The restaurant cook's a Chinee."

"That so? Well, thanks for the tip. I guess you wouldn't know if Mrs. Holcomb's got a room vacant?"

"She has. The town's not all that crowded now. I guess you noticed that when you rode in, though."

"There didn't seem to be much going on," Longarm admitted in a carefully neutral voice.

"It'll pick up in about a month. Roundup time."

"Gets busy then, does it?" Longarm pointed to the barrel.

"Busier than now." The barkeep took away the empty beer bottle, fished another from the barrel, and set it in front of Longarm. "That why you're here? Looking for a job?"

"Not this trip. But I'll be around awhile." Longarm wanted to change the subject. He indicated the bottles on the backbar. "One of them wouldn't hold some Maryland rye, would it now?"

"Maryland rye?" The barkeep stared at Longarm, his eyes wide. "I haven't had a call for that in a year. But it just happens I've got a full case in the back room. It got sent by mistake and I never did get around to sending it back. If that's the drink you favor, mister, I'd say you're in luck!"

"If it's good rye, I'll agree with you. Suppose you bring out a bottle and let me try a taste of it."

Longarm inspected the label on the bottle the barkeep brought from the storeroom. The name on the label wasn't one he recognized, but when the bottle was uncorked and he took a sip of the whiskey, Longarm recognized the quality of the rye.

"I'll buy that case off of you, if you'll make me a reasonable price for it," he told the barkeep. "And when you name a figure, just remember that I ain't one of those rich nabobs."

"You can have it for what it cost me, plus the freight. It'd come to $1.35 a quart, the way I figure it, and I've got eleven quarts left. I only opened the one bottle, and it took me damn near a year to get rid of it. Folks here want bourbon." He dropped his voice and added, "Or moonshine."

"I thought Brother Brigham didn't allow liquor in Utah Territory," Longarm frowned.

"Brigham's a hell of a long ways from here, mister. Not many Saints hereabouts. Land was too dry and water too scarce for them to settle it. Oh, we got a few jack-Mormons, backsliders, but that's all. And that's all we want."

Longarm nodded. He dug out a double eagle and

laid it on the bar. "Take out of that for the eleven bottles. And leave that open one on the backbar; we'll call it my private stock. Buy yourself a drink out of the change, too."

"Well, I guess I can stand another sody, thank you."

"Is soda all you drink?"

"That's my limit. You're new here, of course. Folks around Hanksville call me Sody. Half of 'em don't even know my real name."

"Well, Sody, you done me a few favors, and I won't forget." Longarm picked up his change. "Now I better go see if I can get settled in at Mrs. Holcomb's. I'll be around sometime tomorrow."

The next morning, while he waited for the courthouse to open, Longarm put his time to good use. He got the roan from the livery stable where he'd left it and the mule, and scouted the countryside around Hanksville, ignoring the growls of his stomach telling him that breakfast was overdue.

What he saw of the area around Hanksville didn't impress him. On three sides of the town, in an arc from east to north, the land was gullied and ridged as though a giant dragging a massive garden rake had cut grooves from the Dirty Devil River to the bases of the Southern Wasatch peaks that pushed ten and twelve thousand feet into the sky like the pointed turrets of a castle wall.

Beyond the river, to the east and northeast, the land was less broken but equally forbidding. It stretched in a reasonably level slope as far as Longarm could see as he squinted into the early sun. Distantly, the silhouettes of flat-topped mesas and a few isolated, pinnacled buttes stuck fingerlike above the plain.

If a man was stranded here, it'd be just like he was on one of those desert islands I heard about, Longarm mused as he turned the roan away from the riverbank and headed for breakfast. *One damn sure thing. If I was an outlaw on the run, or a man trying to hide two wagonloads of stolen rifles, this is the kind of place I'd head for. It'd be right easy to get lost in this damn cut-up country, and anybody who was of a mind to could make himself real hard to find.*

It's going to take me a little time to find out where everything's at, and there ain't no use in wasting time looking for those missing rifles until I get the lay of the land firm in my mind. Billy Vail could be right, too. Whatever's going on in the courthouse just might be connected up with those guns that dropped out of sight here. So while I get the land straight, I might as well begin seeing what I can find out about the sheriff and the courthouse crew.

Disregarding the advice given him by Sody the night before, Longarm had breakfast at the restaurant. In spite of the barkeep's warning, he found that the Chinese cook turned out about as good a breakfast steak as he'd eaten anywhere else, and the fried eggs weren't intolerably greasy. With food under his belt, Longarm headed for the courthouse.

A sign on the second door opening off the long hall that ran the length of the narrow frame courthouse told him that behind the door he'd find "Howard Perkins, County Treasurer and Clerk." Perkins turned out to be a narrow-faced, wizened man in his late fifties who wore black cambric sleeve-protectors to keep the cuffs of his shirt from picking up dust from the massive ledgers that filled the shelves lining the office. He was standing behind a counter that ran half the width of the office, making an entry in one of the ledgers, when Longarm entered.

"You'd be Mr. Perkins, I guess?" Longarm hazarded.

"I am. What can I do for you, Mr.—Mr.—?" Perkins searched Longarm's face, as though he expected to recognize him.

"Long's my name. If you don't mind, I'd like to take a look at your court records."

"Why—" Perkins hesitated. "If you'll tell me what it is you're looking for, maybe I can help you find it."

"If you'll just haul out your record that shows cases tried and sentences and fines assessed for the past year or so, I think I can manage without troubling you anymore," Longarm replied.

54

Perkins frowned. "That's a somewhat unusual request, Mr. Long. Usually, somebody comes in to find the details of a specific case. It sounds to me as though you're just fishing for information that you have no right to receive."

"Your records are public property, ain't they?"

"Of course, but—"

"Then I've got the same right as anybody else to look at them."

Perkins still hesitated. "Mr. Long, I'm sure you understand that I'm responsible—"

"Oh, sure. I ain't going to run off with anything. All I want is to look," Longarm replied calmly. He still hoped he'd get what he wanted without using the authority of his badge. The longer he could work without disclosing his job, the easier it was going to be to get people to talk to him.

"Well, I suppose it won't do any harm," Perkins said after a moment of thought. "The last year or so, you said?" Longarm nodded. "I'll bring you the current casebook, then. It goes back about eighteen months."

Perkins went to the back of the room and began running his finger down the shelved ledgers. Longarm glanced idly at the ledger the clerk had left open on the counter, and a column of symbols caught his eye. He recognized them at once as cattle brands. He took a step closer to the ledger and ran his eyes along the columns, noting the brands and the ranches for which they were registered. There were, he thought idly, a lot of brands for so few spreads. His examination was interrupted by Perkins, who returned carrying a thick leather-spined ledger.

"I suppose you'll find what you're looking for here," the clerk said a bit tartly. "If you know what you're looking for, that is."

"Like I said, I just want to see the casebook." Longarm took the ledger and carried it to the end of the counter.

A marker between the pages near the back of the thick ledger gave Longarm his starting point. He began turning the pages, going back chronologically. Dis-

55

crepancies and contradictions showed up at once. While trials for petty offenses were concluded with small fines, criminal cases showed that few trials had been held. Case after case bore the notations "continued" or "dismissed." In most instances, no reason was given. Not until Longarm reached the pages that dealt with a period of more than a year earlier did the entries reflect trials, jail sentences, or fines.

He was no stranger to courts and trials, but even a novice at such matters would have noticed such a glaring record of inaction.

Old son, he told himself as his eyes scanned the pages of the ledger, *either the sheriff ain't got sense enough to pound sand down a rat hole when it comes to getting evidence, or somebody's paying him to overlook what counts. If it ain't the sheriff, then it's the county attorney or the judge. One of them's bound to be in some crook's back pocket. And what you got to do is find out which one it is, and then go after whoever's paying him off.*

Absorbed in the ledger, Longarm failed to notice Perkins as he slipped quietly out of the office. He looked up when footsteps thudded along the bare floor of the hall and Perkins came back in, accompanied by a hulking man a full head taller than the wizened clerk, and twice as wide. Twin pistols dangled from the big man's gunbelt, and a deputy sheriff's star was pinned to his leather vest.

"That's the fellow, Bobby," Perkins said in his reedy voice. "He wouldn't tell me what he's after, but I think you and Jess had better find out."

Nodding, Bobby stepped along the counter to stand in front of Longarm. He said, "All right. Suppose you tell me why you're here, mister, prying into things that ain't none of your business."

"All I'm doing is looking at public records," Longarm answered mildly. "There's not any law says I can't, as far as I know."

"Don't talk smart," the big man snapped. "The law in Hanksville's what we say it is. Who in hell are you, and what's your business? And I better get a straight

56

answer, or you'll find yourself behind bars, wishing to God you was outside!"

While the deputy talked, his hand had been creeping slowly up his side. By the time he'd finished delivering his ultimatum to Longarm, his hand was resting on his pistol grips.

Chapter 5

Longarm saw at once that he wasn't going to be able to avoid disclosing his identity any longer. He said, "You don't need to get riled up, and you won't be needing a gun."

"That depends on you, mister. Start talking."

"My name's Long. I'm a deputy U.S. marshal from Denver. I came in here to look over these county records on official business."

Longarm's explanation didn't cause the big man to relax. He asked, "I guess you've got a badge proving you're who you say you are?"

"Naturally. It's in my inside coat pocket. Just don't let your gunhand get nervous and I'll show it to you."

For a moment, the sheriff's deputy stared fixedly at Longarm. Then he nodded. "All right. Take your badge out slow and give me a look at it."

Longarm pulled his coat lapel aside and brought out his wallet. He unfolded it to show the deputy his federal badge.

"How do I know you're the one this belongs to?" the deputy asked. "You could've taken it off somebody else, or even just picked it up on the trail somewhere."

"Now be sensible," Longarm snapped, "I wouldn't be fool enough to show you a badge I haven't got a right to. All you got to do is send a wire to my chief in Denver, if you've got any doubts."

"That's the first smart thing you've said." The deputy nodded. "I'll just have to do that, won't I, to make sure. Come along."

"Where to?"

"Down the hall, to the office."

"What for?"

"Now look here, Long, or whatever your name really is, it's your idea for me to wire Denver and check up on you." The deputy whipped out his revolver. Longarm, holding his coat lapel with one hand, his wallet containing the badge in the other hand, had no chance to draw his own weapon. The deputy raised his voice, his gun steady, his eyes fixed on Longarm. "Howie!"

Perkins hadn't moved from his place just inside the door. He said, "Yes, Bobby?"

"Go inside the counter and get behind this fellow. Take his pistol out of his holster for me."

"Sure, Bobby." The clerk sidled along the counter, giving Longarm a wide berth, got behind him, and lifted the Colt from Longarm's holster. He asked, "What do you want me to do with it?"

"Just hold on to it, for now," Bobby replied. To Longarm he said, "Now march, mister! Go right past me to the door, and I'll be in back of you with my gun while you walk down the hall to the jail. You try anything fancy, I'll cut you down for sure!"

Longarm said nothing. He obeyed orders, turned as he got through the door, and walked quietly down the hall of the long, narrow building. The hall ended at a door marked "Sheriff."

Bobby said as they approached it, "Open up the door and go on inside. I'm still right behind you."

Longarm went through the door. The sheriff's office was like most of those he'd seen in frontier towns. It contained a couple of desks, a half-dozen chairs, and a rack holding rifles and shotguns. The office spanned the entire rear section of the courthouse, much of its space being taken up by three cells that occupied one entire side. The cells were windowless, but partitions of iron bars divided them and separated them from the remaining space. All three of the cells were empty, and the doors of all of them were open.

"Walk right into that middle cell," Bobby commanded.

Longarm obeyed, and before he could turn around,

he heard the door of the cell he'd entered clang shut. He turned to see Bobby selecting a key from the ring that hung from his belt. The big man locked the door.

"There wasn't much use in you showing off like this, you know," Longarm said with deceptive mildness; inside him, his anger was seething. "I'll only be here as long as it takes you to send a wire to Denver and get your answer."

Bobby holstered his revolver and pulled a chair up to the desk nearest the cells. "Well, sir, I think that's going to take a while. Let's see. It'll be a day or so before the sheriff can send anybody over to Sevier, which is as close to here as they've built the telegraph. That's a two-day ride. Then whoever goes has to wait for an answer; that's another day. Then there's two more days for him to get back to Hanksville. It looks like you'll be calling that cell home for the next week. Longer, if we find out you ain't a real deputy U.S. marshal."

"Now wait a minute," Longarm protested. "Before you start making any plans for keeping me locked up, you better get the sheriff in here and let me have a talk with him."

"Oh, I plan to do that, mister. The sheriff'll be along later in the day. He usually comes in after dinner and goes over things with me before he leaves."

Longarm studied the broad, grinning face of the deputy. "I got a feeling you're trying to let me know that you just about run the place for the sheriff."

"You sure nailed it down. You might be smarter'n I figured you to be."

"Maybe I am, maybe I ain't. But I'm smart enough to be wondering where you'll be setting when the sheriff finds out I'm who I told you I am, and has to turn me loose."

"Oh, I've thought about that. I've thought about a lot of things. Like how plain damn foolish you're going to look to everybody that hears about me slapping you in a cell, a big fancy U.S. marshal—*if* you really turn out to be one. Hell, you'll be laughed out of town in half a day, and out of Utah Territory inside of a week!"

Longarm had already thought about that, and realized that it was a situation he couldn't afford. He said, "Maybe you went off half-cocked, Bobby. By the time the sheriff reads the letter I got in my pocket for him, you're likely to find yourself out of a job."

"What kind of letter?" Bobby demanded.

"I think I'll just save it to show the sheriff, when he comes in. It's addressed to him, anyhow. He wouldn't like it a bit if you found out what was in it before he does."

"How come you didn't say nothing about a letter before now?"

"Because you didn't give me a chance to, damn it! All you had in mind was getting me in this cell."

Bobby stood up and came over to the barred door. "I guess I better have a look at that letter."

Longarm backed away. "Not a chance! I'm handing it over to the sheriff when he gets here."

"If you know what's good for you, you'll hand it over now." The big man brought up his hand to the holstered revolver on his right hip, and fingered the gun's butt suggestively. "You don't know me, mister. I get what I want, and it don't make much difference to me how I get it. Now I don't think you're going to argue too much, seeing that I've got the guns and you haven't."

Longarm said nothing for a moment, then he nodded. "You got a point. Only how do I know you won't draw down on me after I hand over the letter?"

"I guess you don't." Bobby thought things over for a moment, then said, "Tell you what, I'll give you this much. You hand over the letter. I'll read it and burn it up before the sheriff gets here. After it's burned, you can do all the talking you want to, but nobody's going to believe you ever had a letter."

Longarm took time to think now. He let a tone of surrender creep into his reply. "Well, I guess I can trust you that far."

"I guess you'll have to. It beats having me take it off your dead body, don't it?"

"I guess." Privately, Longarm thought that once

61

Bobby found he'd been fooled, the deputy was the kind of man who'd enjoy killing him and claiming he'd been forced to shoot Longarm to keep him from escaping. He said, "Looks like you hold all the cards."

"You're damn right I do! Now hand it over."

Longarm took out the army ordnance map he'd been carrying folded in the inside breast pocket of his coat. He held it out to Bobby through the bars of the cell door. The sheriff's deputy got up and came to the door to get it. Just as his hand closed on the folded paper, Longarm snaked out the derringer that was clipped to the end of his watch chain and jammed its muzzle into Bobby's throat. Bobby didn't need a command to freeze. He recognized the feel of the gun's cold steel muzzle.

Longarm let the map fall and, with his free hand, pulled the key ring from the chain that held it on Bobby's belt. He unlocked the cell door and pushed it slowly open, still keeping pressure on the derringer's barrel. Reaching around the edge of the door, he yanked the revolvers from Bobby's holsters and let them fall to the floor, then toed the guns out of reach.

"Now it's your turn to sample the jail," he told the big man. "Get on inside."

Bobby said, "Wait a minute! Damn it, I was only funning you up a little bit. I wanted to see how good a sport you are."

"Like hell." Longarm's voice was cold. "You never had it in your mind to let me get out of that cell alive, did you?"

"It wasn't like that!" Bobby protested. "I was going to let you out right away! I could see you wasn't enjoying the joke."

"Bullshit. Get on in there!" Longarm commanded.

Bobby quickly found himself in the position Longarm had been in a few minutes earlier. He couldn't argue with the gun pressing into his gullet. Dragging his feet as much as he dared, he went into the cell. Longarm slammed the door.

When the metallic ringing of the closing door had

died away, Longarm said, "You look right at home there. Not the first time you been behind bars, is it?"

Bobby said nothing, but his glaring, angry eyes told the whole story of what he was thinking.

Longarm said, "I guess it'll be safe to let you stew in there by yourself for a few minutes, long enough for me to go get my gun back from that clerk's office." He grinned humorlessly. "You're a damn fool, Bobby. I guess you never figured that a man might be carrying two guns without showing both of them off, the way you like to."

When the sheriff's deputy made no reply, Longarm walked up the hall to the clerk's office. Perkins was sitting at his desk, going over the court ledger that Longarm had consulted. He looked up and his eyes goggled.

"Don't get spooked, Perkins," Longarm told the clerk. "I don't put no blame on you for helping your friend. All I want is the Colt you took off of me."

"It—it's on the shelf under the counter there," Perkins stammered. Then, unable to control his curiosity, he asked, "What happened between you and Bobby? Did you—?"

"I guess you might say we come to an agreement." Longarm stepped around the counter and retrieved his revolver. He pointed to the ledger Perkins had been examining. "You take real good care of that book, savvy? I'll be back here after while, and there's some things in it I want you to explain to me."

"I—I'll do the best I can, Marshal." As an afterthought, the clerk asked, "You really are a U.S. marshal, aren't you?"

"I sure as hell am. You saw my badge."

"Yes. But Bobby didn't seem to believe—"

"What Bobby didn't believe ain't here nor there. You believe I'm the real article, don't you?"

"Oh, yes indeed," Perkins replied quickly.

"Fine. Now there's a little favor you can do for me."

"Anything you say, Marshal."

"You put that ledger away. In a safe, if you got one."

"There's a vault down the hall. I can put it in there."

"That'll be just dandy. And I'll ask you to keep quiet about me being in Hanksville. Folks are going to tumble quick enough that I'm here, but I need a little elbow room to work in, for a day or so."

"Whatever you say," Perkins promised.

Longarm didn't put much faith in the clerk's promise. He had no idea yet whether Perkins was involved in whatever underhanded work was going on in the area, but the smell of corruption hung over the town. It was a smell Longarm knew well; he'd sniffed it before, in other places.

He nodded to Perkins and went back to the sheriff's office. Bobby had settled down on the narrow cot that was the only article of furniture the cell contained.

When he saw Longarm, the deputy said, "Aren't you about ready to call our score even, Long? You turned things around on me, and I guess I can't blame you for doing it. But you can't keep me in this cell forever."

"Oh, I never did figure on doing that." Longarm hadn't stopped to pick up Bobby's guns before leaving the office. He did so now, and placed them on the desk. Then he sat down and lit a cheroot. Bobby's eyes followed Longarm's moves with open curiosity. When Longarm sat down and leaned back, Bobby got up and came to the cell door.

"Well?" he asked. "Don't you figure to tell me what you've got in mind?"

"Why, not much of anything. I'm comfortable. I reckon I'll sit here until the sheriff comes in, unless you know of some way to get him here right away."

Bobby considered Longarm's suggestion. He countered, "Look here. If you'll let me out, I'll take you over to the sheriff's house myself. I—" He hesitated before confessing, "I'd hate to have anybody walk in and see me locked up this way."

"I can see where it'd be a mite embarrassing," Longarm agreed gravely. "Struck me that way, when you had me where you are now."

"I made a mistake," Bobby admitted. Longarm could tell that the admission hurt him. The big man went on, "You know, Long, there's not any reason for us to get our backs up at each other."

"If you'll recall, it wasn't my idea," Longarm pointed out.

"Well?" Bobby asked after he'd waited and Longarm had said nothing more. "I've apologized and made you my offer. You going to take it or not?"

"No, I don't reckon I will, Bobby," Longarm said slowly. "At least not right this minute. I want to think about it some more."

"Think fast, then," Bobby said. "I don't like it in here."

"Oh, I can sympathize with you, Bobby," Longarm smiled. "I didn't like it a bit when I was in there."

With a sour grunt, the beefy deputy went back and sat down on the cot. Longarm finished his cheroot and stood up. Bobby stood too, and hurried to the cell door.

"I figured you'd see it my way," the deputy said. "I'll ride over to Jess's house with you, and we can get this thing straightened out."

"That's not exactly what I had in mind," Longarm told him. "You better stay right where you are for a spell longer. I'll ask your friend up in the front to go get the sheriff."

"Howie?"

"If that's his name. Perkins, the clerk."

"Listen, Long, Howie's as bad as an old granny for spreading tales. Keep him outa this, will you?"

"I'd like to oblige you, Bobby, but I just can't see my way clear to. No, I'll ask Perkins to go fetch the sheriff."

"God damn you, Long!" Bobby exploded. "You're just trying to make me look like a fool! You're making a mistake, rubbing my nose in this shitpile! And I promise you, you'll pay for it!"

"Well, now. That's the chance I got to take, ain't it?" Longarm walked up the hall to Perkins's office. The clerk had gone back to his examination of the

65

ledger. Longarm said, "I guess you know where the sheriff lives?"

"Jess Franklin? Of course. His house is over on the—"

Longarm broke in, "I wasn't figuring on going to look for him. I'd take it as a favor if you'd do that. Tell him I'm waiting here with his deputy to talk a little business with him, and I'd be obliged if he'd come join us."

"Why me?" Perkins asked. "Can't Bobby go after Jess?"

"You might say Bobby's tied up for a while."

"If I leave, there won't be anybody to look after the office," Perkins said with a frown.

"Don't let that bother you. I'll leave the door down the hall open and keep my eye on things. If somebody comes in, I'll ask them to wait. It won't take you too long, will it?"

"No. Twenty minutes or so." Perkins stood up. "All right, Marshal. I told you I'd help you any way I can. I'll go."

Perkins slid off his sleeve-protectors, took his hat off the hook beside the door, and went out. Longarm was reaching for the office door to close it before going back to keep an eye on Bobby, when he noticed the court ledger lying open where Perkins had left it. He stepped over to the desk and glanced at the page.

A series of penciled notations had been placed beside three of the entries of cases dismissed or continued. All of them were among the cases that had drawn Longarm's attention earlier. The first entry was a figure, "$100"; the next was a question mark; the third was another figure, "$50." Longarm whistled silently to himself. He sat down and began turning the ledger pages. Most of the cases that had seemed to him to have been handled irregularly bore either question marks or notes of amounts ranging from $25 to $250.

Longarm still hadn't reached the final pages when he heard the outer door of the courthouse open and close. Footsteps sounded on the bare floorboards of the hallway. A woman came into the office and glanced around. She frowned when she saw Longarm sitting behind Perkins's desk.

"Where's Howie?" she asked. Her voice was husky and well-modulated. "I hope he's not sick."

Longarm replied, "He had to step out to do an errand. He'll be back in just a minute, if you don't mind waiting."

"Well, I'm in sort of a hurry. Why can't I just leave this with you, and you give it to Howie. It's just some brands I want him to register. Just tell him Corinne Gaylord left them. He'll know what to do."

Longarm had been studying the girl while she talked. She was a bit taller than average, her features attractively irregular. Her slightly-too-long nose had a hump in the center that kept its line from being too pronounced. Her topaz-colored eyes were set wide apart above high cheekbones that bore the golden tan of one who spent much time outdoors. Her jawline was a bit long and narrow, but her chin squared off and dipped into a dimple instead of coming to the unattractive point seen on so many long-jawed women. Her lips didn't quite match; the upper one was thin, the lower a bit too full.

She wore a man's denim shirt and a corduroy riding skirt, indicating to Longarm that she was one of the few women who had the courage to ride astride instead of using the more conventional sidesaddle. Her boots came to her knees, and an inch of bare flesh showed between her boot tops and the hem of her skirt, another flaunting of convention. Her hips were slim, and her breasts jutted high and full under the loose, billowing shirt. Her hands and the vee of skin that showed in the open throat of her shirt were less deeply tanned than her face.

When she saw Longarm's hesitation, she said, "Look, here's the brand registry laying right on the counter. I'll just tuck this envelope in the book, and you tell Howie that Corinne left it for him. All right?"

"I guess so, ma'am, if it satisfies you to do it that way."

"Oh, I'm sure Howie'll take care of it. There's no need for me to lose time waiting." She tucked the envelope she'd been carrying into the pages of the brand registry. "Now I'll just run down the hall to the sheriff's office. I've got a message for Bobby."

She'd started for the door as soon as she put the envelope in the book, and was out of the office before Longarm could stop her. He followed her, but she'd gone into the sheriff's office before Longarm caught up with her. He went through the door just in time to hear her exclaim, "Bobby! What the hell are you doing locked up? And who's the dude in Howie's office? What's going on around here?"

Bobby saw Longarm in time to change whatever answer he might otherwise have given the girl. He gulped and stammered, then said, "It's just a joke, Reen. A joke me and Long are playing on Jess."

She sensed Longarm's presence behind her, turned and asked, "You'd be Long, I suppose?"

"That's right."

"Don't get upset, Reen," Bobby said. There was urgency in his tone. "I'll explain about it later."

"Meaning you want me to get out of here now?"

"Well, I'd just as soon you didn't stay," Bobby replied.

"All right." The girl turned to go. "But this whole thing looks crazy to me. I guess you'll tell me what it's all about, the next time I come in?"

"Sure, sure," Bobby said.

"I won't let you forget. I'm curious to know just exactly what's going on, and I don't think I'm the only one who'll want to know."

She pushed past Longarm, down the hall. As soon as her footsteps died away, Bobby said angrily, "God damn you, Long! You've really fucked me up good, now! And you'll pay for it! Just as soon as I get out of here, you'll pay for it!"

Chapter 6

"Don't say anything you can't back up," Longarm advised the fuming deputy sheriff. "You're real mad right now. Wait till you cool off."

"Go to hell! You mark down what I say! U.S. marshal or not, I'll even things up and don't you forget it!"

Longarm had faced stares of venom before. He recognized in the deputy sheriff's eyes the quick and concentrated hatred of a man ready to risk his own life to ge revenge for an injury. He decided the best thing he could do was to fade out of the picture until the sheriff arrived, and let Bobby cool off. As long as he stayed in the sheriff's office, it would only feed Bobby's anger. Without replying, Longarm left and went back to the clerk's office to wait.

On the counter, the brand registry book caught Longarm's eye. He picked it up and began looking at the drawings of brands that were registered to the different ranches in the area. There were a surprisingly large number of them. He reached the pages where Corinne Gaylord had stuck the envelope. Its flap was unsealed, and he opened it out of curiosity. The envelope contained a sheaf of currency and a folded sheet of paper. Longarm unfolded the paper; it bore rough sketches in outline of the new brands the girl had come in to register. There were five of them, labeled "Teepee," "House," "Target," "Circle R," and "Diamond S."

Something clicked in Longarm's memory as he looked at the sheet. He went back to the brand registry and began turning the pages. Now and then he stopped to compare a brand registered in earlier years with one of the new ones outlined on the sheet. Absently, he took a cheroot from his pocket and lighted it. When he'd found the last brand he'd been looking for in the book, Longarm laid the sheet of paper on the counter and rummaged through Perkins's desk until he found a fresh sheet of white paper and a pencil. Then he went to work. When he'd finished, he looked at his work and exhaled a long, low whistle.

He'd drawn the old and new brands in two columns, the old ones in the left-hand column, the new ones on the right. On the left, the old brands were the "Crowsfoot," the "Lazy E," the "Circle C," the "Rocking R," and the "Fork S." He studied the sketches.

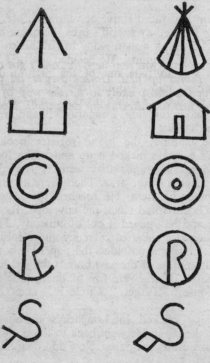

Now ain't that pretty? he asked himself. *Somebody that knows how a running iron's used sure has been studying this book. Why, changing the Crowsfoot to the Teepee and the Lazy E to the House wouldn't take a good running-iron artist two minutes. And the others would be just as easy. Circle C to Target, Rocking R to Circle R, Fork S to Diamond S. Hell, I could have a stab at it myself and do the job as fast, once I got my hand in with a little practice.*

There's only one thing those new brands can mean, his thoughts ran on. *Big-scale rustling. Once I find out where the ranches are that those new brands belong to, I'll have a real deadeye bead on the deal. And two leads to where to start looking—that Gaylord woman and Bobby what's-his-name. As few people as there are around here, it ought not to be too much of a trick to find what I'm looking for. But doing it's going to have to wait until I find out something about those rifles, and dig out what's been going on in the courthouse here. That's what I was sent here for, and I got to clean those two things up first. Unless they're all tied together, which is most likely to be the way of it. It's going to be just like digging up an anthill. You don't see much till you turn over that first spadeful of dirt, then, before you can move away, you're plumb up to your bellybutton in ants.*

Longarm looked at the brand registry again, wondering how many he'd overlooked, but decided there would be time later on to check into that aspect of the case more thoroughly. He restored the paper with the new brands on it to its envelope, and tucked the envelope in the book. He was just putting the paper with his own drawings on it into his pocket when Howard Perkins came in.

"Sheriff Franklin's on his way here," Perkins said. "He ought to be showing up in another five minutes or so. Now, unless there's something else I can do . . ."

"No. I thank you for your help, Mr. Perkins. I know you got work waiting for you, so I'll just go down the hall and wait in his office for the sheriff to get here."

Bobby looked angrily at Longarm when he came in,

but said nothing. Longarm had just settled down at the desk to wait for the sheriff when Perkins poked his head in the door. He said, "I found some money and a list of brands in the registry book when I picked it up to put it away, Marshal. Did somebody—" He saw Bobby for the first time, and his jaw dropped. Staring, he asked the deputy, "Bobby, what're you doing in there? The marshal didn't arrest you, did he?"

Longarm answered quickly, "He's not arrested, Mr. Perkins. You might say he lost a little bet we had between us."

Bobby growled, "Bet, my ass! You pulled a trick on me, Long! You're the one ought to be in here, by rights!"

Perkins looked from Bobby to Longarm, and when neither of them offered any further explanation, he said somewhat uncomfortably, "Well, if it's something between you two, I guess everything's all right. But about that money, Marshal . . ."

"A girl named Corinne Gaylord left it. Said you'd know what she wanted, her brands registered."

"Of course. That's what I thought, but I wanted to be sure. Well . . ." Perkins seemed undecided. "Well, I guess I'd better get back to my work."

As Perkins disappeared, Bobby snarled, "That's another one against you, Long! I told you Howie gossips like an old maid! He'll have it spread all over town that he saw me locked up and you keeping guard over me!"

"Well now, he won't be doing anything but telling the truth, will he?" Longarm asked. "You can't fault a man for that."

Whatever Bobby might have said in reply was lost. Before he could speak, the outside door at the rear of the office opened, and a tall man came in. He was well past his prime, Longarm saw at a glance, and running now to the soft fat that comes so often to big, active men when age slows them down. He saw Longarm sitting at the desk and stopped on the threshold. The opened door hid the cells from him. He said to Longarm, "I suppose you're the U.S. marshal that Howie said was waiting for me?"

72

"That's right, if you're Sheriff Franklin," Longarm replied.

From the cell, Bobby called, "Jesse? That you?"

Franklin came all the way into the office. He looked at his deputy, pressed against the cell door. "Bobby, what the devil are you doing in there?"

"You're the third one that's asked me that fool question, Jesse, and it's starting to get on my nerves. Never mind what I'm doing in here, just get my keys off the desk and let me out!"

Longarm said, "I don't mean to tell you how to run your business, Sheriff, but was I you, I'd hear, first off, why your man's locked up."

"Don't listen to that bastard, Jesse!" Bobby urged. "He's the one that tricked me into this mess!"

"You mean the marshal locked you up?" Franklin asked. His voice wavered with bewilderment.

"He's the only one I see out there besides you," Bobby retorted. "Now will you open this door so I can take care of him?"

"Your man got a few wrong ideas about me, Sheriff," Longarm explained. "I had to lock him up while we got things straight."

"I don't understand what this is all about," the sheriff said to Longarm. "But I sure can't leave Bobby where he is."

"I wouldn't expect you to," Longarm agreed. "And now that you're here, I'd imagine he'll behave himself." He indicated the deputy's matched Smith & Wesson pistols lying on the desk. "But if you don't mind, Sheriff, I'll just make sure that he don't do anything to make more trouble." He pulled the revolvers across the desktop, broke them, and emptied the shells from their cylinders. "Now, seeing as I put Bobby in, I'd say it's only fair for me to let him out." He picked up Bobby's key ring, walked over to the cell, and unlocked the door.

Bobby burst out swinging. Longarm countered his first wild, angry punch with a raised forearm, and before Bobby could set himself for another swing, he grabbed the deputy's wrist and pulled it high behind

73

his back. Bobby was surprised to find that Longarm's strength was more than a match for the muscles that bulged his own big, beefy arms.

"Now, damn it, you two men cut this scuffling out!" Franklin commanded. "Bobby, you cool that hot temper of yours! I want to hear what you got to say, and what the marshal says too!"

Longarm could feel the deputy's muscles relaxing. He released Bobby's arm and stepped away from the big man. Bobby flexed his muscles as though he wanted to keep brawling, but Longarm's grimly set jaw discouraged him after he'd studied it for a moment.

He said in a half-whisper, "We'll wind this up later on, Long. Don't think I'll forget what you did."

Longarm didn't bother to reply. He turned to the sheriff and said, "There ain't much for me to say. Your man threw down on me while I was holding out my badge for him to look at, and shoved me in that cell with his gun in my back. I didn't like it, so I paid him off."

"He played a dirty trick on me!" Bobby protested. "I didn't have a chance!"

"That must've been some trick, Bobby," Franklin said. There was a hint of a smile in his voice, though he kept his face perfectly straight. "You'll have to tell me about it sometime." Turning to Longarm, he said, "I suppose you've got your badge on you, Marshal? I'd like to see it, just in case Bobby's notion was right."

Longarm produced his wallet and flipped it open to show his badge. The sheriff inspected the badge and nodded.

"Seems all right to me," he said. "What district do you work out of?"

"Denver. My chief's Billy Vail."

Franklin turned to Bobby. "You must've had a reason for questioning the marshal's badge. You want to tell me what it was?"

"He didn't act right," Bobby growled. "He snuck into the clerk's office and was trying to pump Howie. If he was legitimate, why didn't he come down here first, and make himself known to me?"

74

"I don't have to account to you for what I do, Bobby," Longarm said. "Or to you, either, Sheriff Franklin. Both of you know that. Now all I'm going to tell you is that I had a reason for doing what I was doing, and we'll just close the book on that."

Franklin nodded slowly. "I guess you're right, Marshal Long. But Bobby's got some right on his side too. Now, if you're here on a federal case, that's fine. You tell us what you want to about it, and we'll forget what went on before."

"Like hell we will!" Bobby snorted.

"You will if I tell you to!" Franklin said.

It was the first assertion of authority Longarm had seen the old man make. It had been obvious to Longarm for quite a while that even though Franklin wore the sheriff's badge, Bobby pretty much ran the show.

Longarm said, "I don't aim to carry things any further. If you're wondering why I'm here, I was sent to track down two wagonloads of army rifles that were stolen quite a while back. I guess you know all about them, don't you?"

"Jesus Christ!" Bobby snorted. "Are we going to have to go back over that damn mess again?"

Franklin shook his head wearily. "We ran out our string on those rifles a long time ago, Marshal. Had the army in here for more than a month. I think it's too late to do anything about them. By now, those rifles have gone down to the Apaches in Arizona, or to the Utes over in Colorado, or maybe down into Mexico, to the revolutionaries. They're not likely to be anywhere close to Hanksville."

"I don't think so, Sheriff. Those rifles were brand-new. Not one of them has turned up, which is pretty likely what would have happened if they'd been sold and put to use."

"That's pretty shaky ground for drawing a conclusion that the shipment hasn't been broken up," Franklin said.

"It's been long enough for some of them to've been put to use. But even if I agreed with you, Sheriff—and I ain't saying I do or don't—I was sent here to try to

75

find those rifles, and this is where I got to start from," Longarm said.

"Go ahead and start, then," Bobby said. The presence of the sheriff had toned down the temper of the bulky deputy. "Just don't look for me or Jess to waste any of our time helping you on a case we closed a long time ago."

"I wasn't figuring on asking you for any help," Longarm replied. "I'm used to handling my cases my own way, by myself."

Sheriff Franklin added hurriedly, "Of course, anything we can give you a hand with, we'll be glad to." He turned to his deputy and cautioned, "Now you remember that, Bobby."

Bobby made no reply, but Longarm hadn't expected him to. The federal man stood up and said, "Thanks, Sheriff. I look to be around Hanksville for a while. If I run into something and need information, I'll drop in and ask."

"You do that," Franklin answered.

Longarm was beginning to feel hungry. His morning had been a busy one, and if he had his way, his afternoon would be equally hectic. He dropped in at the saloon in search of a bite of free lunch to stay him until supper. Sody set out the opened bottle of Maryland rye without asking.

"You feel like joining me?" Longarm asked as he poured a shot for himself.

"Thanks, but I just had a sarsaparilla. Later, maybe," the barkeep replied. He noticed Longarm surveying the interior of the saloon. "You looking for somebody special? Or just looking?"

"Just looking. Thought you might have a bite of food to go with a man's drinks."

"In Hanksville, mister?" Sody chuckled. "Not likely. Free lunch is something a saloon in a big town's got to have, because there's another saloon across the street, or on the next corner, or maybe right next door. All of 'em are selling the same whiskey, so it's the free lunch table that brings the trade in. In Hanksville, they

76

come in here to drink, because there's noplace else to go."

Longarm smiled. "Makes sense. Well, I'll go across the street and get a bite. Then I'll come back over for another sip out of my bottle."

Longarm hurried through his meal. Right at the moment, information was more important to him than food, and the saloon was one of the few places where he could hope to get the kind of leads he was now looking for.

"You lived in Hanksville long?" he asked Sody, when the barkeep poured his after-lunch shot of rye.

"Maybe too damn long," Sody replied. "I'm beginning to feel at home here."

"I guess you're acquainted with the sheriff?"

"Jess? Sure. He was here a long time before I showed up, of course. He's one of the real oldtimers. Been sheriff as long as most people remember."

"It looks to me like he's getting a mite long in the tooth to hold a job like that," Longarm suggested.

"He doesn't get around as much as he used to," Sody confirmed. "But don't ever misjudge old Jess. Why, from what I hear, him and Judge Walton made this place fit to live in."

"Judge Walton? Is he still the judge?"

"Oh no. He put himself out to grass four or five years ago, moved out a ways west of here. Said he didn't want to do anything the rest of his life but loaf."

"But the sheriff stayed on?"

"Why, I don't expect anybody but Jess Franklin could get elected sheriff here. Not that anybody's had the gall to try."

"Keeps a pretty tight rein on things, does he?"

"Well . . ." Sody hesitated before going on, "Maybe not as tight as he used to. But his deputy holds down the lid right tight. Bobby does the hard riding and jobs like that, things Jess is getting too old to handle."

"Are there some folks named Gaylord that own a ranch around here?" Longarm asked.

Sody frowned and shook his head. "No. There's no Gaylord spread that I recall ever hearing of. Why?"

77

"Just curious. I picked up the name somewhere, nosying around town. Got the idea they had a ranch close by."

"There's not all that many ranches for me not to know their name, if they live within twenty miles," Sody said.

"You'd know, I guess." Longarm poured himself another drink. "How about a ranch using the Target brand?"

"Target?" Again the barkeep frowned. "Now that's another name I never heard of."

"Try the Diamond S," Longarm suggested.

Sody's expression brightened a bit. "Sim Haygood's Fork S spread's about fourteen miles south, along the Dirty Devil." Then his frown returned. "There's not any Diamond S, though."

"I guess I misread the brand," Longarm said casually. Then he asked with equal ease, "Most of the ranches lay along the river to the south, I reckon?"

"Some of them. Not all. You'll find some up north along the Muddy, and there's others up that way on Starvation Creek and Last Chance Creek." Sody jerked a calloused thumb in a nebulous direction over his shoulder.

"Not enough water to carry a herd to the east, I suppose?" Longarm pressed. "Riding in, the country to the east looked mighty dry."

"It might surprise you, if you—" Sody stopped short. Longarm waited, but the barkeep did not finish what he'd started to say. Instead, he fixed the lawman with a suspicious gaze. "For a man who says he's not looking for a job, you're sure curious about the ranches close by. You wouldn't be looking for somebody special, would you?"

"No. Just making talk," Longarm replied innocently.

Sody looked around to be sure there was no one close enough to them to hear, then leaned forward conspiratorially. "I'll give you a friendly tip. If I was you, I'd be careful not to act too nosy. Folks here don't like prying strangers. You drop the wrong question in the

78

wrong place, and you just might find yourself with more trouble than you'd want."

"Present company excepted, of course?"

"Sure. In my business, I don't start trouble for anybody. But I try not to get into it myself, by talking too much."

"Stands to reason," Longarm agreed. "Well, I won't bother you with but one more question, Sody. That Judge Walton you spoke of. If I was to look, where do you think I might run into him?"

"Not likely here in town—he just doesn't come into Hanksville any more. But he lives to the west, on Sweetwater Creek, about a mile or two up from the mouth. Just follow the Fremont River trail west. Sweetwater's the first creek."

"Thanks," Longarm said. "If I ride out that way, I might just drop in. He sounds like he might be a real interesting man to talk to."

Chapter 7

Before starting for Judge Walton's, Longarm paid a second visit to the courthouse. He knew he'd risk encountering Bobby, and didn't especially want to meet the deputy sheriff again until Bobby had cooled down from the humiliation of their morning set-to, but there was no other source for the names he needed to learn before talking to the judge. Entering by the front door, Longarm went quickly into Perkins's office.

"Marshal Long. I didn't expect to see you back so soon," the clerk said.

"Didn't expect to be back. But I need to take a look at that brand book of yours."

"Of course." Perkins came up to the counter where Longarm had stopped, reached under it, and groped for a moment. Then his eyebrows rose in surprise and he bent over to look. "That's funny. It doesn't seem to be here."

"It was laying there on the counter earlier."

Perkins scratched his thatch of white hair vigorously. "Yes. I entered those brands that Corinne Gaylord left for registering, and then put the book away."

"You been here in the office all the time?"

"Except for a half-hour or so. I went home to eat."

"You lock your door when you go out that way?" Longarm asked.

"Not at noon. I lock it when I leave for the day, of course."

"Which means just about anybody could've come in and helped himself to it, I guess."

"But who'd want to?" the clerk asked bewilderedly.

"Not much way to tell, is there?"

"No, I suppose not." Perkins brightened somewhat as he added, "Of course, there's no great harm done. Whenever I register a brand, I send a copy of the certificate to the state capital. I can always get them to give me duplicates, and replace the book."

"You sent certificates for the latest brands you registered?"

"No. I was going to do that before I finished today, but I didn't get to it before noon."

Longarm grunted. "How long you figure it's going to take you to get copies from the capital?"

"A month or more. Probably more like six weeks."

"Well, you look around and see if it turns up. I'll stop by in a day or so to see if you've found it. If you ain't, I'll still get along without looking at it." Then, as an afterthought, he asked Perkins, "What about that court ledger I asked you to put away? You didn't overlook doing that, did you?"

"No, Marshal. I put it in the vault, just as you asked me to."

"Good. See that it stays there, will you? I'll look in on you again in a day or two."

Riding along the trail that paralleled the Fremont River west of Hanksville, Longarm pondered the disappearance of the brand registration ledger.

There's three people—four, counting Perkins—who might want that book to up and vanish the way it did. Bobby's the most likely one, but I wouldn't put it past that Gaylord woman to've come back in and lifted it. There's just an outside chance it could've been the sheriff himself, but my money's on Bobby. Now all I got to do is find out if the sheriff put him up to it. Once I get that far, maybe a lot of other things will open up for me to cover before I can pin anything down. But maybe I'll gain a little on them, after I've jawboned a mite with Judge Walton.

From Hanksville, where the vegetation was scanty and the ground stone-hard and a sandy light tan in color, the character of the countryside changed gradually as Longarm rode up the rim of the Fremont River valley. The shade of the soil grew darker by subtle degrees, until it became golden brown streaked with orange yellow, and then light chocolate. Patches of twisted, stunted juniper began to show here and there, and clumps of sagebrush. Where Sweetwater Creek flowed into the Fremont, the earth's tone deepened still more, and low-bowing salt cedars straggled along the water's edge.

Just before he saw in the distance the outline of a low, sprawling house, built, as were those in Hanks-ville, of irregular rectangles chipped from the thin, stratified native stone, the first scattering clusters of grass appeared. Beyond the house, farther up Sweet-water Creek, he could see that the grass grew progressively thicker.

Longarm's approach must have been noticed by those inside the house, for while he was still a half-mile distant, a man came out of its front door and took up his station beside the wide, squat building. For a desert dwelling, the house was surprisingly large, Longarm noted. Behind the house there was a barn, and beyond the barn lay a small corral where several horses and two or three mules plodded aimlessly around. A spring buckboard stood between the house and the barn. At one side of the dwelling, the corner of a garden was visible. Along the banks of the creek, a dozen or so steers grazed.

When Longarm's unhurried pace brought him closer to the house, he saw that the man waiting beside the door was an Indian or a Mexican; he was still too far to tell which. Even when he reined in at the hitch rail in front of the dwelling, he could not pin down the man's origins. He nodded to the man and asked, "Is this Judge Walton's place?"

To his surprise, the man made no reply. Instead, from inside the house, a harsh voice called, "This is it, all right. Who are you and what do you want?"

"My name's Long. I'm a deputy U.S. marshal out of Denver, and if the judge is here, I'd like to visit with him a few minutes," Longarm replied. He scanned the front of the house, trying to find the source of the voice, but the windows were covered with tightly stretched pieces of cheesecloth tacked to the window frames, which effectively concealed the interior.

"I guess you've got identification?" the voice from within the house asked.

"My badge, if that'll satisfy you."

"Hand it over to Mudo. He'll bring it in for me to look at," the unseen man ordered.

Then he said several words in a language that sounded familiar, but was one that Longarm didn't understand. The man who'd been standing at the door came over to the hitch rail. Longarm took out his wallet, unfolded it, and gave it to the man he now supposed was an Indian, who vanished inside. In a moment the Indian reappeared, pushing a wheelchair. In it sat an old man, thin to the point of emaciation. He had a Tennessee hawk nose and a fiercely jutting mustache. His hair was as white as his mustache, and much thinner. A shotgun lay across his knees.

"I apologize for all the mumbo-jumbo, Marshal," he said. "But the reason I'm in this damned wheelchair is because a few years ago a rider stopped just about where you are now. I came out before I'd found out who he was, and got a bullet that broke my spine. I'm Frank Walton. Light on down and come inside where it's cool."

Longarm said, "I'm pleased to meet you, Judge." He dismounted, looped the roan's reins around the hitch rail, and followed the judge inside.

"Sit down anywhere," Walton told him. "You've obviously got something you want to talk with me about, or you wouldn't have ridden all the way out here from wherever you started. Hanksville, I'd imagine it was?"

Longarm nodded. "Guess I better begin at the beginning."

"I've always found that's a good place to start," the judge said affably, handing the shotgun to the Indian, who placed it on pegs driven into the wall beside the door. The pegs were low enough for the judge to reach the gun from his wheelchair. He went on, "It's a dry ride out here. How about a drink before you begin talking? Whiskey, brandy, or coffee?"

"Right now, a cup of coffee'd taste mighty good."

Walton gave a quick command to Mudo, who disappeared through a door at the back of the sparsely furnished room.

"If you're wondering about Mudo," the old man said, "I—well, I guess you might say I inherited him during my last year in office. He was brought in almost dead. His tongue had been cut out and he was wandering around by the forks of the Colorado and the Green. I suppose it was some kind of Indian punishment, but he'll never be able to tell us. He's either Ute or Paiute—he understands Ute. He had no place to go, so I took care of him, kept him on as a sort of man-of-all-work after he recovered. Turned out to be lucky for me. If it hadn't been for him, I couldn't've stayed here after I got shot."

"You never found out who shot you? Or why?" Longarm asked.

Walton shook his head. "I can guess why, of course. I sat on the bench a long time, sentenced more than a few men to hang, and sent a lot more to the pen. I suppose it was a friend of one of them, out for revenge. I never had any way of knowing who. All I got was a glimpse of the bastard before he started shooting."

Mudo came back carrying coffee cups, a graniteware coffeepot, and a sugar bowl on a tray. He set the tray on a table, filled the cups, and offered Longarm the sugar bowl. Longarm shook his head.

Judge Walton said, "You can talk in front of Mudo. I don't know how much he understands, but he'll never repeat anything he hears. Go on, Long. What's brought you here?"

As briefly as he could, Longarm sketched his assignment, then recounted his experiences since his arrival in Hanksville. When he'd finished, Walton sat staring at him, a frown deepening the creases of age that crisscrossed his forehead.

"Jess Franklin's a damned fool," he said flatly. "He should have stepped down for a younger man a long while back. I don't see him very often, you understand, not anymore. It's been seven or eight months since he's come out to visit me, and six months since I saw him, the last time I was in Hanksville. What sort of shape would you judge him to be in, Marshal?"

"Oh, he didn't seem to be in bad shape. Not what I'd call young and spry, but he moved all right, and everything he said made sense. And he snapped the whip good enough at that deputy of his to keep him in line."

"I'm not suggesting that Jess is senile, or anything like that," Walton said. "But I could tell, the last time I saw him, that he'd slowed down a lot. Not as alert as he used to be. Lost his aggressiveness." He grunted sourly. "Happens to all of us, when we get past a certain age. I've seen it. You have too."

"Yes, sir, I suppose I have," Longarm agreed. "Except for being shot up, though, I'd say you've held up better than most."

"Maybe. I don't control my temper as well as I used to. I say a lot of things about a subject before I think them out. But that's beside the point. I've got you wandering away from what you came to talk about, and I guess that's more evidence that I've slipped, just like Jess. Now you say the court records show too many cases being dismissed, too many being continued indefinitely. What are you using as a standard of comparison?"

"I know I don't look on the law the way a judge does, but I've spent enough time in court to know about how many cases get finished up, provided whoever made the arrest did his job right in getting evidence. And in the ledger, I couldn't tell a lot of times exactly why a case was dismissed or continued, or who was responsible for it. But my guess is that about half the cases that come up at a court session ought to be closed."

Walton nodded. "More. Two-thirds, unless the prosecutor and arresting officer are incompetent." As an afterthought, he added, "Or crooked."

"One other thing struck me about that record too,

85

Judge. It was the *little* cases that got closed. Petty theft, little five- and ten-dollar burglaries, fights and stuff of that sort. The big ones, the murders and horse and cattle stealing, they're the ones that got put over."

"When you say 'closed,' I assume you mean by a defendant being found guilty and sentenced, or innocent and released?"

Longarm nodded. Then he said, "Maybe not everybody in my kind of job feels like I do, Judge Walton, but I don't arrest a man until I've got hard evidence that'll stand up in court. It might be that's what's wrong in Hanksville. That deputy the sheriff's got working for him—"

"Bobby Mason?" Walton interrupted. Longarm nodded. The judge went on, "Not worth a damn, Mason isn't. Jess wouldn't have had a man of his sort working for him a few years ago."

"Mason seems to be pretty much in charge of everything, but he did toe the line when the sheriff called him down. And feeling like I do about him, I don't want to misjudge him, not until I've found out about the prosecutor and the judge."

"And that's what you've come to me to find out?"

"I figure you're about the only man I *can* find out from. Nobody there in Hanksville seems to want to talk about anything."

"They always have been that way, tight-mouthed where strangers are concerned. Well, Marshal," the old man said after a thoughtful pause, "if you're worried about Jess Franklin being tied up in anything that's not strictly legal and right, you don't need to be. I can't say the same for Bobby Mason, but then, I've never had much use for him. I feel about like you do, though. I'd hate to let my personal dislike lead me to misjudge a man."

"Which leaves me the prosecutor and the judge. And the clerk, Perkins."

"Howard Perkins is a born go-alonger. He's with whoever's on top, or in charge. He's not a leader, and that's what you're looking for. I'd be inclined to trust Judge Harris. He's not part of Hanksville, never has been. He lives over in Torrey, which is far enough away from Hanksville to make him independent of the town. As I understand it, Harris only goes into Hanksville on court days."

"Well, you've narrowed it down to the deputy and the county prosecutor," Longarm said when Judge Walton fell silent. "I got my own opinion about Bobby Mason. What about the prosecutor?"

"I think you might look at him pretty closely, Long. I don't suppose you'd be familiar with the plays of William Shakespeare?"

"I don't have much time to watch play-acting," Longarm admitted.

"No, I suppose you wouldn't. Well, in one of his dramas, Shakespeare described one of the characters as having 'a lean and hungry look,' and went on to add that 'such men are dangerous.' That's about the way I'd speak of Victor Jensen."

Longarm chewed pensively on the edge of his mustache, then said, "If this Jensen and Bobby Mason was to be working as a team . . ."

"They'd be able to manipulate the evidence in a trial to make it go just about the way they wanted it to," Walton said, "given the situation there in Hanksville. A judge who's in town only when court's in session can't always see much outside his courtroom. And a sheriff who's retired for all practical purposes, who leaves the actual operation of the job to a deputy, can't always see past the deputy."

Longarm took his time in replying. He tried to frame his words carefully. "What you're saying to me is that you think the judge and sheriff don't know what's going on behind their backs. Ain't that about the size of it?"

Walton smiled. "You're a plainspoken man, aren't you, Marshal? I used to be myself, but I told you I was feeling my years. Yes, I was saying just that, in a roundabout way."

"As long as I understand you, that's what I'm interested in."

"How much my opinion's going to help you is something I don't know," Walton went on. "You've got other business here than trying to straighten out local problems."

"Meaning I'd be better off putting my time into running down those missing rifles than mixing into the court and the rustling I suspect is going on?"

"I had that in mind, yes. Not that I'm trying to discourage you . . ."

"I wouldn't say I'm wasting my time on those other things, Judge. I've got a real strong hunch all of it ties up together."

Squinting thoughtfully, the old judge said, "What that leads to is a pretty obvious conclusion. There must be a good-sized gang of criminals with headquarters somewhere close to Hanksville."

"That's the only thing I can see that'd fit," Longarm agreed.

"If there is a gang of any size, I never did see any evidence of it when I was on the bench," Walton said.

"You said you've been retired five years," Longarm pointed out. "And spent most of your time right out here, since that fellow shot you. There's no reason you'd have heard about it."

"I suppose not. I do know about the Outlaw Trail; it's been there as long as I can remember."

"Sure. I don't guess there's an outlaw or a lawman west of Kansas who don't know about that. Starts up at the Milk River in Canada and swings through Montana to the Devil's Roost. Goes around Bozeman and down to the place they call the 'Hole in the Wall,' around where Wyoming and Utah and Colorado all come together. Goes along then to Green's Hole, and south along the Green east of Hanksville, on down into New Mexico's Cimarron country, and then into Texas, someplace close to Tascosa. Branches off there. One leg goes east into the Indian Nation, the other one down to Hell's Half-Acre in the Big Bend country. Then it peters out across the Rio Grande, in Mexico."

"You know more about it than I do, Marshal," the old judge said, smiling. "But you know, too, that it's always been just a trail, and aside from the Hole in the Wall and Green's Hole, and I'd guess the place you named Hell's Half-Acre, the men using it never have stopped very long anywhere else."

"One thing I've learned in my business, Judge. It don't make much never-mind how hard a man on the run's being pushed, he can't keep on a hard trail all the time. There's got to be places where he can stop to rest—places where he's safe."

"God knows, there are plenty of places around here where a hundred outlaws would be safe," Walton said. "They could hole up in some canyons I know about, where there's a creek flowing the year around, or in a box canyon that's got a good spring in it."

"You'd know the country better than I do," Longarm told Walton. "You've been here a long time."

"Yes. I was active when I was younger and could get around. Spent a lot of time in the saddle. I'd say I know the country around Goblin Valley as well as anybody, better than a lot."

Longarm took out his army ordnance map. "You remember it good enough to mark some of those valleys and box canyons for me, Judge? It'd save me a sight of time I'd have to waste looking for them."

"My memory's still good, Marshal. Let me see your map."

Judge Walton unfolded the map and spread it on his knees. He studied it for a moment, then gestured to Mudo, who'd been hunkered down against the wall, and made a motion with his hand to indicate writing. The mute brought him an inkwell and a pen. Walton bent over the map, tracing distances with a forefinger, stopping now and then to dip the pen in the inkwell and mark a spot. He gave the map a final look and handed it back to Longarm.

"I just marked the places that seemed most likely," he said. "And I'd better warn you, some of them aren't going to be easy to find."

"I didn't expect they would be. The kind of spots I'm looking for are the ones a man could pass by within a pistolshot and never suspect they were there." Longarm stood up. "Judge, I do thank you for your help. I'll try not to bother you again."

"It's a pleasure, not a bother, for me to have a visitor, Marshal. You come back anytime you feel like it." Walton glanced out the nearest window, where the sky was beginning to show pink. "If you're not in a hurry to get back to Hanksville, why don't you have supper and stay the night?"

Longarm smiled regretfully. "I'd be honored to, Judge, except that I feel like I'd best ride on back tonight, so I can get an early start in the morning."

"Maybe next time, then," Walton said. There was clear disappointment in his voice.

"If that's an open invitation, I'll take you up on it." Longarm walked over to the wheelchair and shook hands with the old man. "If you have anything that calls you to go into town soon, I'm staying at Mrs. Holcomb's."

Longarm took his time in riding back to Hanksville. Shortly after he started, he took out the map Judge Walton had marked, and guided the roan with the pressure of his knees while he studied it. There were a dozen places the judge had marked with crosses, places that the Army topographers who drew the original map hadn't identified with any specific details of landmarks or formations. He gave up when the failing light caused the lines to blur and swim, and put the map into his pocket. Darkness overtook him shortly after he reached the river, and he let the roan set his own pace until three or four pinpoints of brightness indicated the town.

By then his stomach was grumbling, and he sped up to get to his boardinghouse before the supper hour ended. Mrs. Holcomb was clearing the table when he walked in. The landlady looked up and sniffed, then her dour expression changed into a smile.

"You sit down, Marshal," she said. "I told you when you come here that I keep regular serving hours in my dining room, but I'll make an exception for you. I heard about you giving that Bobby Mason his come-uppance, throwing him in a cell in his own jail. I'll just be happy to serve you dinner, even if you are late."

"Sounds like you don't have much use for Bobby,"

Longarm said as he hung his hat on the rack inside the door.

Mrs. Holcomb sniffed again. "Not just me. I don't know anybody in Hanksville who does. Now you sit right down, and I'll get some hot gravy and meat from the kitchen, and some fresh biscuits."

When the landlady came back in, Longarm asked her, "How'd you happen to hear about the run-in I had with the deputy?"

"My lands, it's all over town! And everybody's just laughing up their sleeve about it. Why, you're the most popular man in Hanksville tonight, Marshal Long."

"Well, it really wasn't such a much," Longarm said, spearing a piece of steak with one hand and reaching for a hot biscuit with the other. "I'd be obliged if you and the rest of the folks didn't blow it up into something bigger than it was."

"Never you mind about that. There's nobody around here who really likes Bobby. He's been riding for a fall for a long time, but you're the first man who's come along who could give it to him." Mrs. Holcomb gave the table a final inspection. "Now I've got chores to attend to in the kitchen. You make a good meal. If you want anything else, just call me."

Longarm ate his solitary supper in contemplative silence. He'd been concerned that the brush he'd had with the deputy might create talk, a stir that would keep Mason's anger hotly alive. Still, he didn't see any other course that he could have followed. If he hadn't reversed their positions, Hanksville would be laughing at him instead of Mason. He finished his meal, stood up, and put on his hat.

Well, old son, he told himself, *looks like you got a mean one coming up. And putting off facing a mean thing never made it go away. If it's going to happen, it might as well be tonight as tomorrow or the next day.*

He left the boardinghouse and walked along the edge of the unpaved street toward town and the saloon.

Chapter 8

When Sody saw Longarm come into the crowded saloon, the barkeep hurried to the front corner of the bar and motioned for Longarm to join him.

"Where in God's name you been, Marshal? And why didn't you tell me who you are and what you're doing in Hanksville?" Sody asked, without drawing breath between the two questions.

"I been out in the country. And I didn't figure there was much reason to say anything about my job. I figured everybody'd find out about that soon enough."

"Well, I won't say I didn't begin to suspect something, what with the kind of questions you been poking at me," Sody said.

"Does it make that much difference?" Longarm asked.

"It don't to me. It might be different to some folks."

Longarm looked around the saloon. The bar was fairly solidly lined, and most of the tables in the long, narrow interior were occupied by two or three men. There were more people in the place than Longarm had seen in his previous visits.

He asked Sody, "Word got around, did it?"

"That's all I've heard since right after you left today. How in hell did you get Bobby in that cell? Unless you mind telling me."

"Talking's dry work," Longarm replied, evading an immediate reply. "You might reach that bottle of mine off the backbar and get yourself a sarsaparilla, if you want one. Maybe after I've wet my whistle, I'll feel more like gabbing a bit."

"Sure." Sody took a step away, then turned back

long enough to say, "I'd keep an eye on the door, if I was you. Bobby's been in here twice this evening. I look for him to try again."

"Thanks. Maybe I'd be better off sitting at one of those tables in the back."

"Why don't you? You'll get a clear look at the door from back there." Sody brought the bottle of rye Longarm was working down, and a glass, and put them on the bar. "I guess I can wait for you to tell me how you corralled Bobby."

"You don't act like the idea of him coming in looking for me upsets you much," Longarm commented.

"I'm not enjoying the idea of trouble, if that's what you're hinting at," Sody told him. "But if something's going to happen between you, it might as well be here as anyplace."

Longarm nodded. He took the bottle and glass and walked slowly back to the one unoccupied table at the rear of the saloon. He sat down, facing the door, and poured himself a drink.

From the moment Longarm had entered the saloon, whispers had begun to circulate along the bar and around the tables. In isolated, ingrown towns like Hanksville, strangers stood out, and it was obvious that the word of the clash between the U.S. marshal from Denver and the local deputy sheriff had sped through the community via the backyard grapevine.

For a few moments after Longarm sat down at the back table, nobody moved. Then, almost imperceptibly, the men began shifting. Those close to the door moved away from it. Those between the door and the back table Longarm now occupied began edging their tables back to clear a wide aisle down the center of the building. Conversation died away. The loud voices and frequent laughter that had filled the air when Longarm first came in were no longer heard. The atmosphere was like that of a church during the few moments of restless movement and diminishing conversation when the minister walked to the pulpit to begin his sermon.

Longarm was unruffled by the movement and the silence. He'd been in similar situations before. He paid no attention to the crowd, but took his time in lighting a cheroot and savoring his rye between puffs. He emptied his glass in slow, deliberate sips, and refilled it. Without making it obvious that he was doing so, Longarm never let his eyes leave the open door of the saloon completely. Even when he seemed to be looking to one side or the other, a corner of one eye was always watching the doorway.

After the first few minutes of waiting, time stopped having any meaning. There was no wall clock in the saloon, and Longarm was too experienced to have a hand engaged in something as unessential as taking out his watch; he closed his mind to the passage of time, and sat waiting imperturbably. Sooner or later, Bobby would show up.

It might have been a half-hour, or it might have been two hours after Longarm sat down at the back table, before the big deputy appeared in the doorway. The aisle down the middle of the saloon gave Longarm a clear view of the door, just as it gave Mason an unobstructed view of Longarm sitting at the table. The deputy took the step that brought him inside.

"Long!" he called.

There was not a whisper in the saloon.

Longarm nodded calmly. "Good evening, Bobby."

A look of surprise began forming on Mason's face. It was evident that he'd expected Longarm to leap up, and that he'd been set to draw the moment he saw Longarm start moving.

"You did your best to make a fool out of me today," Bobby said loudly. "I don't aim to stand for it, Long!"

"Well, if you're tired of standing up, come set down and we'll talk about it," Longarm replied.

On the deputy's face, the look of perplexity grew.

"Damn it! You know what I mean!" he said. There was smothered anger, but bewilderment as well, in his tone.

"Guess maybe I got a case of the stupids tonight," Longarm said. His voice was casual. He might have been commenting on the weather. "Maybe you better explain what you mean."

"You got a sixgun on under your coat," Bobby said. "I know that much. And any man that wears a pistol knows what it means when he gets called."

"Are you real sure you want to call me, Bobby?" Longarm asked solicitously. "Because I sure don't want to have to kill you."

"You stand up and move to draw, and we'll damn quick see who's going to kill who!" Bobby grated.

"I don't feel like standing up right now," Longarm said.

"Damn it to hell! You're just inviting me to shoot you out of that chair!"

"Now you wouldn't want to do that, Bobby," Longarm said in a tone that a schoolteacher might use in chiding a mischievous pupil.

"You're forcing me to!" Bobby retorted.

"No, Bobby. You're wrong about that. I ain't forcing you to do one single blessed thing."

"You've got all of Hanksville laughing at me behind my back!" Bobby said. A querulous note had crept into his voice. "Next thing, they'll be laughing in my face! I can't have that!"

"Just take a look around you," Longarm invited. "You won't see anybody in here laughing." He decided it was a safe time for him to move.

Very deliberately, he picked up the cheroot he'd placed on the table and put it in his mouth. He took no chances, though. His movements were as deliberate as though he were underwater, and he kept Bobby's eyes locked with his own. He picked up the match he'd laid beside the cheroot, and flicked his thumbnail across its head. He was careful to keep his hand well away from his eyes and to slit his eyelids against the glare of the flame as he drew on the cigar until its tip glowed. He flipped the still-burning match off to one side. Bobby's head turned involuntarily to follow the arc the tiny flame made through the air.

Longarm said sadly, "You made a mistake then, Bobby. If I'd wanted to cut you down, I'd've had time to draw and kill you while you were watching that match drop to the floor."

"Like hell you would!" the muscular deputy blustered. His loudness didn't hide the worry that underlay his words.

Longarm pressed his advantage. He hoped nobody in the place would move or laugh and spoil things. He risked a quick look at the tables and along the bar. Every man he saw was standing open-jawed and frozen, too engrossed in what was going on to move, almost too engrossed to breathe.

He said quickly, "You might as well make up your mind to it, Bobby. I don't aim to get into a shootout with you. I wasn't out to make you look little. And I don't think that little dispute you and me had this morning's enough to get either one of us killed over."

"I've got my pride to hold up!" Bobby almost shouted.

"Now you sure as hell won't build up your pride by shooting me while I'm setting down and telling you flat-out I won't draw against you," Longarm said quietly.

"Then stand up and face me like a man!"

"That wouldn't prove a thing," Longarm told him in a flat voice. "Now let's put an end to this palaver. You don't want to draw on me, and I've said loud and clear that I won't draw on you. Why don't you just walk over here and set down with me and have a drink, and we'll talk to each other sensible."

For a moment, Longarm was afraid he'd rushed things too much. Bobby's lips twitched and his eyes slitted. He opened his mouth to say something, then reconsidered, and closed it. He glared down the length of the room at Longarm, his Adam's apple jerking nervously in his bull-like throat. Longarm knew that in that moment Bobby was closer to drawing than he'd been when he first came through the saloon door.

Then the moment passed. Bobby shouted, "How in hell can you fight a man who won't fight back?"

Whirling, he ran out of the saloon into the darkness.

Slowly the tension ebbed away. Conversations were resumed, half-finished drinks gulped down. Longarm had his drink already poured. He swallowed half of the liquor in the glass, took a quick puff on his cheroot, and swallowed the rest of the rye. Then he refilled the glass. At the bar, Sody was working furiously to refill everyone else's glasses. Longarm sat calmly, sipping his whiskey, and ignored the stares that were turned his way.

Well, old son, he was telling himself silently, *you pulled that one off, but it got a little bit flukey there toward the end. And when you step outside, you better remember to look both ways, and to keep an eye over your shoulder whenever you walk out in the dark. And you'll likely have to kill him later on, when it sinks in how you talked him out of a showdown. But you can cross that bridge when and if you come to it.*

Longarm reined in when the dropoff appeared directly in front of the roan. The horse was tired, and so was he. He'd been in the saddle four days now, and there hadn't been a water hole where he'd stopped for the night, so the desert dust lay thick on his face.

Below him, at the bottom of the wall of the canyon that dropped almost vertically, he could see the gleam of running water. Longarm scanned the canyon wall, looking for a place the horse could navigate to the bottom. He didn't see one, so he turned the roan and rode slowly, paralleling the rim, looking for a place to descend.

Longarm had left Hanksville early on the morning following his facedown with Bobby Mason. Even if he hadn't planned to go, he'd have gotten away from Hanksville for a few days after forcing Mason to back away from a shootout. He didn't want another confrontation with Bobby until the sting of his retreat had faded from the big deputy's mind.

Longarm had set his course by the markings Judge Walton had made on the ordnance map. He'd set out to circle the oval saucer of Goblin Valley, the shallow saucerlike depression that lay between the southern spur of the Wasatch range, which jutted down the middle of Utah Territory, and the deep canyon carved by the Green River just before it merged with the mighty Colorado. Goblin Valley lay between the rounded, bulging rise of the San Rafael Swell at the foothills of the southern Wasatches, and the river canyons to the west. Around the valley's rim, the Fremont and Big Muddy Rivers cut their courses to the southwest, and on the opposite side, the San Rafael flowed into the Green.

Longarm's course had been an erratic one, dictated by the flow of the rivers and the markings on his map. While he'd prudently stayed close to water, some of the springs and box canyons marked by the old judge were three or four miles from the rivers. He'd been forced to zigzag back and forth as he'd followed the base of the San Rafael Swell in an irregular path to the northeast after leaving the Muddy. To his right, as he rode, the saucer of Goblin Valley dipped down in a series of ridges that looked more like the half-open pleats of an accordion than they did like formations of sand, earth, and rock.

In the early morning when the air was cool, Longarm could see all the way across the valley and beyond the canyon of the Green River, which lay thirty to forty miles distant. On one dawn that had been especially cool, he'd seen far past the river valley's eastern edge, and had gotten a glimpse of the low, jagged escarpment of the wide canyon where the waters of the Green and the Colorado Rivers mingled. The sawtoothed canyon rim had been silhouetted against the dawn for a short while; then, as the sun came up, the heat-haze returned. The air began to swirl and dance with rising cross-currents, creating a shimmering curtain that cut off the vista and reduced his horizon to the ragged floor of the Goblin Valley, and often to just a hundred yards from the dim trail he followed.

Longarm's visits to the ranches along the Fremont and the Muddy had fallen into a pattern. The ranchers had been friendly enough, but strangely uncommunicative about their neighbors. He'd always begun by asking if any of them had seen the army wagons carrying the stolen rifles, but none of them had, of course. He hadn't expected anyone to have seen them, nor had he expected to pick up the trail of the guns so easily. The army had covered the area earlier, and so had Sheriff Franklin.

When Longarm had casually turned the conversation to missing cattle, he'd drawn a similar blank. All the ranchers admitted that they missed a few steers now and then, but most of them put the blame for their losses on the country itself. As one of them remarked, it was a place that was hell on women and livestock. That there were steers killed by accident was something Longarm could easily understand. An unwary animal, thirsty and smelling water, could walk right off the edge of a sudden dropoff like the one he was following along the San Rafael River.

It was some of the roughest country he'd ever ridden over. There were buttes piled on top of buttes, abrupt rises from a featureless plain. There were pillars too small to be called buttes—strange vertical-sided colums, cut by wind or water, that jutted straight up from level ground. Sometimes there would be a cluster of these pillars covering a mile or more, and sometimes a single column stood isolated on a piece of land as flat as a tabletop.

Longarm had encountered a number of strays along the way, mavericks that had wandered out of one of the valleys or box canyons where the ranchers tried to keep their herds concentrated close to water. He'd also run into little bunches of steers, too few to be thought of as a herd—six or eight animals that had somehow found their way into one of the isolated box canyons marked by Judge Walton, a canyon with a slit of a mouth that, from all but one direction, looked like nothing more than another crease in the side of a butte. In the box canyons where he'd seen cattle, a spring always rose to form a little pond—enough water for a few steers and enough to create a patch of green where a handful of animals could graze for a short period of time.

There were plenty of such canyons. Longarm had stumbled into a few the judge had either forgotten about or hadn't thought were big enough for him to mark. A half-dozen steers could easily be overlooked by a ranch hand seeking strays, and they'd never be missed at roundup because neither the rancher nor his hands had ever seen them.

Or steers could be driven by rustlers into those isolated spots and gathered later into a herd big enough to drive to market in Colorado or Wyoming, or even to New Mexico or Texas. If their brands had been altered by a running iron to form one that could be offered with a legitimate bill of sale—say a brand like the Circle R or the House or the Teepee—the buyer would never suspect that he'd paid his money for stolen cattle.

Longarm thought about the brands used by the ranches he had visited along the base of the San Rafael Swell, before he'd turned east. They included the Rocking R and the Circle C on the Fremont, the Crowsfoot on the Muddy, and another, the V Bars, a few miles up the Muddy from the Crowsfoot. He'd seen how three of those four brands could be doctored by anybody who knew how to use a running iron. The hunch that had begun to form after his inspection of the missing brand book grew into a certainty.

Somewhere in the area he'd traversed after leaving the base of the San Rafael Swell and heading due east, Longarm realized that he must have crossed his own trail, the one he'd followed when riding south from the ford on the Green River, on his way to Hanksville. He hadn't seen any trace of his earlier passage, of course. The baked soil didn't hold hoofprints. The only way he'd known he had crossed the southward trail was that he had spotted the marks of wagon wheels. The wheelmarks hadn't been ruts, just sets of parallel scratches in a spot or two where the soil softened enough to allow the iron rims to dent the ground.

Crossing the trail had lifted Longarm's spirits. Half of his trip now lay behind him. He'd picked up the

San Rafael River and followed its course until it curved north to enter the Green. At that point, Long-arm had turned south. There were still canyons and water holes marked on his map, enough of them to assure him that he'd be safe in riding almost due south along the rim of Goblin Valley, a dozen miles from the winding course of the Green River, and about twenty miles east of Hanksville. The stream that flowed at the bottom of the canyon he was now following didn't show on his map. It must, he decided, be a creek that plunged into a sink somewhere between where he was now and the Green River, or just the flow from a big spring that ended in a pool somewhere along the canyon floor.

A short while later, he found that his second guess was correct. Ahead, the canyon widened in an abrupt, fan-shaped slope that ended in the green crescent of a pool—almost a small lake. Longarm held the roan in when the horse smelled the water and started to speed up, going down the slope. He let the animal drink sparingly before he dismounted, then led it away from the water long enough to take off his saddle and saddlebags. There was no danger, now, that the horse would founder.

He hobbled the horse and let it go back to drink again, while he walked along the pond to the point where the creek entered it, and drank from his cupped hand. He stood gazing at the water while he lighted a cheroot. It was too inviting to pass up, he thought, rubbing a hand over his dust-thick cheeks. He stripped quickly and waded out into the water. The bottom was clean, and the wet, warm sand that formed it felt good to his boot-weary feet.

Wading out until he was chest-deep—about as deep as the pool was anywhere, as far as he could tell—Longarm stopped. He began lifting water in both cupped hands and letting it splash down over his head and shoulders. As the warm, clean water trickled over his skin, he could feel it washing away the sweat and trail dust that had caked his face. The last thing he was expecting was the voice that spoke from the bank.

"A bath sure feels good after you've been riding around in Goblin Valley for a while, doesn't it?"

It was a woman's voice. Longarm whirled around, blinking to clear away the drops of water that clung to his eyelids. The woman who'd spoken stood beside his clothes on the bank of the pond. The late-afternoon sun was in his eyes, and her face was shaded by the wide brim of her Stetson, so he could see her only as a skirted silhouette. What he could see clearly was the rifle she held cradled in the cook of one arm.

Between eyeblinks, Longarm said, "First bath I've had in a few days. It feels good, all right."

"Riding through? Or just riding looking?" she asked.

"South for a ways. Then I aim to cut on west to Hanksville." Longarm started for the bank, but stopped as he felt the water level at his waist. "You sort of surprised me. I didn't figure there was anybody close by."

"If you're wondering where I came from, my place is just a little way to the south." She hesitated for a moment, then said, "I'm Verda Blankenship."

"My name's Long, and I'm pleased to meet you. Even if you did surprise me out of a year's growth."

She measured with her eyes the expanse of Longarm's chest, his broad shoulders and well-muscled arms. "Looks to me as though you've got enough growth so you won't miss any more. You planning to stop here for the night, or are you in a hurry?"

"I was figuring I'd stop. There's no reason for me to be in a rush. Nobody pushing me, if that's what's worrying you."

"I didn't think there was, or you wouldn't have taken time for a bath. But I wanted to make sure. Well, if that's the case, and you'd like a hot meal, you're welcome to stop for supper."

"A hot meal would go down good. I'll take your invitation, Mrs. Blankenship." Longarm took a step forward without thinking, then stopped abruptly as the water lapped at his hips. "If you'll just stand a little bit away and turn around, I'll come out of here and get my clothes on."

102

"You don't have to be bashful," she told him. "I know what a man looks like naked. As a matter of fact, I'd like to take a look at what you've got, to see what I can expect from you later on."

Chapter 9

Longarm hesitated for a moment, then he said, "You sure do speak out plain, don't you?"

"There's no reason for me to be mealymouthed. You'd find out I'm not later on, so you might as well know it now."

"If that's how you want it to be, it suits me just fine." Longarm started wading to the shore.

"Well," Verda Blankenship said when he stood beside her on the bank of the pond, "if the ground here wasn't so hard and rocky, I'd be tempted to take a sample from you right now. But I guess we'll both enjoy it more in bed, after supper."

Longarm started pulling on his trousers, not bothering to put on his balbriggan underwear. He asked, "Is your place far from here?"

"Only a few steps. You'd have seen it if you hadn't been so taken by the water. It's around the slope, right up against a bluff. No need to ride, just throw your gear on your horse and lead it."

Longarm put on his shirt, vest, and coat, and worked his feet into his stovepipe cavalry boots. He tucked his balbriggans into his saddlebags and cinched the roan's saddle on loosely. Verda watched him working, her eyes following the swift economy of his movements.

"You handle your saddle gear like an old ranch hand," she commented as he took the hobbles off the roan and pulled the reins down over the horse's nose.

"Which I was, for the little while it took me to learn I didn't want to chase steers for a living," he replied.

"Your job now keeps you in the saddle, though,"

she said as she led the way around the foot of the slope.

Longarm didn't respond to her hint. Instead, he said, "I sure don't see how I could've overlooked your place when I was riding up. Of course, I wasn't really looking for any kind of house out here."

"You might not have seen it even if you'd been looking at anything but the water," she replied. "You'll see what I mean in a minute."

They rounded the bottom of the slope, and Longarm saw at once why he'd missed the house. It was nestled up into a vertical cliff. It looked as though part of its interior was cut right into the base of the cliff. In front of the house rose the uprights of a well, and at one side, a small pole corral had been put together. It was only big enough to hold a dozen head of stock at most, and there was only one animal in it, a dappled mare, which he supposed was his hostess's saddle horse. Saddle gear hung on one of the poles.

Longarm studied the layout for a moment before he said, "I sort of figured you had a little ranch. You mean you live here all by yourself?"

"I sure do. Oh, now and then I do a little trading, get myself a few calves or yearlings and finish them up to market size. The pond back there gives me year-round water, and there's enough graze up the creek to feed maybe twenty or thirty head. I do it more to keep busy than anything else."

"I see," Longarm replied. He was being polite; he didn't see at all. He'd started talking just to make conversation, to give him a chance to study Verda Blankenship while they walked from the pond. Something stirred a memory in Longarm's mind. He told himself it was probably just that he'd encountered women very much like her before, but the feeling still persisted that it was more than that. He kept glancing at her covertly while they walked.

Except for her nose, which was a little bit too long, and her chin, which was a trifle sharp, she was an attractive woman. He judged her to be in her middle thirties, but the kind of life she was now leading hadn't caused her to neglect her appearance. Her skin was tanned but not leathery, and her hands were fairly smooth, not gnarled and wrinkled as would be those of most women doing the kind of work required by one maintaining herself alone on a desert homestead.

Her mouth was a rosebud that went incongruously with the rest of her face, giving it a softness that the firm set of her chin belied. Her brows were thick, but smooth. There were small lines etched into the corners of her cat-green eyes and from the rims of her nostrils to the corners of her mouth, but they hadn't formed into deep creases as yet. From the color of her eyebrows, he judged that her hair would be dark blonde. A few moments later, after he'd turned the roan into the corral and she'd led him into the house, she took off her hat and he found that his guess about her hair shade was right.

"Well, what do you think of my place?" Verda asked, as Longarm stopped just inside the door to take stock of his surroundings.

"Looks real nice. Sure beats the outside, for cool."

"Drop your saddlebags off anywhere and sit down," Verda invited. "You look to me like a man who'd take a drink. I've got some whiskey on the shelf back of the stove, there. And I'd like a sip myself, if you feel like joining me."

"It'd be my pleasure."

She started for the shelf, and Longarm used the moment or so to look around some more. The house did extend into the cliff face; only the big front room stuck out. Behind a partition in which a door stood ajar, he could see another smaller room at the back. The only two windows in the room where he stood were in its front wall, and they were shuttered against the heat. Big exposed beams spanned the room, with the bare shingles that covered the gabled roof exposed above them. The walls were of the same flat stones that seemed to be the most popular—or the only available—building material in that part of Utah Territory.

Verda came back with a bottle and two glasses. She

106

said, "I hope you don't object to rye whiskey. It's all I've got on hand right now."

Longarm smiled. "I'd sooner have rye than bourbon. Matter of fact, I was just wondering how I could drink out of the bottle of rye in my saddlebags without hurting your feelings."

"And I was just feeling good that you'd take a drink. It proves to me you're not one of the Saints."

"Mormons?" Verda nodded. He went on, "I don't go in much for churches and preaching. Not that I've got anything against them, or against folks that enjoy them, but I never could get stirred up."

"I thought I could, once." she said as she handed him a glass. "It turned out I was mistaken. And that mistake's been dogging me for a long time. But that's ancient history now—or at least I hope it is. Drink up, Long. And for God's sake, sit down. You act like you're going to run off any minute."

"You invited me to supper, didn't you?" Longarm sat down in a big, leather-covered easy chair. "I don't aim to leave before I've been fed."

"I'd better warn you, I don't have any use for a man who'll eat and run."

"We'll see about that later."

"I think we ought to see about it before dinner. It's early. Unless you're starving?"

"I'm not all that hungry. And I guess I know what you've got in mind."

"You'd have to be deaf, dumb, and blind if you didn't. Come on."

Longarm followed her into the bedroom. Verda turned toward him, and her arms went around him. She held up her face. Longarm kissed her, meeting her extended tongue with his. She put one of his hands on her breast, sliding it through the low-cut neck of her dress. Her breast was firm and soft, and sagged a little. Its aureole stiffened as Longarm stroked across it with his fingertips. Verda shivered.

She broke off their kiss to say, "If you think I'm as randy as a she-goat, you're right. We'll have all the preliminaries the next time. It's not that I don't enjoy

107

them, but I just can't wait. Feel how wet I've gotten without anything more than a kiss and a good look at you back there at the pond."

Longarm lifted her dress. She was wearing only a petticoat under it. She spread her thighs a bit, and he slipped his hand between them, letting it slide upward.

"Do you need more time to get hard?" Verda asked. She felt the bulge in the front of his trousers. "No. You don't. I had an idea you wouldn't be that kind." She unbuttoned his fly and would have pulled his trousers down, but his gunbelt kept her from carrying out her plan. She said, "Get rid of that damned belt, will you, while I take off my dress."

Longarm still wasn't quite sure Verda was real, but there was only one way to find out. He stepped over to the chair that stood beside the bed and shrugged out of his coat and vest. He hung them over the chair-back, then hung his gunbelt over them. He carefully arranged the holster so that the butt of the Colt could be grasped quickly from the bed. He became aware that Verda was not moving, and looked at her. She'd stopped, with her dress pulled up around her waist, to watch his preparations. Her white thighs gleamed below her dark pubic hair in the dim light of the windowless room.

"You're a careful one, aren't you, Long?" she asked. "What's the matter? Do you think you've run into something like the Bender family?"

He knew who Verda was talking about. The Benders had taken in travelers at their roadside stop in Kansas in the seventies, killed them for their belongings, and buried their bodies under the dirt floor of their one-room cabin.

Longarm shivered involuntarily as he recalled his own encounters with two of the deadly Bender clan, a little while ago. One of the pair—Kate—had been fried by a lightning bolt in the Sand Hills of Nebraska; and the other—Junior—had tried to split Longarm's head with an ax in a Denver saloon. They had been a bloodthirsty, conscienceless crew, and he didn't care to run up against the likes of them anytime soon.

He said, "It did cross my mind that you were right eager."

Verda grinned. "Maybe a little too eager?" She finished taking off her dress and rubbed her breasts luxuriously. "You can believe what you want to, Long. The truth is that I'm a woman who needs to be loved hard and often. If I'm not, I turn into a nasty, spiteful bitch. As for being eager, well, I came to believe in one thing from reading Victoria Woodhull and Tennessee Claflin's paper. If it's all right for a man to invite a woman to bed with him, a woman's got the same right. Now, if you've still got any doubts, you're free to go. If you're satisfied, get out of your pants and get on top of me."

Longarm grinned. "Like I said when you first asked me, you're honest enough about it. I'll admit, I got to wondering for a minute. But even if you were up to some Bender tricks, I guess I'd gamble on being able to take care of myself."

He sat down and struggled out of his boots, then stood up to step out of his pants. Verda was standing by the chair, waiting for him. She grasped his erection. "Damn! I knew when I saw you coming out of the pond that you'd be a big one, but I didn't expect all this much! Oh, but this is going to feel good!"

Verda stood on tiptoe, but found she couldn't raise herself high enough to take Longarm in. She put a foot on the side of the bed and levered herself up, her arms around his neck. She grabbed his erection and buried it inside her, then swung free and wrapped her legs around him to pull him in deeply.

"Good, good, good!" she gasped. "Oh, how I've needed this!"

Longarm held her in place while he stepped to the bed. He leaned forward, letting Verda's weight pull him down on top of her. She exhaled through clenched teeth as he went in deeper than had been possible while they were standing up. Longarm braced his feet on the floor and began driving. Verda's excitement had set him off, and he'd been without a woman for a while, too. He held back nothing as he plunged into

109

her, long withdrawal and deep stroke following one another as fast as he could move.

"That's it!" Verda panted. "That's how I love it! Go on! Don't hold up, even if I am—" She began to cry out in short, sharp moans that came faster and faster until she inhaled deeply with a huge, sobbing shudder. She said quickly, "Don't let me put you off. That was just my first time. Go on, Long! Don't stop! I'll be ready to meet you when you let go!"

Longarm was far from being ready. He kept on driving, but slower now, more deliberately, still plunging deep. Verda twisted beneath him, tossing her hips from side to side, rising to meet him as he ended his thrusts. Her throaty sighing and the soft pounding of their bodies when they met were the only sounds in the dim room.

Verda came to climax quickly again. Her moans started and changed to sobs, her upward thrusts became fiercer, the pauses between them shorter. Longarm speeded up to match her tempo, and after a few furious moments, she uttered the same long, shuddering sob he'd heard her loose earlier, and her frenzy relaxed a bit.

It did not leave her completely, even as she shook in the grasp of her climax. She kept meeting Longarm's deep-driving penetrations, and the little animal-like yelps she loosed each time he plunged full-length into her soon began to work on him. He sped up. Verda matched him, upward lift for downward thrust. She must have sensed that he was getting close. She said, "Go on, if you're ready. I'm right with you. Or will be in just another minute or two, if you can hold out that long."

"I can hold out," he said, carefully conserving his breath.

He was very near when Verda began to tremble for the third time. He knew her signs now, and paced himself, holding back until he felt her going into her final climactic spasm, then let himself go while she writhed below him, shaking furiously and letting her sobbing moans fill the quiet room.

Longarm fell forward on Verda's relaxing body. She wrapped her arms around him. Together they rolled over until Longarm could lie on the bed beside her. They lay there in a daze that stretched for minutes until they were breathing normally again.

Verda said with a contented sigh, "I don't know about you, but I feel like a different woman."

"I feel set up pretty good, too." Longarm fumbled in his vest for a cheroot, and in his coat pocket for a match, and presently began puffing into the blue-dim air even bluer clouds of smoke. "Another drink and a bite of supper, and I'll be in right good shape."

"You'll have both," she promised. "Just as soon as my legs get strong enough to hold me again."

Verda got up after a few minutes, and pulled on her dress. She went into the main room and began rattling pots. Longarm slipped on his pants and followed her. She waved at the whiskey bottle and he poured them drinks. They said little until they sat down at the table, to the stew she'd reheated. Longarm was no admirer of stews of any sort, but he ate hungrily.

When the edge had been taken off his appetite, he asked her, "How'd you happen to wind up out here in the middle of noplace, Verda?"

"It wasn't because I wanted to. And it wasn't by accident, either. Since you're not a Mormon, I guess it's safe to tell you. I'm hiding from my husband until I can get further east."

"He's a Mormon?"

"Yes. And I was just one of his five wives. He'd stay with me one night a week. We'd do it just one quick time, and he'd turn over and start to snore. And when I tried to wake him up, he'd slap me away."

"So you left him?"

"Not exactly. He came on a different night once, and caught me with his hired man. He beat the hell out of me and shut me up in a closet. I was in there for a week, until he made the mistake of forgetting to throw the bolt on the door. I waited for him with a bed-slat and broke it over his head. Then I took all the money he had tucked away and ran like hell."

111

"You figure he's still looking for you, then?"

"I'm sure he is. He almost caught up with me while I was trying to hide up in Provo. I got away and started running. This is where I finally wound up. I was raised in these parts—over in Caineville, to the west of Hanksville—and I figured that knowing the lay of the land hereabouts might give me the advantage if my husband was to trail me here."

"You sure ought to be safe here. It's far enough from anyplace."

"No. I don't feel safe. I guess you noticed I was carrying a rifle today, at the pond?"

"It would've been hard to miss it. You handled it like you know how to use it, too."

"I do," Verda said grimly. "And I will, if he catches up with me again before I can get out of here, out of Mormon territory."

"What's to keep you from getting up and going anytime you feel like it?"

"Money, for one thing. I've spent most of what I stole. And I'd like to find somebody to travel with."

"There'll be somebody come along one of these days."

" 'One of these days' might not be soon enough. I've been here now for more than a year. Sometimes I wake up in the night, thinking I hear footsteps, and shake like hell before I realize I'm just dreaming." Verda shook her head. "Hell, Long, you don't want to hear my tough-luck story. What about you? You said you're not running from anything. You said you're not a ranch hand. What're you doing out here in noplace? Prospecting? Land-scouting?"

"Right now I'm just traveling."

Verda was caught up in her guessing game. "You could be a gambler, you've got the looks. Or a professional gunfighter, you'd fit into that frame too, the way you took care of your gunbelt just so at the head of the bed. What the hell are you, anyhow?"

"Like I said, I'm just traveling."

"All right. No more questions from me. I've learned, out here, it's not wise to ask too many." She stretched luxuriously. "How do you feel by now? Did I drain you too much before supper?" Her smile left Longarm no doubt of her meaning.

"About one more drink will give my supper time to settle down. But if you can't wait, I'm ready now."

"I can wait. Not too long, though. I know you'll be riding on, tomorrow. I want all of you I can get tonight. Have your drink. I'll clear away and put the dishes to soak. No use wasting time washing them tonight. I won't have anything else to do tomorrow, and I've sure got something better to do now."

Longarm made his drink last until Verda had attended to the supper dishes. She came and stood before him, feet apart, hands on hips. He stood up and followed her into the bedroom.

"Oh my!" she exclaimed in mock dismay when Longarm took off his pants. "You're not as quick on the trigger as I thought you'd be."

"It won't take but a minute or two," he promised. "You sort of took me by surprise, finishing up so fast."

Verda lay down on the bed. The lamp she'd left burning in the front room, its soft yellow light flooding through the open bedroom door, gave her skin a rich golden glow. The dark, round rosettes of her bulging breasts, the triangle of her pubic hair, accented the glow of her smooth skin.

"Come to bed," she said. "I'll get you up. It's something I enjoy doing."

Longarm lay down, and Verda knelt above him. She started with his lips, rubbing the stiffening nipples of her breasts along them, twitching when the stiff hair of his mustache scratched their tips. Her tongue explored his ears, and he felt her gently gently nipping at his neck and earlobes. Her fingers brushed through the hair on his chest, and when she moved them, it was to drag her breasts the length of his body, from his chin along his chest and the corded muscles of his stomach, down to his groin. She took his growing erection between her breasts and squeezed it, buried in the softness of their warm flesh, pushing her breasts together with her fingers to hold him firmly.

Then Verda went back to Longarm's throat and retraced with her tongue the path her breasts had followed down his body. He had begun to stiffen, and the moist caresses of her tongue brought him up fully. Verda shifted her hips and straddled him, impaled herself, and sank down. She began to rock her hips back and forth, slowly at first, in a lazy, measured rhythm, then faster and faster until she moaned and shook and Longarm felt her hot juices trickling down his thighs. She did not stop, but kept up her furious rocking, pressing hard upon him, until she quickly climaxed for a second time.

Longarm had expected her to stop then, but she did not. She kept on working furiously, a fine film of moisture springing from her skin. Even her breasts, under Longarm's kneading hands, grew damp and slick while she drove herself to yet another climax.

"It's your turn now," she told him. "But I hope you won't hurry too much. I'd like to keep you in me the way you are right now, big and hard and deep, for the rest of the night."

"I don't know as I can go that long without *some* rest," he said, turning with her to lie on top of her, without breaking the bond of flesh that connected them. "But I'll hold out as long as I can."

Verda spread her thighs wide, bending her knees, and braced her feet flat against Longarm's hipbones. "You can go deeper now," she said, "All the way in, as hard and fast as you can!"

Longarm plunged, and Verda clung to him with her feet, holding herself in place while he pounded hard. She climaxed again before he was ready, and then once more when Longarm reached his own peak.

He lay drained on her, her arms wrapped tightly around his torso, her face buried in the curve of his shoulder. Longarm felt himself drifting into sleep. Verda heard his deep, regular breathing and slid from below him. He was too tired to do more than turn on his side, his back to her, before he lapsed more deeply into slumber.

Once during the night he woke up. He was still lying

on his side, Verda spooned up to his back. One of her arms was draped across his hip, her hand grasping him firmly. He smiled drowsily and settled deeper into the soft bed. His movement roused Verda but did not wake her. She sighed and her hand closed more tightly around him. Longarm pressed closer to her, her breasts warm and soft on his back. In an instant he was asleep again.

Chapter 10

A pounding on the door woke him. The first loud knock drove sleep instantly from his brain. By the time the second knock sounded, he was on his feet beside the bed, his Colt in his hand.

Verda was slower to awaken. She began to stir when the second rap echoed through the house. Her eyes opened at the third and she looked at Longarm standing by the bed, naked, but with his gun ready. Then there came a series of repeated knocks. Verda sat up and shook her head, compressing her lids to squeeze the sleep from her eyes.

Once again, Longarm got the feeling of familiarity that had bothered him before, but couldn't connect it with anything. He asked her, "You expecting company?"

"No. But I have a few friends who don't always let me know in advance when they're going to stop in." She got up and pulled her dress on over her head. "You stay here. I'll see who it is."

Longarm positioned himself in the doorway. He was aware of his nakedness, but didn't stop to pull on his pants. Verda was nearly to the door.

"Who is it?" she called, without opening the door.

"Me." The voice was a man's. It had a rasp like a file in it. "Open up, Verda!"

"Wait just a minute. Take your horse up to the corral. I'll be ready to let you in when you get back."

"To hell with the horse! Open up!"

"Do what I say, Mose! I need a minute to myself."

Footsteps scraped on the gravel outside the door.

116

Verda turned to Longarm. "It's all right, I know who it is. Close the door if you like."

"You sure it ain't somebody who'll make trouble for you?"

"I'm sure. Mose might feel like making trouble when he sees you, but he's got no claim on me. Get dressed and come on out when you're ready."

Longarm closed the door, leaving a crack wide enough to allow him to hear what was said in the front room. He began dressing. He heard Verda take the bar from the door, and the rough voice that had called said, "Whose horse is that in the corral, Verda?" Then, after a moment's pause, "You got somebody here with you, ain't you? That's why it took you so long to open the door for me!"

"Yes, I have got someone here, Mose. And that's no business of yours," Verda replied tartly.

"It is if I make it my business!"

"Oh, cool down, Mose! You know what I told you from the beginning. You've got no strings on me, and I've got none on you."

"Maybe I don't feel that way anymore."

"Then you'd better change the way you feel. I don't want any man to feel like I belong to him, not ever again."

Longarm was strapping on his gunbelt when Verda said this. He checked the set of his holster quickly, and opened the door. A tall man stood just inside the front door, wearing Levi's, a green-and-black checked shirt, and a loose vest. The door was still open, and against the soft sunrise light flooding in from outside, Longarm couldn't see the man's face as clearly as he'd have liked to. He got an impression of a twisted nose, a wide mouth, and a closely trimmed black beard that obscured the new arrival's cheeks and chin.

Mose asked, "Who the hell might you be?"

Longarm didn't answer.

Verda said, "He's a friend of mine. That's all you need to know."

"You laid up with him last night, didn't you?" Mose demanded.

"Of course I did. Damn it, Mose! You know you're not the only man that's welcome here! You know that I've had Red and Chesty in bed with me."

"That's different. They're my friends. But I don't like you fucking every two-bit saddle tramp that passes by!" Mose glared at Longarm. "All right, mister. You're through visiting here. Get saddled up and ride."

Longarm said in his mildest voice, "I'll be ready to go when Verda tells me to."

"Don't start something you can't finish, Mose!" Verda warned. "Get off that high horse you're riding and come down to earth. This is my house. Anybody I welcome here stays until I tell him to go."

"Damn it, Verda! I rode thirty miles out of my way, going back to the Roost from Hanksville, just to stop in and see you! This ain't no way to treat me!"

"You're welcome to stay for breakfast," she said, "as long as you act halfway decent."

"I don't know as I care to," Mose replied sourly. "There's a limit to what a man can stand!"

"All that's wrong with your feelings is that hard-on you brought here, now that you see I won't work it down for you," Verda snapped. "Get over your gripe, and sit down and have some breakfast. You've still got a ride ahead of you to get to the Roost."

"It's more than that, by God! Here I come by to give you some good news about our scheme and what the Kid's ready to do, and look at what I walk into!"

"Your news will keep, Mose. I'll listen to it later. Right now I want to eat. I think you do too, and so does Long."

"Long!" Mose exploded. "Is that who that bastard is?"

Longarm had braced himself to draw the moment he heard Verda mention his name. He cut Mose down with a slug from his Colt while the bearded man's hand was closing on the butt of his own revolver. Mose crumpled slowly to the floor. Verda stared, wide-eyed, frozen in place.

Mose was not yet dead. He made a futile effort to bring up his revolver. Longarm, his Colt still in his hand, saw that the attempt would fail. He didn't waste another shot on the dying man.

Mose rolled his head, trying to focus his eyes on Verda. He muttered something indistinct, then, in a final burst of strength, said clearly, "You fixed me good, you fucking slut! Laid up with a federal marshal behind my back, and stood there doing nothing while he finished me off!"

His voice failed suddenly. His lips kept working, but no words came out. Then his jaw fell slack and his body slumped and lay still.

Verda broke the silence. "I guess you had to kill him, didn't you?"

"There wasn't much else I could do, once he tumbled to who I was. If I hadn't shot, he'd have killed me."

"Are you really a U.S. marshal?" she asked. When Longarm nodded, she frowned. "But how did Mose know your name?"

"I suspicion he heard about me when he was in Hanksville. He said he'd just come from there."

"Were you after him, then?"

"No. He must've thought I was, though. Men on the owlhoot trail get right edgy and suspicious."

"And I had to mention your name!" Verda sighed, a deep, heavy sigh, almost a moan. "I'm beginning to think I'm a jinx to men."

"That's a fool way to talk." Longarm went to the table and poured her a glass of rye. He held it out to her. "Put that down, and you'll feel better. It was a hell of a way to get a day started."

He poured himself a drink and lit a cheroot. When he saw that Verda had downed half of the whiskey, he refilled her glass. She lifted it and took another big swallow. Longarm watched her closely. The glazed look was fading from her eyes.

"What's done is done, Verda," he said softly. "Now the best thing you can do is keep busy. You were about to fix some breakfast. Go ahead and do that. We both need some grub and coffee. While you're cooking, I'll get him—" he jerked a thumb at Mose's body— "out of the way."

Verda moved slowly to the stove. Longarm pushed aside the revolver that had fallen from Mose's hand, worked his hands under the dead man's armpits, and pulled the body outside the house. The smell of frying bacon soon filled the air.

When Longarm returned, Verda had set the table and was beating pancake batter in a big bowl.

"Long, why didn't you tell me you're a U.S. marshal when you first got here?" she asked.

"Would it have made any difference if I had?"

"Yes. I might not have been so quick about inviting you to stay." She stopped stirring the batter, looked searchingly at Longarm's face for a moment, then said, "Thanks, Long."

"For what? I don't see as I did anything for you to thank me about."

"Not for anything you did. For something you didn't do."

"How'm I supposed to take that, Verda?"

"Thank you for not telling me I'm lying to myself. I am, and we both know it. After I saw you naked, coming out of the pond, I'd have invited you to stay if you'd been the devil himself, complete with horns, hooves, and a tail. Of course," she added, "you had a tail, only it was hanging down in front of you."

Longarm said, "You ain't to blame for what happened, you know. Mose whatever-his-name-is was on the wrong side of the law a long time before you ever run into him."

"Oh, I know that." Verda gave the batter in her bowl a final flurry of whackings, and started ladling it in dollops onto the griddle that had been heating on the stove. "And it was my choice to go along with the scheme Kid Manders worked out. You know why I did, I suppose?"

"Sure. You needed the money. And you don't even try to make a secret of it that you want to have a man around most of the time."

"Not just *most* of the time. *All* the time. Damn it, if you crooked your finger at me this minute and

120

started for the bedroom, I'd follow you and let these griddlecakes burn."

"And the money? Ain't I right about that? You need the money so you can move on, get to where your husband can't find you?"

"Yes." She began turning the pancakes. "I bought this homestead from a man and his wife who were pretty desperate to get out. I paid more than I should have, I know that now. I guess I knew that when I bought it, but it seemed to me I had a lot of money then."

"Money's got a way of not lasting as long as you figure it will," Longarm observed.

He sat down at the table as she started lifting the pancakes onto plates and covering them with strips of crisply fried bacon. She brought the plates to the table and put them down, then sat opposite Longarm. They began eating. Longarm noticed that Verda's appetite hadn't been much affected by what had happened such a short time before.

Halfway through the meal, she looked at him and said, "You'll stay long enough to help me bury Mose, won't you?"

"Sure. And a while longer, if you don't object to having a U.S. marshal around."

"Not if the marshal is you." Verda grimaced. "I'm a little surprised you'd stay, though. You must think I'm pretty much what Mose said I was, there at the very last, a slut."

"No. I think you're wild for loving. You already showed me that side of you. That don't make you dirty or lazy or anything else. I enjoy it too."

"But you don't have to have it all the time, the way I do."

"No. I've known women who do, though. Men too, as far as that goes. I don't think it's something a person can help."

"It's not. I call myself all kinds of names at times, when I come right out and ask a man to take me on. But I keep on doing it."

Longarm finished his hotcakes and bacon, and

pushed his plate away. Verda got up silently, went to the stove, and brought back the coffeepot. She refilled both their cups and sat down again.

"Are you going to arrest me, Long? If you are, I'd like to know it now, instead of later."

"What gave you the idea I was going to arrest you? You ain't done anything that's against the law, as I see it. Not yet. You've talked about it, but if we could arrest folks for talking or thinking about breaking the law, half the people in the country would be in jail."

Verda nodded. "Thanks. I feel better, knowing you're not."

"I am going to ask you to help me, though," Longarm told her. He spoke very seriously to impress on her the importance of what he was going to ask her to do.

"I think I already know what it is," Verda said. "And I'll make a deal with you. I'll tell you everything I know about Kid Manders and what he's planning, if you'll stay around for another day or two."

Longarm had anticipated her request. "You've got a deal. I wasn't real anxious to move on anyhow, after last night."

Verda leaned back in her chair and sighed with mingled relief and satisfaction. Then she sat erect, and a frown began to form on her face. "Damn! I forgot about Mose lying out there. We'll have to—"

"Bury him, before we do anything else," Longarm finished for her. "I'll take a look in his pockets first, though. I guess you've got a shovel?"

"There's one outside," Verda said.

Longarm bent over Mose's body. He unbuckled the dead man's gunbelt and holstered the unfired pistol that had dropped from Mose's dying hand, before going through the dead man's pockets. There were some scraps of paper that he put aside for later inspection, and a gnawed-at chunk of cut-plug tobacco. There were a few crumpled bills and two double eagles.

"You go ahead," he told Verda. "I'll be right behind you."

"Wait. I just thought of something, Long. There's a

little gully just beyond the corral. It's about the right size, and if we put—put him in there, it'd save a lot of digging."

"All right. You lead on, then, and show me the way, if you don't feel too squeamish about it."

They made a small, grim procession to the gully. Verda led the way, carrying the shovel. Longarm followed her with the corpse across his shoulders. The dead man's head, arms, and legs hung down and swayed in rhythm with Longarm's steps. Verda stopped and pointed.

"Right there."

Longarm nodded as best he could with the corpse resting against his neck. "I see it. Turn your back while I put him in."

Verda faced away from the gully. Longarm backed up to the shallow, narrow gash in the soil, and let the body slide into it. He took the shovel from Verda and threw earth over the corpse. The entire job took little more than ten minutes.

Walking back to the house, Verda came up close to Longarm and put an arm around his waist. She said, "I feel a little bit blue. Let's go inside and have a drink and go back to bed."

"You figure that'll make you feel better?"

"I know it will. It always does. Oh, I'm not randy like I was yesterday, not after the way you took care of me last night. But when I've got a man on top of me, I don't think about anything except how good I'm feeling."

"If that's what you want, that's what we'll do."

When they got in the house, Verda barred the door and windows and lighted the lamp. She turned it low and left it on the table in the front room, then went into the bedroom. Longarm saw the scraps of paper he'd taken from Mose's pockets lying on the table, and picked one of them up. He unfolded it. The paper bore a rough sketch of three of the brands Corinne Gaylord had come in to register at the courthouse in Hanksville. He was still examining the sketches when Verda called from the bedroom.

"Aren't you coming, Long? I thought—"

"You said you wanted a drink," Longarm called back. He picked up the whiskey bottle and glasses and carried them into the bedroom. Verda had already undressed and was lying on bed.

"Yes," she said. "A drink might make me feel better."

Longarm undressed while he sipped his drink. He was completely flaccid. Verda looked at him and shook her head.

"You're not real eager, from the looks of that."

"Don't worry about me. I'll come up without any trouble."

"Oh, I know you will. Especially with me helping you. You know how much I like playing with a man. And I want this to go on for a long time. Come here and stand by the bed a minute."

A bit puzzled, Longarm did as Verda asked. He thought he'd shared in almost every sexual experience an eager woman could dream up, but Verda's request was, for him, the first of its kind. He found out quickly what she had in mind. Kneeling, she backed up to his groin. Her hand slipped between her outspread thighs and grasped him. She began massaging herself gently, rubbing him up and down and across her moist crotch.

Using Longarm as a tool excited Verda quickly. She began twisting her hips to bring untouched spots into contact with her rubbing strokes. She made no effort to place him inside her, but seemed contented with the sensation the rubbing was creating. The breath began to whistle in her throat, and her body started to tremble. Longarm's erection had begun to grow soon after Verda started her massage. She speeded it up by squeezing him gently as she probed. When she began trembling, Longarm lunged into her. She gasped when he penetrated her, and shoved her buttocks back against him. Within seconds, she was moaning and writhing in climax.

Longarm had just begun. He stroked with slow deliberation, his hands holding her hips firmly in place. Even though Verda's face was almost buried in the tangled bedclothing, her whimpers of delight reached his ears. Her back arched and the volume of her cries increased. Longarm speeded up. Verda twisted her hips in spite of the pressure of his hands, and rotated them furiously. He felt her flooding him, and began to slow his tempo.

"No!" she cried. "Faster and deeper!"

Verda's inner muscles were gripping Longarm, trying to hold him in her when he drew back for his lunges. He felt himself building faster than usual. Verda sensed his feeling when he speeded up.

"Not yet!" she said urgently. "Not much longer, but not yet!"

Longarm was in the grip of his own drive to climax now. He tried to move more slowly, but his body demanded that he hurry. Verda's hips were working furiously now, as she raced to catch up with him. She was still moving them when Longarm let go, then, as he held her to him, pressing hard into her while he came, she went into her own climax and writhed against him. Then he felt her muscles ripple and relax as she dropped away from him and sprawled on the bed. Longarm was glad enough to lie down beside her and close his eyes in semi-slumber while his breathing slowed to normal and strength returned to his legs.

Verda was quicker to recover than Longarm. She stretched and sighed and said, "That was the best ever. Why didn't I run into you years ago, Long?"

"I guess because we never were at the same place at the same time," he replied, sitting up. He lit a cheroot and poured them each a drink. After he'd taken a sip or two, he said, "It's about time we had a serious talk, Verda."

"You're sure you don't want to put it off a while longer?"

"I don't see much way that I can. Half the day's gone, maybe more. I've sort of lost track of time, but I do know it's been passing."

"All right," she sighed. "What do you want to know?"

"Everything you can tell me. Even if I happen to

know part of what's going on, I'd like to be sure what I've figured out is right."

"I guess you already know that there's a bunch of rustlers working around the edges of Goblin Valley," she said.

"I suspicioned it. And I've figured they're working up a scheme to sell a whole big herd of stolen cattle."

"That's a pretty good outline of their plan," Verda agreed. "It's Kid Manders's idea."

"Wait a minute. Who's Manders? I never heard of him."

"He's been up in Montana Territory until just recently. He did something there just about like he's planning here." Verda paused thoughtfully. "The Indian bureau's planning to start a new reservation for the Utes and Paiutes over in western Colorado. They'll need a lot of beef. They're also pretty particular about being sure it's sold by legitimate ranchers, so they'll be checking brands. The Kid's idea is to register a bunch of new brands that are close enough to those used by the ranches around the valley so that the original brands can be altered without too much trouble."

"Like turning the Crowsfoot into the Teepee? And the Circle C into the Target?" Longarm asked. "I found them and one or two more on some papers in Mose's pocket."

"Yes. That's the scheme."

"Where did you get roped into it?"

"I'm supposed to own two or three of the new brands. This place of mine's in the right location, and I'd be expected to swear they're my cattle being sold, to kill any suspicion before it gets started. The Kid thinks the plan can be worked for two or three years, maybe longer."

"There's others besides you in on it, ain't there?"

"Oh, I'm sure there are. I don't know who, or where their places are located, though."

"You ever hear any names?"

"Just those in the gang that'll steal the cattle and drive the herd to market when the time comes."

"How many of them are there?"

"I don't know, exactly. Fifteen or sixteen, maybe more. And Corinne. She's Kid Manders's girl. I've never seen her."

"Corinne Gaylord?"

Verda shrugged. "I suppose. I don't think I've ever heard her last name. I don't think Gaylord's her real name."

"When will they start getting that stolen herd together?"

"Sometime soon. I'm not sure exactly when. The Kid and his bunch have been around the valley for the past seven or eight months, getting everything up."

"Where do they hang out?"

"Over on the southeastern edge of Goblin Valley. There's a big box canyon over there with a good spring in it and some caves they've been living in. The Kid's had them build a little cabin for him and Corinne. I don't know exactly where it is, though."

"Is that the place Mose called the Roost?"

"Yes. It started as a joke, calling it Robber's Roost, but the whole gang calls it that now," Verda said.

"How about landmarks around it?"

She shook her head. "If there are any, I've never heard anybody mention them." She yawned and stretched. "You know, Long, you're one hell of a man, the first one in a long time who's really worked me down. Can we sleep a while before you ask me any more questions?"

"Sure. I'm not in any hurry to leave now."

They slept as they had during the night, Longarm on his side with Verda spooned against his back, her hand gripping him. With the shutters and the door barred and the lamp burning, it was as peaceful by day as by night. Hunger woke Longarm. He stirred. Verda was not beside him. He got up and slipped on his trousers and boots, and went into the front room. Verda was standing by the stove, stirring something in a pot. The smell of freshly brewed coffee was in the air.

She said, "It's almost sundown. I thought we'd better eat before we starve."

"Good idea. I think being empty woke me up."

Longarm started for the door. "I need to go to the outhouse. Be right back."

When he came out of the privy and headed back to the house, Longarm looked across the ridges to the south. The light was fading fast, but he could see clearly enough the two riders who were approaching. They were still two or three miles distant. Keeping in the shadow cast by the cliff, he went inside.

"You expecting more company tonight?" he asked Verda.

"No. Hell, Long, I wasn't expecting any last night, either. Who is it now?"

"I couldn't make them out, they're still too far off."

Verda went to te door and gazed at the horsemen. "I can't tell who the other one is, but one of them's Kid Manders. I'd know that paint pony he rides if he was twice as far off." She turned to face Longarm. "Well? I'll let you decide what we'll do. But if I didn't tell you before, Manders is a mean, suspicious bastard. If we don't play this just right, there's going to be trouble."

Chapter 11

"There's noplace else they'd be heading for but here, is there?" Longarm asked.

Verda shook her head. "No. They might be heading somewhere else and swinging by here to tell me something. But they'll be here in a little while, you can be sure of that, Long."

"Maybe they're stopping by for pleasure instead of business."

"Damn it, Long, I'm not whoring out here. Sure, I've bedded Mose and a couple of the others in Manders's gang, but it was because I wanted to, not for money. Anyhow, Manders is so gone over Corinne that he wouldn't be interested in me."

"I sure wouldn't want anything to happen to let them know I'm after them." He looked at the two riders, then at the darkening sky. "It'll be dark by the time they get here. Chances are they won't notice there's two extra horses up in the corral—not unless they're aiming to stop here for the night."

"It'd be the first time, if they did," Verda said. "But we can take Mose's horse and yours around to the pond and hobble them. if you think it's too risky to leave them where they are."

"Might be a good idea. I'll tend to it as soon as it gets a mite darker."

"What about you? Are you going to stay in the house while they're here? Or hide outside?"

"That's what I've been trying to decide. How much chance is there that they'd come into your bedroom?"

"Not much," she replied. "Do you intend to stay in there while they're here?"

"I'd sure like to hear what they say to you. And that's the best place I can think of. Close the door all but a crack, then I can hear what goes on. I'll be on hand if trouble starts, too."

"If you think it's safe." There was doubt in Verda's voice, though.

"I ain't thinking as much about a safe place to duck into as I am one where I can hear what's said between you and them," Longarm told her. "Let's do it that way, then. You think you can handle it without giving me away?"

Verda smiled. "Did you ever have a woman hide you under the bed when her husband came home unexpected, and talk to him as though she'd been an angel while he was away? Don't worry. I can handle things."

"All right. It's settled," Longarm said. "Now, we got a few minutes to spare. Let's eat a bite while we're waiting for it to get dark enough for me to move the horses. I'm starved."

They ate hurriedly. His hunger satisfied, Longarm went to the door and looked out. Only the dying glow of sunset's afterlight gleamed faintly in the west. The riders were invisible.

"If I can't see them, they can't see me," he said. "I'll take care of the horses now. You better look around and make sure there's nothing that'll catch their eyes in this room here."

"Mose's gunbelt," Verda came to the door and picked the belt and holster up from the floor where Longarm had put it. "And your Winchester, in the corner there. They'd know it's not my gun."

"Look around good, and clear out anything else," he said. "I'll be right back."

By the time Longarm returned, the sky was totally dark. Verda told him, "I've cleared away everything I can see that might catch their eyes. Hadn't you better go in the bedroom now? They ought to be getting here soon."

"Be a good idea. And if trouble breaks out, Verda, you find a corner and stay where you're safe. Let me handle those fellows."

130

Longarm had only a short wait after he'd gone into the bedroom. He closed the door, leaving only a crack wide enough for him to hear Verda moving about in the front room. Lighting a cheroot, he stretched out on the bed. He was just settling down comfortably when hoofbeats reached him from outside. The thudding stopped, and a sharp rapping at the door echoed into the bedroom. Longarm snuffed out his cigar and sat erect. He swung his legs off the bed to get his feet on the floor, and heard Verda's quick footsteps as she went to the door, followed by the scrape of the bar being lifted.

"Well," she said. She sounded genuinely surprised. "If it's not the Kid himself. And Lance. Come on in and rest yourselves. I'll fix you some coffee. Or supper, if you're hungry."

A man's voice said, "Don't bother, Verda. We just rode over on the chance that Mose might be here."

"Look around, Kid," Verda answered calmly. "You can see he's not."

"Somebody else is, then," the other man said.

Longarm told himself, *That'd be the Kid's segundo. Lance, Verda said his name was.* Then he kicked himself mentally as the second outlaw went on, "I sure as hell smell cigar smoke."

"Oh, that's just some old scraps of Mose's cut-plug I swept up and threw in the fire," Verda replied quickly.

Longarm swore silently at himself for his carelessness in lighting the cheroot he'd just snuffed out.

"You missed a piece," Kid Manders said. "There it is, on the table."

"Damned if I didn't forget that one," Verda said coolly. "I'll just throw it in with the rest. It's so dry Mose couldn't bite a chew off of it." The stovelid clanged. Verda went on, "Now what's got you stirred up about Mose, Kid?"

"I sent him into Hanksville yesterday evening. He was supposed to be back today, and he still hasn't showed up," Manders said.

"Ah, Kid, you're just getting edgy," Lance said before Verda could comment. "Mose had a few too many and stopped to sleep it off."

"Damn it, Lance, it's not like Mose not to show up when he says he will," Kid Manders replied. "He might've got into a jam of some kind in town there."

"I wouldn't worry," Verda put in. "Mose can look out for himself."

"That's what I told the Kid," Lance said. "Mose couldn't get into a jam if he tried. Not in Hanksville, the way the Kid's got the town hogtied."

"Well, he's sure not here," Verda repeated. "And I haven't been expecting him. Not that I know when he's likely to ride over, of course."

"Let's backtrack, then, Lance, and ride toward Hanksville," the Kid suggested. "Might be he had trouble with his horse."

"Hell!" Lance replied. "He'd have had plenty of time to *walk* to the Roost if he started when he said he did. Anyhow, we can't see nothing now. It's dark."

"We ought to've started when I first wanted to," the Kid said. "If we had, we could've hit Hanksville by sundown and maybe found out something by now."

"Look here, Kid, I don't plan to worry about Mose until daylight. If he hasn't showed up by then, we can start looking," Lance said firmly.

"Damn it, he was supposed to bring me word from Jensen about them cattle orders!" the Kid grated. "After Corinne missed seeing him the other day, we don't know where we stand, how fast we'll have to move, or anything else!"

Longarm had sharpened his ears when Kid Manders mentioned the name Jensen. He recalled Judge Walton's telling him that Jensen was the county prosecutor in Hanksville. He was disappointed when he heard nothing from the front room except a shuffling of feet and a scraping of chair legs, indicating that the outlaws were getting ready to leave.

"All right, Lance," Kid Manders said. "Let's get on back to the Roost. Mose might be there by the time we ride in. But I'll tell you this—if he don't show by daylight, we're all going to turn out and start looking for him!"

"Whatever you say, Kid," Lance replied. "You're the boss."

Verda said, "I don't look for Mose to stop by here, I told you that. But if he does, I'll tell him you're anxious about him."

"You do that, Verda," the Kid replied. "But Lance might be right. Mose could've just bent his elbow too many times. Or maybe it took him longer to get things straight with Jensen than we'd figured on. We'll wait out the night at the Roost, and start worrying in the morning."

Longarm heard the hoofbeats of the outlaws' horses start up, then faded into silence. He came out of the bedroom. Verda was barring the door. She saw that Longarm had on his hat and coat, and was carrying his rifle.

"Where're you going?" she asked him.

"I'm going to trail them back to that Roost, wherever it is. It's the best chance I've got to find it fast."

"That's too dangerous!" she protested. "You'd be taking an awful chance of them spotting you!"

"That's the kind of chances I get paid to take," Longarm reminded her. "I'm going to have to take your horse. If I go get the ones tethered at the pond, I'll run the risk of losing them."

"Go ahead." Verda smiled. "That's one way I can be sure you'll be coming back, I guess. If you don't bring my horse back, I'll turn you in as a horse thief."

"You do that."

Longarm started for the door. Verda grabbed him as he passed, and kissed him.

"Be careful, Long. I do want you to come back, you know."

"I will. Now I've got to hurry. You'll be all right, won't you?"

"Of course. I'll be right here."

Longarm hurriedly put his own saddle on Verda's mare. He knew the general direction the two outlaws would be taking, and trusted that he'd be lucky enough to see them in the starlight before they spotted him. If it hadn't been for the cigarette one of them was smoking, though, he would have run into them. Kid Manders and Lance were letting their horses walk, arguing as they rode.

"Damned if I'll agree with you, Kid," Lance was saying. "This fancy scheme you've dreamed up don't do anything except waste a lot of time that we could put to good use just plain stealing a few head here and a few there and selling 'em wherever we found a buyer who'd wink at whatever brand they had."

"What you've come to call my 'fancy scheme' worked just fine up in Montana Territory. It'll work just as good here."

"Maybe it will, maybe it won't. That ain't what I'm driving at, Kid. Shit, we've been sitting on our asses now for more than two months, not doing a damn thing but scratching up little pieces of paper and shuffling 'em around. None of us has made a dime except what you've handed us. The boys are getting pretty damn edgy, I tell you."

"They'll get over that soon enough, Lance. Jensen ought to have everything just about ready now. Once we start moving on this new scheme, they'll settle down."

"Something else they don't like, either, is you having your woman at the Roost and them not having anything to fuck but old lady thumb and her four daughters."

"Well, I'm real sorry about that, but I can't bring everybody a woman. Christ, if there was a woman for every one of the boys, all we'd have would be one big hen fight."

"You could send Reen back home. That'd end a lot of their bitching."

"Goddamnit, let 'em bitch! What the hell's the use of being boss if you can't have a little something special?"

"All right. Just don't say I didn't warn you."

"You warned me and I listened. Whether I do anything about it or not is up to me."

Longarm pulled up the mare as the two men ahead fell silent. If his horse made a misstep that they could hear above the faint thudding of their own mounts' hooves, they'd turn on him at once, and his chance of finding the hideout would be lost.

He almost lost them, as it was. He'd been holding the mare back, straining his ears in the dark, trying to follow the pair ahead of him by sound; straining his eyes too, trying to keep their silhouettes in view against the starlit sky. Suddenly he realized that both silhouettes and sounds had vanished. He reined in and held the mare in check, looking and listening. The night was totally still. He caught the faint grating of a shod hoof clicking over rock, and kneed the mare toward the sound. A wall of stone unexpectedly loomed in front of him, and he pulled up just in time to avoid running into it.

Longarm turned the mare and rode along the base of the butte. When he found no opening after a reasonable time, he backtracked. A few dozen yards from the point where he'd encountered the almost vertical base of the butte, he found what he was looking for. A narrow slit, barely wide enough to admit a single horse and rider, cut the butte's wall. Longarm tethered the mare a few steps away from the opening. He dismounted, slid his Winchester from its saddle scabbard, and entered the slit on foot.

Feeling his way with his boot toes in the dense dark inside the cut, Longarm followed the winding passage. He must have been able to move faster than the riders he'd been following, for he heard voices ahead and stopped to listen.

A man whose voice he didn't recognize said, "So you didn't run across Mose's trail, Kid?"

Manders's now-familiar voice replied. "No. The woman says he didn't stop at her place."

Lance cut in, "I keep telling the Kid that Mose will show up. He's just late getting back, is all."

"Some of the boys are getting a mite uneasy," the strange voice said. "I'd like to see some action start, myself."

All right, come on over to the fire," Manders told the man. "We'll have ourselves a talk, all of us."

Longarm held his position without moving until he heard the horses move away and the footsteps of the third man die out. Then he edged ahead. A dim glow in front of him warned that the end of the cleft was near. He slowed down. The glow grew brighter as he advanced cautiously. When he could see the edges of the slit outlined ahead, Longarm slowed again. He crept forward to the spot where the towering sides of the passage ended and opened out into an oval box canyon perhaps a quarter-mile or a bit more across at its widest point.

A small, roughly built cabin—little more than four walls covered with a pole roof—stood near the center of the oval floor. On all sides, the walls rose almost straight up, though the dark gash of another cleft showed beyond the spot where the cabin stood. Dark blotches on the walls at two other places along the canyon floor indicated the presence of caves. The fire that Longarm had seen glowing was near the center of the canyon, at some distance from the cabin. A group of men stood around it; they kept moving and shifting, and Longarm was unable to count them. Beyond the fire stood the horses Manders and Lance had been riding.

Longarm was too far from the fire to hear what the men were saying, but from their quick gesticulations and the attitudes in which they were standing, he could tell without hearing their words that their discussion was serious. From the way one or another of the outlaws waved an arm for emphasis, he judged that there might even be some angry words being exchanged between members of the band and their leader.

A woman came out of the cabin and walked toward the fire. Even though the distance and the bad light reduced her features to a blur, Longarm recognized her by her walk and what she wore; there couldn't be two women in that part of the Territory who'd be wearing a riding skirt. It was Corinne Gaylord, the girl whom he'd encountered registering false brands at

136

the courthouse in Hanksville. She reached the fire, and the men shifted around to make room for her to stand close to one of them.

That one she went to is Kid Manders, for sure, Longarm told himself.

Corinne Gaylord's arrival must have interrupted whatever kind of discussion or argument was going on, for the men began straggling away from the fire. Longarm had his first chance to count them accurately. He tallied a dozen, not including the two leaders and the woman. Verda Blankenship had estimated the gang's strength fairly closely.

Most of the men had now left the fire and were heading for the caves. Kid Manders and Corinne started toward the cabin. Three of the men still remained hunkered down by the fire. Longarm caught a glimmer of light flickering from the cabin into which Manders and Corinne had disappeared. The flickering grew brighter; yellow light from a lamp or lantern spilled from the cabin door and window. The cabin was set at an angle that kept Longarm from seeing through either opening from the mouth of the split where he stood in deep shadow. He turned his attention back to the fire.

All three of the men who'd been squatting beside the blaze were standing up now. One of them picked up a rifle, its shape unmistakable in silhouette against the dying coals. Cradling the gun in an elbow, he started toward the dark line of the cleft that cut the vertical wall almost directly across from the passage that provided access to the box canyon. The man was soon lost to sight in the darkness beyond the fire. Soon, Longarm heard a muted scrabbling sound, and the patter of gravel and small rocks being dislodged. As the faint sounds continued, he realized that the cleft must provide a path up to the box canyon's rim, and the man carrying the rifle was going up there for sentry duty.

Longarm weighed his chances of getting close enough to the cabin to hear what was being said inside. He surveyed the oval enclosure minutely, looking for brush, trees, boulders, or even shadows that might give him cover if he tried to reach the shack. There were none. The ground between the entrance and the cabin was bare. Regretfully, he talked himself into discarding the idea.

Old son, that's not a smart thing to try. The place is bare as the town dude's jaw after his Saturday-night shave. Besides, there's still two of them by the fire, and the others ain't been gone long enough to be sound asleep yet. It'd be right risky to try a sneak now; later might be different. You're stuck here till daybreak anyhow. You sure can't leave till there's light enough to spot whatever landmarks you'll need to find this place, but it'd sure be interesting to hear what's being talked about in that cabin.

He heard fresh noises coming from the direction of the cleft across the canyon. They stopped after a few minutes, and a man walked into the diminishing circle of light cast by the coals. He wasn't the same man who'd left earlier. The other had worn a hat with a cavalry crease; this one had on a Stetson with a broader brim and a high crown worn uncreased, Montana-fashion. The three now at the fire talked briefly, then the newcomer turned away and walked toward the caves. The other two started for the slit where Longarm was hiding. He watched them for a moment, then stepped back a bit deeper into the concealing darkness. Within a few seconds, he could hear their voices becoming louder as they drew closer.

"So if you know any of the other boys, besides Strang and Bynum, who don't like this waiting any better than you and me, you talk with them on the quiet, Matt."

Longarm recognized the voice. It was the nasal, high-pitched twang of Lance, Kid Manders's segundo.

"There's one or two who ain't satisfied," the other outlaw said. "But if it's only you and me and Strang and Bynum against the rest of the bunch . . ."

"There's bound to be others," Lance said confidently. "Shit, we been sitting on our butts here, getting hornier and hungrier every day. The Kid's got

138

that girl in bed with him every night, and I've got a hunch she brings him some special grub that they hide in the cabin every time she comes back from town."

"Now that's one thing I don't think any of us likes," Matt said, "her going off into Hanksville every few days. It's too damn dangerous. Seems to me that people there have got to start wondering about her, sooner or later. But the Kid don't seem bothered."

"That's right," Lance agreed. "And he's sure upset because Mose hasn't showed back here yet. Made me ride all the way over to Verda's place to see if he'd swung by there. Which he hadn't, of course."

Lance and Matt were at the mouth of the slit now. Longarm could hear them clearly. They stopped just outside the opening.

"You think Mose has pulled out?" Matt asked.

"No. I halfway looked to find him putting the prong to Verda. But there wasn't—" Lance stopped short.

"What'd you start to say?" Matt asked.

"I started to say there wasn't any sign of Mose at the Blankenship woman's place. But I just remembered something. There was a hunk of cut-plug laying on the table there, and Mose always has a cud of that stuff in his jaw. And when me and the Kid first went inside, I thought for a minute I smelled cigar smoke."

"Damn it, didn't you search the place?" Matt asked.

Lance said thoughtfully, "No, we didn't. Hell, Matt, Verda's supposed to be in this job with us. I guess me and the Kid both figured she wasn't lying about Mose not having been there. But if his chewing tobacco was on the table, it sure hadn't been laying there for very long."

"What do you think happened?"

"Damned if I know. But I'm beginning to wonder."

"You mean the Kid might be right, something's happened to Mose?"

"I don't know, but I think maybe I better go talk to him. You recall what Corinne said a few days back, after she'd been in Hanksville—that there was something funny going on at the courthouse?"

"Sure, I remember. But—"

"Never mind any buts right now," Lance said. "I better go over to the cabin and palaver with the Kid. There might be something going on that none of us has tumbled to yet."

Longarm heard the grating of footsteps on the hard soil as the outlaw left hurriedly. He risked looking out. Dimly, he saw Lance's silhouetted form moving in the direction of the cabin.

You better figure out something real fast, he told himself. *If those two get their heads together and decided to take another trip to Verda's, the fat's going to be sizzling in the fire.*

Chapter 12

Left to himself, the outlaw called Matt began settling himself at the opening of the passage. Longarm could interpret the moves the man made by the sounds that came to his ears. There was a scraping of dirt under booted feet, then the satisfied grunt of a man easing into a sitting position, then a low, tuneless humming. Longarm knew he needed to hurry, but forced himself to bide his time. He waited long enough for the sentry to feel relaxed and comfortable, then started inching back to the mouth of the cleft. Matt was leaning against the canyon wall; Longarm could see a corner of his shoulder sticking out beyond the irregular line of the opening. He started trying to figure out a method of luring the sentry into the cleft without giving him a chance to rouse the other outlaws. Longarm discarded each ruse that occurred to him as so risky that it was unusable.

Then he decided to quit trying to be fancy. Drawing his Colt, he hissed sibilantly, hoping Matt would forget that snakes rarely venture from their dens in the cool desert night. When the sentry failed to react to the first hiss, Longarm hissed again, louder. Matt moved quickly, this time. He jumped to his feet, drawing his revolver as he stood, and stuck his head around the edge of the opening.

Longarm clubbed the man hard with the barrel of the Colt. Matt dropped without a sound. The only noise that broke the silence of the night was the small thud his pisol made as it fell to the ground.

After dragging the unconscious outlaw into the darkness of the cleft, Longarm took out his jackknife and cut the sleeve from Matt's thick denim shirt. Split into halves lengthwise, two of the strips knotted together made a lashing for the sentry's booted ankles. One of the other strips tied his hands behind his back, and the last one made an efficient gag.

Leaving Matt lying in the darkness of the entrance, Longarm picked up the revolver the unconscious man had let fall, and tossed it into the darkness of the passageway. He didn't need any extra guns weighing him down; the added firepower they might give him wouldn't compensate for the fact that they'd impede his ability to move fast. He gave Matt's rifle the same treatment. Peering out of the opening, he saw that the window and door of the cabin still threw rectangles of yellow light on the ground. There was no sign of movement from either of the caves. The glow of the fire had died to a dim reddish purple.

He left the protection of the cleft and began working his way around the base of the canyon wall. He'd be a target for the sentry posted high on the rim, but he gambled that the man would be chiefly concerned with watching the approaches to the hideout, and would pay little attention to the box canyon's floor.

He moved slowly and silently. When he'd gotten to the point where the distance from the canyon wall to the cabin was shortest, he stopped again to look and listen. The night stayed noiseless. He half-ran, half-walked to the corner of the cabin.

Inside, Kid Manders was saying impatiently, "All right, Lance! You say you seen a chunk of cut-plug on Verda's table; that don't mean it belonged to Mose, or that he'd been there lately. And maybe you did smell smoke when we first went in, but I sure as hell didn't. You ain't said a thing that'd make it worthwhile for us to go back there and poke around."

Longarm flattened himself against the cabin wall and sidled along it to the window. He peered inside cautiously, a quick glance, to get its features fixed in his mind. The little shack was sparsely furnished: a raw wood table in the center, a narrow bed along one wall, three or four chairs, a bench on which stood a washbasin and a pail of water. Pegs on the wall held a mixture of men's and women's clothing. Manders's gun-belt hung on one of the pegs, and his rifle rested across two others. Corinne Gaylord was sitting on the bed. Kid Manders and Lance faced each other across the table.

Lance replied to Manders, "You ain't said a thing that's changed my mind about Mose getting into trouble, either. Listen here, Kid, if you want me to go on straw-bossing this outfit for you, I expect you at least to listen to me."

"I listened, didn't I?" Manders demanded. "Even if you didn't say anything worth listening to."

"All you seem to come up with anymore is 'shut up and follow orders,'" Lance snorted. "You act like nobody's got horse sense but you, Kid."

Before Manders could reply, Corinne said, "It might be a good idea if you did listen to Lance, Kid."

Manders wheeled around to face the girl. "Whose side are you taking in this fuss, Reen?"

"Yours, of course," she answered quickly. "But don't forget, I told you almost a week ago about that federal marshal being in Hanksville. Well, the last time I was there, a couple of days ago, Jensen said the marshal had dropped out of sight."

"What am I supposed to get out of that?" Manders asked.

"Maybe that Blankenship whore's been in cahoots with the federals all along. Maybe she knows more than she let on about what happened to Mose."

"You're gonna keep harping on what you thought you seen and smelled?" Manders asked.

"Damn right I am!" Lance retorted. "And I don't intend to let you talk me out of it. If you won't go back with me to Verda's and kick the truth out of her, I'll go by myself!"

"It might not do any harm to look into what Lance suspects, Kid," Corinne suggested. "You can't be sure unless you do."

"You've got more sense than the Kid has," Lance

told Corinne. He turned back to the gang leader. "Well, Kid? Do you or don't you?"

Manders gave in, though his surrender was anything but graceful. "All right, damn it!" he growled. "Take a couple of the boys and see what you can drag out of her. It'll just be time wasted, but you won't be satisfied until I let you do it, I reckon."

"You're right about that, Kid. And I'll get the truth out of that Verda bitch, no matter what I have to do to her to start her jaw wagging." Lance started toward the door.

Manders said, "Wait a minute! You're not aiming to go back there tonight, are you?"

"I don't see why not. If we bust in on her and grab her before she wakes up good, it might be easier to get her to talking. It's late, anyhow. Be full daylight by the time we get there."

"Who you figuring to take with you?"

Lance scratched his head, pushing his hat back. "Strang and Bynum, I reckon. Why? Does it make any difference to you?"

Kid Manders hesitated a moment, then shook his head. "No, take whoever you want to. But you better get a little shut-eye before you take on another long ride."

It was Lance's turn to hesitate. Watching the segundo from his vantage point at the window, Longarm could almost read Lance's mind. He'd made his point with Kid Manders, and won a minor concession. Now Lance was debating whether to push his luck, or give the Kid the satisfaction of having had the final word of command.

Finally Lance nodded. "Maybe you're right. I'll roll up in my blankets until daybreak. That'll give me a couple of hours of sleep."

Longarm slid around the corner of the cabin just in time to avoid being seen by Lance as the outlaw came outside and headed for the caves. As soon as the grating of the segundo's footsteps faded, Longarm returned to the window where he could watch Kid Manders and Corinne, and listen to what they were saying.

"I halfway hope Lance finds out something about Mose from that Blankenship woman," Manders said. "Even if it does give him another chance to poke it at me for being wrong."

"Jensen promised he'd have the papers all fixed up," Corinne said with a frown. "Damn it, Kid, I wish you'd let me go in after them, instead of sending Mose. Jensen can stall him. He couldn't put me off as easy."

"I wish I'd sent you, too, Reen. But you been seen too many times lately in Hanksville. You can't risk getting the sheriff curious about why you come in to see Howie and Bobby so much."

"Oh, you don't have to worry about old Jess Franklin. He's half drunk most of the time. He hasn't the slightest notion what's going on."

"Just the same, we can't afford to have anything upset our plans, not this late."

"We could always move out as soon as we've cut the bunches we want from the ranches," Corinne suggested. "If we had to, we could change the brands at Peters's place, after we get across the Green."

"It'd slow us down too much. We'll just about have time to do the running-iron work here in the canyon and get the herd away before the ranchers around Goblin Valley begin their tally. As soon as they do, and see how short they're coming up, all hell's going to bust loose. We want to be over the Colorado line by then."

"You still don't think the Indian agents would buy the herd if we didn't change the brands?" she asked.

"I'm not worried about the agents; they don't give a damn what steer carries which brand. The army paymasters are the ones I'm thinking about. That damn Charlie Goodnight talked the army into the system he worked out to keep his own cattle from being sold if they got rustled. Them paymasters are going to want a bill of sale for every single steer by the brands the critters have on 'em."

"Change the brands on the trail, then."

Manders shook his head. "Too risky. We'd have no

way of knowing who might come up on us while we was stopped."

"I still say Peters's place is the best bet, then," Corinne said.

"Jim's spread's just too damn little for the size herd we'll have. It was all right until we decided we had enough men to handle a bigger herd than we'd figured on. If we stopped there now, the damn critters would scatter, and we've got no time to chase strays." Manders bent over the lamp. "Hell, Reen, let's go to bed. Jawing won't help." He blew out the lamp.

In the sudden darkness that followed, Longarm ducked back quickly to keep his head from being silhouetted against the cabin window. He hadn't realized that, while he'd been watching and listening, the moon had risen, and the sky had turned almost daylight-bright. Pressed against the cabin wall just outside the window, he could still hear what the Kid and Corinne were saying indoors.

Over the soft rustling of clothes being removed, Manders said, "Looks like I might have to put Lance in his place. He's getting too damn uppity lately. Seems to me he's getting ideas."

"He's been doing a lot of talking to some of the men," Corinne said. "Bynum and Strang, especially. And Matt too. I'd keep an eye on all four of them if I were you, Kid."

"Damn it, we can't afford to have anything upset our plan, not this late. We're going to need every man we've got to gather critters off the spreads we've picked out to hit, and trail them over to Colorado. And Strang's one of the best and quickest I've seen with a running iron."

"I don't think you'd have to worry about Strang and Bynum, if it wasn't for Lance egging them on." Then Corinne added, "Lance has started looking at me again, the way he did when you first brought me here."

"Now, by God, I won't stand for that!" Manders exclaimed. "He hasn't made any moves, has he?"

"No. Just looked at me. But he gives me the creeps, Kid, when he looks at me that way."

"If Lance ever puts a hand on you, it'll be the last thing he ever does!" Manders told her.

"Don't stir up trouble with him as long as he just looks at me, Kid. I can stand that for a while, until we finish this job. But I don't think I could stand having him feel of me. You're the only one I want to do that."

"You mean feel of you this way?"

"Yes. And between my legs."

"Like this?"

"Oh, like that all the time! And with something besides your fingers, too."

"I'll be ready to do that pretty soon."

"Here, I'll help you make it even sooner."

Longarm heard the bed creak as they moved around. He waited until the creaking settled down into a steady rhythm, then decided the Kid and Corinne were going to be too busy for a while to notice much of anything but themselves. He could see the sky lightening into the gray of dawn as he zigzagged from the cabin to the canyon wall. Then, taking his chances that the sentry posted on the top of the butte was either looking away from the canyon or asleep, he dodged along the wall to the entrance.

Matt was still lying where Longarm had left him. The outlaw's sentry was conscious now. He stopped struggling with his bonds when he heard Longarm approaching, and his eyes, above the gag, glared when he saw Longarm approaching. The outlaw would be found soon enough, Longarm knew. He stopped long enough to check the denim strips before dragging the man a few yards into the blackness that still prevailed in the passageway.

Lance and his cohorts would be sure to find the man when they left, but there was no point in giving them the few extra minutes they'd gain if the bound and gagged sentry was clearly visible. Longarm wanted all the lead-time he could get on the trio that would be riding to Verda's. He'd have to make a wide sweep around the base of the butte to keep the sentry from spotting him and rousing the whole outlaw band.

Three-to-one was long enough odds; there was no use in making it a dozen to one.

By the time Longarm reached Verda's mare, untethered the animal, and swung into the saddle, there was enough dawn light for him to be able to spot landmarks he could use to find the entrance to the canyon when he returned. He rode east far enough to be lost to easy sighting on the rough slope of the drop into Goblin Valley, then turned and set off to the northwest. He figured by this time that he must be almost halfway back to Verda's house, and somewhere close to the trail Kid Manders and Lance had followed from the house to the box canyon the night before.

He slowed the mare to a walk, and began looking for signs of a trail. In that unpopulated and untraveled country, any path taken by even a few riders more than two or three times would stand out like a pencil line drawn across a sheet of virgin paper.

He spotted the trail with less difficulty than he'd thought he'd have. In the strict sense of the word, it wasn't a trail at all. A casual traveler encountering it might have thought that a group of perhaps a half-dozen riders had passed that way at one time going north, and that another small band might have retraced the same route heading south, for there was no well-beaten path, just a scattering of hoofprints visible now and then on the softer stretches of baked soil.

Longarm reined in the mare and lit a cheroot. The fragrant smoke rolled with a welcome harshness over his tongue.

He studied the terrain. The line of prints ran along the edge of the shallow saucer that was Goblin Valley. To the east the land stretched level—alkali flats broken only by shallow undulations, with an occasional small butte rising above them. To the west, the crisscross gullies of the valley unrolled in a bewildering maze. It wasn't, he thought, the best place in the world for a man alone to meet up with three outlaws who, from the nature of their business, would know how to use their guns.

A horseman in the saddle in country like this could

148

see seven miles in any direction as long as the air was cool and clear. He would not be able to distinguish details of the terrain, but he'd be able to see moving objects that showed dark against the landscape. By raising himself in his stirrups, he'd add a mile to the distance he could scan, perhaps even a bit more if he was tall.

Longarm took advantage of the knowledge he'd gained on many a chase. He stood up in the stirrups and looked south toward the outlaws' hideout. There were no riders in sight, and he was far enough from the butte to see it only as a mass jutting above the horizon, its outlines blurred by the shimmering heat-haze already beginning to form as the sun climbed higher in the morning sky. He settled back and nudged the mare south along the faint trace that led from the hideout.

Almost two miles from the point where he'd picked up the trace, Longarm found what he'd hoped for. The rim of Goblin Valley dipped down in a narrow gully deep enough to hide a horse and wide enough to accommodate one. He reined the mare off the trace into the gully, and settled down to wait.

Patiently, Longarm sat in the saddle while the sun moved higher into the sky. He'd been prepared for a long vigil, allowing time for Lance and his two companions to discover the tied-up sentry, to realize their hidden lair had been successfully invaded, and to spend a certain amount of time palavering.

But if I got that Lance figured out right, he told himself, *he ain't going to give up on his idea that the answer to what's happened is back at Verda Blankenship's. He's going to start out for there, and it won't make much difference what Kid Manders tries to do to stop him. So all I got to do is keep my pecker in my pants, and sooner or later, Lance and those other two are going to come riding along on their way to Verda's.*

Longarm had set noon as the time past which he'd know his judgment had been wrong, but long before the sun reached its zenith, his patience was rewarded and his judgment proved sound. Through the haze that

149

hung above the parched, hard ground, he caught sight of three riders approaching his hiding place.

Longarm slid out of the saddle, taking his Winchester out of its boot as he dismounted. He'd already spotted a big rock a few paces away in the bottom of the gully, and rolled it over the dropped reins of the mare. He backtracked along the gully until its bank was at shoulder level. Stopping, he raised his rifle and pressed his cheek to the stock as he sighted through the dancing haze. All that he could see was the shimmer of heated air. The three shapes that he'd watched coming up from a distance were blurred to a point that made accurate aiming impossible.

After waiting what seemed to him plenty of time to bring the outlaws within sighting distance, Longarm raised the Winchester again. When he lowered his eyes and tried to catch the trio in the sights, nothing had changed. All he could tell was that there were three men on horses in front of him. He had no way of judging their distance, for at one moment the three looked bigger than life-size, while at the next instant they had shrunk to the size of dwarfs astride ponies.

Resigning himself to a still longer wait, Longarm brought the rifle's muzzle down once more. The uncertainty of the situation was getting on Longarm's usually relaxed nerves. If he let the riders get too close, if the element of surprise he'd been counting on was lost, he faced odds of three to one. Under normal conditions, Longarm's justified confidence in his own marksmanship wouldn't have wavered. Now, with long-range shots proving to be impossible, he was courting extra danger by letting the three get too close. When shooting became a matter of chance instead of skilled gun-handling, three rifles against two were a fool's odds.

This time he waited even longer to shoulder his rifle. His extra time allowance improved the sight-picture a little, but not enough. He was almost able to tell now where horse ended and man began. Time was running out; he'd reached the point where losses had to be cut. Longarm chose the man in the center. He sighted on him as best he could in the thick, shifting haze, and squeezed off a shot. The rider did not fall, but his horse stumbled and began to hobble on three legs.

Dense as the air was, Longarm could see the riders whip out rifles from their saddle scabbards. He ducked instinctively, even knowing that they could aim no more accurately than he could, as bullets from two of the rifles raised puffs of dust in the dirt in front of him and a third slug whistled above his head. When he looked up again, two of the horses had left the trail. He could see them cutting to right and left. The wounded horse was still directly in front of him, still limping on three legs.

Longarm began lifting his rifle for another shot, but with the butt halfway to his shoulder, he suddenly realized that a crippled horse in his present situation was worth as much as a dead horse or, for that matter, a dead rustler. The realization gave him a new strategy to follow, one he needed now that the trio had separated. It was the outlaws now who had the advantage. With one on each side of him, they could catch him in a crossfire, and whipsaw him with ranging shots until their two rifles against his one brought him down.

Old son, he muttered, *there's a time to stand still and a time to move.*

Chapter 13

Hurrying to the mare, Longarm freed the reins and levered himself into the saddle. He kicked the horse's flanks, and she picked her way unwillingly along the bed of the narrow gully, where there was barely room for her hooves to meet solid ground, up to the hump that marked the rim of Goblin Valley.

As Longarm topped the rounded rise, a rifle cracked. He ducked by instinct, but heard no bullet whistle past, saw no dust cloud raised by a short shot. He looked back along the trail. The horse he'd wounded had fallen to the ground. The man who'd been riding it stood over the animal, his rifle muzzle pressed to its head.

One down and two more to go, Longarm thought as he let the mare pick her own way over the seamed earth, with its maze of wrinkles and ridges.

He looked around him, trying to locate the other two riders. He saw one almost at once. This man, like Longarm himself, had ridden into the valley's saucer and was cutting an arc that Longarm guessed was designed to bring him up in the rear of the gully from which the shots had come.

Of the second rider there was no trace, but Longarm's line of sight to his rear was cut short by the valley rim. Since one man had ridden into the valley toward the west, Longarm guessed that the other outlaw had gone east in a maneuver designed not only to flank the gully, but to catch it in a crossfire.

Longarm turned his attention to the rider he'd glimpsed before. He was coming at Longarm in an almost straight line. Just as Longarm saw him, the outlaw brought up his rifle and fired. The slug fell short. It plowed into the earth, and a puff of whitish dust rose about ten feet away from the mare's hooves. Longarm jerked the reins in a quick change of direction, but did not return the shot. He still faced odds of two to one, and a final showdown with the whole gang lay ahead. He needed to conserve ammunition.

Apparently the outlaw had all the shells he wanted to use. He fired again, and this time Longarm felt the slug. It seared like a hot branding iron along the top of his thigh, leaving a neat hole in his trousers where it entered, and a small slit where it came out. Longarm's leg began to hurt, but only a little blood seeped out of the bullet crease. The burning sensation told him that the bullet had not entered his leg, but had just scratched a shallow groove in the skin.

It was a wound that could slow him down, though, if the outlaw succeeded in what he was now trying to do. He'd obviously adopted Longarm's own tactics: aim for the horse, a bigger and more certain target, instead of trying to knock off the rider. Longarm fixed his eyes on his antagonist, who'd turned his horse to ride at right angles to Longarm's path. Longarm was tempted to try another shot, but the haze in the valley was even thicker than it had been on the rim. Instead, Longarm switched his direction and cut at right angles to the line he'd been riding.

Seeing the change, the outlaw altered his own course. Now he was chasing Longarm, riding behind him, and Longarm was moving parallel to the trail on which the fight had started. This wasn't at all to Longarm's liking. He was at a disadvantage now, being chased by a rider who could take his time aiming and firing at Longarm's back. He reversed his course in a tight circle and charged at his pursuer. The outlaw veered away. Longarm persisted until he foced the other man to change the sharp angle he'd chosen to a wider one. Then Longarm turned the mare and became the hunter instead of the quarry.

By now, the mare's chest was heaving. Longarm reined in and released the leathers in order to bring his rifle up. The air in Goblin Valley was thicker, but the distance to his target was shorter. Longarm aimed for the flank of the outlaw's horse. He could tell his slug had gone home. The animal reared, throwing its rider, and dashed ahead for a few steps before collapsing. Longarm turned the mare quickly, and had ridden out of certain range before the outlaw could pick himself up, find the rifle he'd dropped, and get off a vengeance shot. The slug was harmlessly wide. The man did not fire again. Longarm looked back and saw him standing, gazing down at his dead horse.

Now the game had become one of hide-and-seek in the gullied slope on the far rim of Goblin Valley. Longarm did not hurry to pursue it. He was contented, after getting far out of range of the unhorsed outlaw, to let the mare walk. After she'd cooled down and her panting had stopped, he let her drink scantily, pouring water from his canteen into his cupped hands and bringing them to the horse's nose before it all trickled out. The horse got little except moisture, but the little she got was better for her than a deep drink would have been, in her present condition.

Remounted, with the mare breathing regularly again, Longarm rode up the slope of Goblin Valley and over the hump of its rim. In front of him, the land stretched to the east in a cross-stitched maze of ravines and cliffs and more ravines, broken here and there by small rainbow-painted buttes. There was barrenness everywhere except for a rare patch of green atop an occasional butte, where the windborne sand had gouged out a cup big enough to hold a bucketful or so of water for a few days following one of the occasional rains that passed quickly over the arid land.

There were canyons of all sizes, some big enough to swallow a herd of elephants, others so small a mouse would have trouble hiding in them. Longarm pulled up the mare, trying to decide which direction might have been taken by the outlaw still to be accounted for. During the chase in which he and the second rider had been engaged, Longarm had lost his bearings. He tried to orient himself now by looking along the valley rim and locating the dead horse that lay somewhere

154

along its circular sweep. A buzzard wheeling high above gave him the clue he sought. Keeping the black speck in sight, he started north for the area over which it was flying.

Preoccupied with watching the buzzard, setting his mind to ignore the shallow crease in his thigh, which was beginning to itch as sweat trickled into it, and with the heated air shimmering even more thickly ahead as the day went from uncomfortably warm to unpleasantly hot, Longarm missed seeing the horse that came around the curve in the rim ahead. His first hint that the man he was looking for was anywhere nearby was the thudding of a rifle slug into the baked ground at one side of him, followed instantly by the sharp crack of the rifle that had fired it.

Longarm's own rifle was ready. He'd had a bit more experience now in sighting through the haze. He took quick aim and sent a shot to the dead center of what he was reasonably sure was the chest of the horse ahead. Then, as quickly as he could lever fresh shells into the Winchester's chamber, he placed bracketing shots on either side of his first point of aim. The triple effort was not wasted. The horse lurched and fell forward. Only then could Longarm see that the animal was being ridden double. He deduced that the outlaw who'd ridden off to the west had circled back to pick up his companion, and had started his overloaded horse back to the Roost.

Longarm turned off the trail onto Goblin Valley's raddled surface, and looped out of reasonable aiming distance to go around the stranded outlaws. Both of them fired at him, but he'd urged the mare into a trot and, though under normal conditions he'd have offered an easy target, the hazy atmosphere confounded the men firing at him. He ran the gauntlet without harm. When the two dismounted outlaws were swallowed up in the haze, he rode back to the trail and let the mare drop into a walk again. He had no worries about the outlaws behind him. There was no way they could overtake him; their only choice was to return to the

Roost. On foot, carrying their saddles, they couldn't possibly get back to the box canyon until dusk.

His eyes automatically searched the trail ahead, and the terrain on both sides. A dark figure approaching through the haze drew his instant attention. He couldn't yet make out the features of the man on the horse, but anybody who was heading in the direction of the rustler's hideout was automatically marked in his mind as a suspicious character.

Slowly the deliberate pace of their horses brought them together. Longarm drew his Winchester from its saddle scabbard and rested it across his arms. Just before they came within hailing distance of one another, the approaching rider spread his arms wide. Longarm didn't sheathe his rifle at the gesture, though. He waited until he could make out the man's features, and presently he recognized Jim Peters, the ex-convict turned rancher. Longarm's original suspicions about Peters came back the instant he recognized the approaching rider. He reined in and waited for Peters to reach him.

"Marshal," Peters said when he got close enough to greet Longarm, "I'm surprised. You didn't mention that you were heading this way when you stopped at my place."

"I never know where this job of mine's going to take me," Longarm replied. "But I came real close to not getting here."

"Sounds like you ran into trouble."

"You could say that. The night after I left your spread, a fellow tried to bushwhack me. Took a couple of potshots into my bedroll where I stopped to sleep by the trail. Lucky I wasn't in it."

Peters's startled jump and the surprised look that appeared on his face were genuine enough to satisfy Longarm that he'd known nothing about the effort to kill him.

Peters said, "The hell you say! I hope you caught the fellow."

"I killed him," Longarm said bluntly.

156

"That must've happened close to my place, Marshal."

"It did. But I don't figure you had anything to do with it."

"You're damned right I didn't!" the young rancher exclaimed. "I don't want any part of killing somebody."

"Most folks don't," Longarm nodded. "I guess your foreman—Bailey, ain't that his name?—I guess he's still with you?"

"Of course. Clem's a good foreman." Peters tried not to show that he caught the association of Bailey's name with Longarm's remark about the assassination attempt, but his voice was far from firm.

Longarm said, "You're sort of far from home, ain't you?"

"Quite a ways." Peters's efforts to hide his confusion at the question didn't quite succeed. He added, "I'm heading over to Fort Cameron, to see if I can sell some cattle to the army."

"Funny you'd range this far. I'd think those Mormon towns up north would make an easier place to drive to market."

"Oh, those folks are too hard to bargain with. I'll get a better price from the army without a lot of dickering."

"I see. But there's forts closer to you, over in Colorado, it seems like to me."

"I'd like to sell to them, sure. But I'm told the army quartermasters have orders to buy from ranchers in the same territory the forts are in."

It was a clumsy lie, and Peters's expression showed he knew it.

Longarm let it pass. "Must be a new regulation I ain't heard about." Then he stared hard at the young man. "I guess you've thought about selling to some of the Indian reservations? I hear they're paying top prices now for beef cattle."

Peters's face tightened, but he managed to meet Longarm's eyes. "Now that never occurred to me, Marshal. I'll have to look into it."

"You do that. There's one thing the government's real fussy about when they buy reservation beef, though."

"Oh? What's that?"

"They want a bill of sale that proves where the steers come from. If a man was to try to run in some brands that'd been changed with a running iron, like turning a Circle C into a Target, or a Lazy E into a House, he might find himself in deep trouble."

Peters flinched when Longarm mentioned the brands. He said, "I've had all I want to do with running irons, Marshal."

"I'm glad to hear that. You know, Peters, I've noticed something about judges. They'll go light on a man who claims he got into a spot of trouble accidental, but if he gets himself into a jackpot again and says that was an accident too, the judge just plain won't listen to him."

Peters was keeping his features composed, but his lips were pressed together so tightly that a line of white outlined them. He finally said, "I think I've had all I want of standing up in front of a judge, Marshal. I don't intend to do it a second time."

"That's good." Longarm took out a cheroot and lit it. He said after his first puff, "You've got a nice little wife. You be sure to give her my respects when you get back home."

"Thanks. I'll sure do that."

Longarm went on, "If you're on the way to Fort Cameron, you'll save some time by cutting straight across Goblin Valley instead of taking this old trail around it."

"Thanks. I—I really don't know the trails all that well in this part of the Territory." Peters picked up the reins that he'd let fall loosely on his horse's neck. "I guess I'd better be getting on. The day's half gone, and I've still got a long way to ride."

"Good luck to you, Peters." Longarm said.

"Same to you, Marshal."

Longarm watched Peters ride away. The young rancher cut off the trail and started due west across the valley. Longarm let him get forty or fifty yards away before calling, "Peters!"

Reining in, Peters turned in his saddle. "You forget something you wanted to say to me, Marshal?"

"Just one thing. I figure you'll make a pretty good rancher. But you make a damned poor liar."

For a moment, Peters hesitated. Then he touched his hatbrim and kneed his horse into motion again. Longarm watched him until he disappeared into the heat haze, then resumed his own interrupted ride.

"Long!" Verda Blankenship exclaimed when she opened her cabin door to Longarm's call and knock. "Goddamn! Am I glad to see you back!" She caught sight of his torn trouser leg. "I always knew you'd tear your pants one of these days. I'll have to fix that for you." Then she looked at the two rips more closely. "That's not just a snag you got by accident, Long. Those are bullet holes! Are you hurt?"

"No, just a graze. It stings a little bit, is all."

"Well, let's get your pants off, and I'll see if it needs to have a bandage on it."

Longarm followed her inside. The bedroom door was open wide, the bed still rumpled. He let Verda help him take off his vest and gunbelt and hang them on a chair, then sat down to remove his boots. When his pants and shirt and balbriggans had followed the boots, and she looked at the wound, she shook her head and grinned.

"You're lucky, Long. A little bit closer to center, and that bullet would've ruined the best part of you," she told him.

Longarm looked at the bullet-graze. The slug had traveled between his underwear and skin, tracing an angry red line from just above his knee almost to his hip. The skin over the crease was crusted, but only a few drops of blood had flowed.

"It don't amount to anything," he told Verda. "I've had a few that was worse."

She looked at his naked body, and the scars it bore. "I saw that when you waded out of the pond the other day, but I didn't think you'd want me asking questions."

"I didn't. Talking about old scars never does any good."

"Well, this won't scar, but I'd better wash it clean, just the same. You're not in any hurry to leave again, are you, Long? What I mean is, is there time for me to get some water hot?"

"Sure. It's just past noon. There's not any hurry."

"Good." Verda busied herself filling the kettle and putting a few thin sticks of scrub cedar in the stove. Over her shoulder, she said to Longarm, "I got so excited when I saw you'd been shot that I haven't even asked if you found the Roost."

"I found it, all right. And I've got to go back there later on, toward evening. But like I said, there's not any hurry."

"Have you had anything to eat?" she asked. "Because if you're hungry, I can fry some bacon and hotcakes while the stove's hot."

Longarm had reached for the bottle of rye, still standing on the table where he'd put it the day before, and was pouring himself a drink. He said, "I can stand to eat something, sure enough. About all I've had today's a few bites of jerky and parched corn."

"Then you'll need food. And if you're not in too big a hurry, you can rest in bed awhile. If you feel like it, that is."

Longarm looked at her over his glass. "You'd be resting with me, I suppose?"

"Of course," she said innocently.

"I know about how much rest I'd get, then. Not that I'd complain."

Verda smiled. "We'll get around to that later. First, I'll wash off that bullet-graze and feed you."

She had the food ready before the water boiled. Longarm hadn't realized how hungry he was. His mind had been too busy to listen to any messages from his stomach. Verda set a plate of hotcakes covered with strips of thick-sliced crisp bacon on the table in front of him.

"Go ahead and eat," she said. "I'll sit down and sew up your pants, and you can tell me what happened at the Roost."

Between bites, while Verda took neat, almost invisible stitches in the small rips the bullet had made in Longarm's trousers, he told her what had happened.

"So those three men who were coming to get you— Lance and whoever the others were—are still hoofing it back to the Roost," he concluded. "I figure they'll get there about sundown, which is a little bit before I aim to show up there myself."

Verda shuddered. "I'm sure glad you were here, Long. I keep on telling myself I can handle any trouble I might get into, but this would've been a lot more than I could've faced alone."

"You sure picked out a rough bunch to throw in with."

"I guess I knew it, but wouldn't let on to the truth to myself. You seem to be a lot rougher than they are, though."

"Maybe I just had a lot of luck."

Verda snorted—an unladylike, unmistakable snort. "Don't talk about luck to me. I saw you face Mose, remember? Well, it looks as though you're going to have a busy night, if you plan to take on a dozen or more just like him. Or is that what you've got in mind?"

"More or less. You see, Verda, if I move just right, I can bottle up that whole gang in the canyon, with that narrow passageway the only way in or out. And they won't be looking for me back there. After Lance and those other two pull in and tell Kid Manders what happened to them, they'll figure I've gone looking for help."

"But you don't intend to," she said flatly.

"No. Which don't mean I won't *need* some help. But first I've got to make sure about one thing."

"What's that?"

Longarm sat silently for a moment. He'd tried to plan what he would say to Verda while riding in after he'd said goodbye to Peters, but no matter how he

161

twisted words and phrases around, he hadn't succeeded in finding quite the right words. Finally he said, "You see why you can't keep on staying here by yourself, don't you?"

She nodded somewhat reluctantly. "Much as I hate to admit it, you're right."

"And you're done with Kid Manders and his bunch, too," he went on. Again Verda nodded agreement. "So it don't look to me like you've got but one way to go."

"Oh, stop beating around the bush, Long!" Verda snapped. "I've already argued that out with myself, while you were gone. I had it in mind to ask you— even beg you, if I had to—if you'd give me a hand getting out of the mess I've gotten myself into. I'm through with Manders and his kind for good. Now, if you've got something in mind, come out with it in plain words. But I suppose you know in advance that whatever you want me to do, I'll say yes."

Chapter 14

For a silent moment, Longarm studied Verda's face. Satisfied, he nodded. "That's all I wanted to hear you say. We'll go over the ins and outs later on. This place on my leg keeps stinging me a little bit. I was sweating pretty good out there on the trail. Maybe if you wash the salt out of it, it'll quit bothering me, and I can put my mind on things better."

"Now that's an idea that appeals to me," Verda said. She stood and draped Longarm's mended clothing over the back of her chair. "I'll fix the hot water."

Longarm stepped gingerly into the washtub Verda dragged out of the corner behind the stove. She poured in cold water and then added hot from the steaming kettle until Longarm could feel the heat all the way up to his waist. Verda knelt in front of the tub and began to wash the bullet-crease. She soaped the angry red welt, then rinsed away the soap with a cloth. The stinging that had been plaguing Longarm eased almost at once. She began to rinse the crease a second time.

"It feels fine now," Longarm told her. "You can stop, and I'll dry off."

"Stand still, Long!" she commanded. "While you're wet, I might as well do a good job of washing."

Verda soaped her hands and ran them, slick and warm, up Longarm's unwounded thigh. She didn't stop there, but went on to soap his crotch. Her touch was soft, her fingers caressing. Longarm began to grow hard even before she started rinsing away the soap. Cradling his swelling erection in her moist hands, Verda looked up at Longarm. "You're not as tired as I was afraid you'd be."

163

"It sure don't look that way, does it?"

"And I don't think this will tire you too much."

She pushed his hardening flesh against her cheek and stropped it gently against her soft skin. Lifting her head, she moved her hands around her neck, below her chin, stopping now and then to rub his tip back and forth. Then she spent several moments stropping her other cheek before bringing the tip across her eyes. Sensitized ·by the soft caresses, Longarm could feel each eyelash prickle as Verda worked his tip from one eye to the next. His buttock muscles tightened involuntarily as he looked down and saw Verda's upturned face, her lips curved in a smile of sensual bliss.

Keeping the pressure on her skin as soft as the brushing of a butterfly's wings, Verda traced the swollen tip down her cheek again, across her neck, and up her chin. She moved it slowly along her closed, pursed lips before opening them and nibbling up and down his swollen, fleshy shaft. Then she pushed her tongue through her lips and repeated the caresses.

Longarm was throbbing even before Verda opened her mouth and took him in. Her lips closed over him, and inside the hot cavern of her mouth, he could feel her tongue rasping over and across and around him.

She released him once to ask, "How long can you last, this way?"

"About as long as you'd like for me to."

"That's good. I'd like to enjoy you this way for a while."

Verda returned to her caresses. She varied them to prolong her pleasure by shrugging her dress off her shoulders and letting it fall to her waist. By stretching, she could rub his erection over her breasts, pushing it hard into their roughened rosettes, cradling the shaft between her soft mounds, pushing and molding with both hands to enclose it in their pulsing warmth.

Once, while she was holding him this way, Longarm said, "It ain't that I don't like what you're doing, Verda, but hadn't we better go get in bed now?"

"If that's what you want to do. I'm just at the point of going off, though. It wouldn't be any good for you.

164

Wait just a few more minutes, Long. I love this so, I hate to stop so soon."

She moved him from her breasts, dragging the tip up her neck and chin to pull him into her mouth once more with eager lips. Longarm was beginning to hold himself back when he felt her mouth close tighter around him and her body began quivering. She jerked and writhed while holding him motionless, her hands grasping his thighs to pull him to her. When her trembling subsided and came to an end, Verda released him. She stood up, leaving her dress in a wrinkled ring on the floor.

"Now, take me to bed," she urged him. "Hurry!"

She moved aside to let Longarm step out of the tub, and started for the bedroom. He hurried after her, and reached her while she was bending over the bed, throwing the coverings aside. Grabbing her by the hips, he entered her from behind in one swift, forceful lunge.

"Oh God!" Verda cried. "Keep it there awhile! It feels bigger than ever when you put it in that way!"

Longarm lifted her hips and stepped forward to let her get her knees on the bed. "You got me real worked up, Verda," he told her. "Hang on now. I aim to give you all you want and maybe a little bit more!"

Longarm had left his fatigue behind, in the bath water. He felt fresher than he'd thought he could be, after a hard and sleepless night and the pounding of several hours in the saddle. He held his first thrusts deep, pulling hard on Verda's hips, her softly rounded buttocks flattened against his muscular belly.

When he began stroking, Verda started to sigh. He was pulling back, almost leaving her, then pounding in with such ferocity that his hips smashed into her buttocks with a sharp, fleshy slap. She buried her head in the bed, raising her hips as high as they would go, to let him reach even deeper inside.

He felt Verda's muscles tighten and her body begin to undulate. Her sighs became moans and her moans grew into animal-cries as she shook into her orgasm, and continued to shake in rhythmic rippling as he went on driving.

Longarm was reaching his own point of no return now. Each time he went pistonlike into Verda's ready body, his spine arched, pulling his shoulders back and thrusting his hips forward. He was conscious of Verda, but now his own feelings were taking over, sending him into a series of shorter, faster, almost spastic thrusts until at last there was no more delaying. He felt himself going over the edge, and slowed his strokes to prolong the shaking that rippled over his body. Verda's ululations were ringing in his ears. They rose to their highest pitch and ended in a sobbing, moaning decrescendo while her paroxysmic shudders reached still another peak and then subsided with low, keening moans, and both she and Longarm were motionless and shaken, and the only sound in the room was the rasping of air in their throats as they gasped for breath.

Slowly Longarm withdrew from her, and stretched out across the bed beside her. Verda was lying on her face. Now and then she shuddered involuntarily. As the minutes passed, the shudders came less often and finally stopped completely. Longarm was only half aware of her. He lay with his eyes closed, conscious of nothing except his drained relaxation and the occasional current of air that passed over the drying moisture on his groin and thighs.

Verda finally raised her head. "You really did what you said you would. You gave me all I could take, for once."

"You're about the readiest woman I ever did see," he told her. "But I'll say this—you sure make a man feel like he's appreciated."

"Oh, I appreciate you. I guess you're the first man I've really appreciated in a long time, though. Most of them give out while I'm still ready to go again."

He sat up. "This one time's going to have to last you for a while. There's not anything I'd like better than to stay right here in bed, but I've got things to do that won't wait until I'm ready to do them."

"Kid Manders and his gang?" she asked.

"Yes. Now, we better get our clothes on and sit down in the other room and have a long, sober talk."

166

"I suppose so. If we try to talk lying in bed, the first thing that's going to happen is that I'll be reaching over there and taking hold of you, and then we'll be off again." Verda stood up and stretched with a purely animal litheness, a stretch that brought her full breasts high and taut, and flattened her stomach.

Longarm said, "Go on and dress. I'll be right there."

He followed her into the main room. Wordlessly, Verda motioned for him to come to where she was standing beside the tub. He hesitated. She said, "Don't worry, I'm not going to try to get you hard again. But you need to be sponged off."

Longarm nodded and stood beside her while she wet the washcloth and rubbed it over his belly and legs. "Now," she said when she'd finished, "you'll feel better when you go to put your clothes on."

While Longarm dressed, Verda sponged herself off and pulled her dress over her head.

Longarm looked up from the chair where he'd sat to put on his boots. "You'll want to wear more than that," he told her. "I've got something I want you to do for me in Hanksville."

She looked at him, her eyes questioning. He shook his head. "Go in and get on what you'll be wearing to town. Then I'll tell you."

Verda disappeared into the bedroom. Longarm lighted a cheroot and poured two drinks from the bottle of rye. He sipped from one glass while he waited. In less time than he'd thought possible, Verda came back. She now wore a long wool skirt and blouse, and carried a jacket that matched the skirt. She was wearing boots instead of the heavy work shoes that were usually on her feet.

"All right," she said. She picked up the shotglass and sat down. "I'm as ready as I'll ever be. What is it you want me to do?"

"I already told you what that place Manders and his bunch call the Roost is like," he began. Verda nodded. He continued, "I aim to get back there about a half-hour after it gets dark. They'll have lookouts posted,

167

same as they did last night, but I'll figure out a way to bottle the whole gang up in that box canyon."

"You're taking on too big a job," she protested. "Listen, Long, I'm a good shot, and I'm not afraid to stand up and have it out with somebody. Let me go along and help you!"

Longarm shook his head. "No. Bottling up the Kid and his crew's not all that much of a job. Keeping the stopper in the bottle's what bothers me. I can't hold them inside the canyon forever, but I can keep them in there long enough for a posse to get there from Hanksville."

"And that's where I come in," Verda said.

"That's where you come in," Longarm confirmed as he looked searchingly at her. "Can I depend on you to ride into town and get a posse started out?"

"How am I supposed to do that? I know there's some officials there who're mixed up with the Kid—the sheriff's chief deputy, maybe the sheriff himself, for all I know. And the county prosecutor. And maybe some others. The Kid hasn't really said anything except to brag now and then that he's got the town under his thumb. Damn it, Long, I wouldn't know who to turn to. And if I went to the wrong man, you'd be in one hell of a fix!"

"I know that, Verda. I only know one man I feel like I can trust. I aim to send you to him. He's old, and crippled up right bad, but when you tell him what I'll pass on to you, and explain what's going on out at the Roost, I'm gambling he'll do something about it."

"Who is he?"

"I don't imagine you'd know about him. He's a retired judge, and he don't live right in Hanksville, but I can tell you how to find his place."

Verda was smiling. She asked, "Would his name by any chance be Frank Walton?"

"That's the one. You saying you know him?" Longarm asked her incredulously.

"I ought to. He's my uncle. And I know where he lives. My mother and I used to visit Uncle Frank when he first moved out there, right after he retired."

168

Longarm kept himself from showing surprise and relief. For the first time, though, he felt it was safe for him to trust Verda to carry out the job he'd hesitantly planned for her. He said, "I don't aim to pry into your family life or your private affairs, Verda, but there ain't any reason why you'd shy away from going to Judge Walton, is there?"

She shook her head. "No. Oh, I guess I'll feel a little bit ashamed, or maybe embarrassed, having to explain to Uncle Frank how I got tangled up with Kid Manders and his gang, but that's not going to keep me from going to him." She took a deep breath. Longarm could see that she wanted to tell him more, and said nothing. Verda went on, "I guess it'd be hard for you to understand, Long, but—"

"Try me," Longarm broke in. "Maybe you'd be surprised."

"It's a long story."

"We got a little time to spare." Longarm glanced out the open window in the front wall. "It'll only take me about an hour or so to get to the Roost, and I don't have to leave right now."

"Well," Verda began, "Uncle Frank won't be surprised when I go to him with this, I guess. He'll remember what a crazy, wild fool I've always been. He tried to keep me from getting married, did his best to show me that Mormon ways are different from ours. I found out he was right, of course, but I've been too stiff-necked to go to him and admit it."

"He might even be glad to see you, then," Longarm suggested.

"Oh, he will be. Uncle Frank's always been able to see the other side of things. And I've missed him. I do love him, you know."

"Sure. Well, then, if you're sure I can depend on you to get there and tell him what's going on—"

Verda said angrily, "I promised you I will, Long. What more do you expect me too say?"

"Nothing, Verda. I wasn't aiming to insult you."

"I didn't take it as an insult. I was surprised, that's all. Don't you think I'm smart enough to see that I'll

169

never be able to draw an easy breath until Kid Manders and Lance and that whole gang of theirs are behind bars?"

"I had to be sure," Longarm apologized.

"One thing bothers me," Verda frowned. "How's Uncle Frank going to find the Roost? Remember, I don't know where it is. I've never been there. All I'm sure of is that it's somewhere south of here."

"I'd bet the judge will know," Longarm told her. He fished out the map Walton had marked and measured distances with a practiced eye. Then he fumbled the stub of a pencil from his vest pocket and marked a small circle in the area where the Roost had to be. He handed the map to Verda. "Here. Show your uncle this. And when you explain to him the kind of situation I'm in, tell him I said old judges are like old soldiers—they never do retire. And they can always be called back to duty if they're needed. Make sure he understands how bad I need him to help out."

"If I know Uncle Frank, he'll jump at the chance. He never did want to retire, you know. I don't think he would have, if it hadn't been for his back." She studied Longarm's face for a moment, then said, "You're an awful lot of man, Long, but I don't see how you can handle as big a gang as the Kid's got, all by yourself."

"You let me worry about that," he told her. "I'll manage."

Verda's frown changed to a smile. "Yes. I guess you will."

Longarm stood up. "I'll go get the horses from the pond. I'll put your saddle on the horse Mose was riding, instead of on your mare. She needs to be rested, but the other horse is fresh."

"All right. I'll be ready by the time you get the horses up to the corral."

Verda was waiting at the pole corral when Longarm rode her mare back from the pond, leading the big gray Morgan that Mose had ridden, as well as his own cavalry roan. She helped him put her saddle on the Morgan, and was starting to give him a hand in trans-

170

ferring his own gear from the mare to the roan when he stopped her.

"Leave this for me to do, Verda. You get on to Hanksville and find Judge Walton. It's going to take a while for you to do that, and more time for you and him to put a posse together. Even moving as fast as you can, you can't have a posse to the Roost before sometime about noon tomorrow."

"Can you hold the gang bottled up that long?"

"I sure as hell aim to try."

Verda was still reluctant to mount. She asked Longarm, "Suppose I run into some of the gang on the way to town?"

"I thought you said only three or four of them know you?"

"That's right. Besides Mose, I know the Kid and Lance and Chesty and Bowers. There might be more of them who've seen me, though, spied on me when I didn't know about it."

"You ain't getting cold feet on me, are you?"

"No, damn it, I'm not! I'm just trying to think of anything and everything that might come up!"

"Well, you've got your rifle there. Use it if you got any doubts. Now mount up and ride. You can't get that posse to the Roost a minute too soon to please me."

Verda clung to Longarm for a moment when she kissed him goodbye. "Take care of yourself," she whispered. Her hand sought his crotch in a brief caress. "I wouldn't want anything to happen to you, you know."

"I'll be fine. Now you get going!"

Longarm watched Verda until she was lost to view in the glare of the westering sun and the shimmering heat-haze. Then he turned to making his own preparations to return to the Roost. His guns drew his attention first. He emptied the spare boxes of ammunition he always carried in his saddlebags; his .44-40 Colt, his derringer, and his Winchester were all chambered for the same shells. He inspected each cartridge, looking for signs of corrosion around the primers that might cause a misfire, for deformed noses on slugs that might cause even a well-aimed shot to miss. He distributed the shells in the pockets of his pants and flannel shirt. They made a heavy but surprisingly compact load.

Turning to his guns, Longarm checked out the Colt. There was a small amount of hot water left in the kettle; he swabbed the barrel and cylinder with it to remove any powder residue that might have escaped his careful previous cleanings. Then he gave the weapon a light rubbing of gun oil, wiped it with a clean handkerchief, and slid it back into the holster that had been shrunk to fit the revolver's contours.

His Winchester received similar treatment. From butt-plate to front sight, it was inspected, cleaned, and oiled. Finally, he took out the wicked-looking little derringer that was clipped to one end of his watch chain and went over its simpler mechanism as carefully as he'd checked his other weapons.

Longarm's final chore involved a visit to the corral. He took a rein-strap off the bridle that had belonged to Mose and, with the addition of a pair of saddlestrings from the dead outlaw's saddle, improvised a sling that would allow him to carry his Winchester across his back, army-style. The result looked clumsy, but it worked. He tested the sling a few times until he found the angle at which it hung most comfortably and did not interfere with his draw. His coat had long ago been folded and added to his bedroll.

Longarm had worked neither hastily nor slowly, but at a deliberate pace. He checked the sun's position occasionally as he went about his chores, gauging its angle against the time he knew it would take him to ride to the Roost and arrive just after dark. When the time came for him to leave, he had no idle waiting to do.

Without looking back at Verda's deserted house, he rode south until he reached the rim of Goblin Valley, then started around the sweep of its shallow bowl.

Chapter 15

When Longarm reached the carcass of the dead horse on the rim of the valley, the bottom edge of the red sun was just touching the jagged horizon. As he got closer, three buzzards flapped clumsily up from the carcass and began circling, rising into the cloudless sky. Longarm watched them leveling off, waiting for him to move on. He did not stop. There'd be nothing he could tell from the horse's carcass unless he turned it over to inspect the brand, and that was a job he didn't intend to take on.

He was in no hurry. His timing was working out. If he kept the roan at a fast trail-walk, he'd sight the butte into which nature had cut the outlaw's box canyon at just about dusk. When he sighted the steep walls of the big butte on the horizon, though, there was still too much light to suit him. The sun was gone, and the fitful twilight breeze was beginning to stir and cool the air. The heat-haze was dissipating, which meant that a lookout atop the butte could see much farther. It wasn't part of Longarm's plan to be seen approaching. The kind of action he had in mind must be carried out with quick, unexpected strokes. He stopped to wait.

While the light faded to blue dusk in the quick transition from day to night that occurs in desert country, Longarm lighted what he knew might be his last cheroot before things were decided at the Roost. The first stars were appearing, and he marked the butte's location in relation to the three brightest, then set his course by them as he rode through the early darkness. With night to cover his approach, he toed the roan to a faster gait. Soon the black bulk of the butte's sheer rise was blotting out the stars in the southern sky. He reined in and dismounted. He led the roan to the base of the towering butte, and when he reached it, he walked with the horse plodding behind him until he found a shelf that would hide the animal from above. A big rock laid on the grounded reins of the cavalry-trained gelding was enough for a tether; the roan would stand until Longarm returned.

Rising above him, its rim black against the night sky, the butte looked to Longarm as though it were ten miles high. He slung his canteen over one shoulder by its strap, his rifle over the other by its improvised sling. Setting his jaw, he began to scale the wall.

Longarm was no mountaineer, but in the hard-scrabble hills of West Virginia where he grew up, his boyhood had been spent in hunting over the rough mountain terrain. He knew that even the sheerest rises never shot up straight, but were seamed with shelves and cracks that would give a determined man hand-holds and toeholds. The butte at the edge of Goblin Valley was no exception.

Rockslides at its base had angled out from the high walls to form a loose scree over which he picked his way, testing each step with his forward foot before taking his other foot off the ground. The scree shifted and slid at times when it took his weight, but the slanting course he chose eventually got him to the massive wall itself, fifty feet above ground level.

He scrambled along the edge of the scree until he reached a long crack that zigzagged up the wall. The soft sandstone of the butte's side was layered between strata of earth almost as hard as the stone—almost, but not quite, Longarm learned before he'd gone up the crack more than a dozen yards. In his eagerness to mount the wall quickly, and having found the going this far so easy, he grew overconfident and raised himself in a footrest without testing it thoroughly. The earth that had seemed so solid was eroded here. It gave under his weight, and for a moment Longarm hung in precarious balance, one foot sliding down the narrow slit, the other behind him over empty space.

174

Somehow, he managed to throw his body forward and grab at the slit with his hands. His clutching fingers found nothing to grasp except crumbling earth. The weight of his body dragging against the cliff-face did little to slow his descent. He lost twenty feet before the foot that was still wedged into the crevice hit a layer of sandstone firm enough to take his weight. Motionless at last, Longarm pressed himself to the rough surface and rested for a moment before starting up once more.

His near-fall taught him caution. He traversed the section of soft sandstone by wedging his lower leg in the crack and, in effect, climbed with his knees until the edges of the crack became solid once again.

Suddenly, the crevice ended. An expanse of unbroken wall stretched above his head. Craning his neck backward, he looked for protruding rocks or shelves of earth that would give him something to cling to and hoist himself upward. There were none.

Longarm clung to his place for several minutes while he studied his position. There were cracks on either side similar to the one he'd used to ascend this far, but all of them were beyond the reach of his arms, no matter how far he might stretch them. Straining his eyes to the utmost in the darkness, he tried to pick out the crack that rose highest on the wall, but his field of vision was limited. He finally made a random choice of the slit on his right.

Fishing his jackknife from his pocket, Longarm stretched and bent to gouge out a toehold in the wall beside him. The soil, baked by countless thousands of years of sunny days, resisted his blade stubbornly. He pecked away until he'd dug a niche three inches wide and two inches high and perhaps six inches deep. Stretching his leg, he fitted his booted toe in the hole and tested it carefully by letting it take his weight a little at a time. The toehold held. Longarm swung his body sideways and hung with one toe in the hole until he could gouge out a smaller niche for his hand.

He could not test the handhold as thoroughly as he had the toehold, by letting it take his weight gradually. He flexed his arm, pulling down on the small groove, and it seemed solid enough. Bit by bit, he shifted his weight until he could swing sideways and hang with a hand and a foot in the precarious supports he'd dug.

There was still a greater test, a bigger risk. Longarm took his foot out of its niche and hung by his right hand while he groped with his other foot for the toehold. It seemed to him that he'd never find it. His right hand was beginning to grow numb before his left foot at last slid into the hole and he could stand on it while bending to dig another toehold at knee level.

Then he had the same agonizing process to repeat. Dangling by his left hand, he planted his right foot in the new toehold and clung long enough to peck out a hole for his right hand. Clasping his knife between his teeth, Longarm balanced with his left foot in the toehold and brought his left hand as near his right as possible.

He slid his right hand from its shallow notch in the wall and, by leaning a bit more precariously, got the fingers of his left hand into the notch while still holding his balance. One more shift after cutting a third toehold, and he could wedge his right foot in the new crack that gave him a path up the wall the rest of the way to the top.

For a moment, after he'd gotten both feet firmly anchored in the crevice, Longarm rested. The strain of crawling like a crab across the sheer face of the butte, supported only by a single hand or foot, had taken a toll of even his use-toughened muscles. He looked down, but could not see the base of the butte, more than a hundred feet below him. Leaning back as far as he dared, and gazing upward, he saw the top edge outlined against the sky and estimated that he'd covered nearly half the distance. Thus far, he'd caused only minor disturbances, dislodging small earthslides and a few pebbles that made little or no noise as they trickled to the bottom. He hoped he'd be as lucky during the remainder of the climb.

After his crabbing cross-traverse from one crack to the other, the rest of the way to the top was relatively easy. It was a matter of wedging a foot into the sandstone crack, his knee cross-braced at an angle on the side of the opening opposite the foot, and pulling himself up with hands grasping the sides until he could raise his other leg and wedge it into place.

When his last upward push brought his eyes level with the rim of the butte, he wedged his leg more firmly in the crack than usual, and began looking for the sentry. A fire on the floor of the box canyon outlined the inner wall with a faintly flickering glow. Longarm could see no moving silhouette in any direction. He waited until his legs were beginning to tire, and pulled himself over the rim to lie flat on top of the butte.

Longarm had hoped to find a few clumps of sagebrush, or perhaps even a scrubby, stunted cedar, growing in the streaks of soil that lay thinly in cracks of the sandstone. He was disappointed; the top offered no such cover. Except for a few tall boulders, carved by centuries of windblown sand into cones or columns or low humps shaped like toadstools, the top was as barren as the walls. The closest boulder was a column taller than a man; it rose a dozen yards away, and Longarm belly-crawled to its base.

He stood up carefully, trying to merge his silhouette with that of the boulder. Standing erect, he could now see the sentry. The man had been hidden before by the curves that rose and dipped across the rim like undulating sea-waves. The outlaw on lookout duty sat thirty feet away. His back was propped comfortably against a boulder, his rifle rested across his upraised knees.

Longarm debated his dilemma. A shot from his Colt or Winchester echoing from the top of the butte would alert the entire band, and bring at least one of them up from the canyon floor to investigate. On the other hand, he could not risk letting the sentry use his gun. To get within reach of the outlaw meant a silent sneak. On the hard sandstone that layered the rim, even the smallest noise would echo like thunder in the sentry's ears.

Longarm prepared to move silently by taking off his rifle and canteen and placing them on the ground beside the boulder that concealed him. No accidental clink or clatter of rifle against canteen would take place. He kept his booted feet parallel with the rock underfoot as he lifted them in slow, deliberate steps and planted them firmly and silently while he crept up behind the outlaw. As he moved, Longarm slid his derringer out of his vest pocket and cradled it in his palm.

He reached the rock against which the outlaw leaned, without the man hearing him. Thrusting the cold muzzle of the derringer into the sentry's throat, Longarm said in a half-whisper, "You make a sound, and you're dead." The man froze.

Longarm went on, "Lay your rifle on the ground and stretch out on your face." The startled outlaw let the rifle down carefully. He straightened his legs as though to obey Longarm's second command, but turned instead and tried to knock the derringer aside with his left hand while his right hand clawed for the revolver holstered on his hip.

Longarm pressed the derringer's muzzle hard against the outlaw's head and squeezed the trigger. The ugly *splat* the wicked little weapon usually made was smothered by contact into a subdued cough that would have been inaudible twenty feet away. The outlaw slumped to the ground. His legs twitched once, and then he lay still.

While he put a fresh cartridge in the discharged barrel of the derringer, Longarm stood thoughtfully beside the body. He'd planned to tie and gag the man and leave him on the butte's rim.

But maybe it's better this way, old son, he thought as he snapped the breech of the derringer closed and dropped it back into his vest pocket. *There's enough of them down below there in the canyon to tilt the odds pretty heavy. Now you got one less to worry about.*

He squatted behind the boulder the dead outlaw had been using for a backrest, so that the flare of the match he struck to light a cheroot would be unseen below. Cupping the cigar in his palm and shielding it with a hand when he puffed, he walked to the inner rim of the butte and looked down into the canyon. The fire burned in the same place as on the night before. Across the canyon, he could see one man standing sentry duty at the passageway that led to the outside. In one of the narrow ends of the canyon, he saw something he'd missed in the darkness the previous night. A pole fence had been thrown across the canyon to form a corral for the gang's horses. The window and door of the cabin were dark.

It was the fire that drew most of Longarm's attention. The entire band, except for the two men who'd been posted as lookouts, stood or sat or hunkered down around the dancing flames. Their faces glowed dark red in the reflected light. Silhouetted against the blaze, two men stood facing the others. Longarm counted the seated men. There were thirteen, the same number he'd counted the night before. One of the seated figures must be that of Corinne Gaylord, he thought. With one guard dead and one still on duty, that made sixteen he'd have to hold off until the posse got there.

With a shrug, Longarm went back to pick up his rifle and canteen, then started down the zigzag path in the cleft that led to the canyon floor.

Steep as the path was, it had been tamed through its use by the outlaw sentries going up and down it. Longarm found it easy going, compared to the job of scaling the butte's face. He was halfway to the canyon floor when the group around the fire started to break up. He stopped, not wanting to risk having one of them look up and catch sight of his moving figure.

As had been the case the previous night, most of the gang straggled off to bed down in the caves, while three or four stayed talking by the fire. Longarm saw the door and window of the cabin light up, telling him that Kid Manders and Corinne had gone inside. He waited to see if one of the men standing by the fire was going to come to relieve the sentry he'd killed, but none of them made any move toward the canyon wall.

After he'd waited several minutes to give the group time to settle down, Longarm continued his descent to the canyon floor. He stood at the foot of the trail. The black outline of the cabin was in front of him, only a few paces away, and the temptation to hear what was being said inside was too great for him to overcome.

Keeping in the shadow of the cabin, Longarm walked up to it and slipped along the wall to the window.

He heard Kid Manders saying, "I want you out of here tomorrow morning early, Reen. Ride into Hanksville for the day."

"What do you want me to do?"

"Nothing. Just make yourself scarce around the roost, is all."

Corinne's voice held the shadow of the frown that Longarm couldn't see. "What're you setting up to do, Kid?"

"I ought to've known I'd have to tell you, Reen. I ain't going to put up with Lance any longer. I'm going to kick him out tomorrow, and it's likely there'll be trouble."

"If there is, I want to be here."

"Damn it, Reen, I don't want you to be! After what you told me last night, I watched Lance off and on today, after him and Strang and Bynum come dragging in with their saddles over their backs and their tails between their legs. He's hot to get at you, for sure."

"That's all he'll ever get, is hot," Corinne said angrily. "Don't let Lance worry you where I'm concerned."

"Oh, hell, you know I won't, Reen." The Kid paused and added, "I can't keep on worrying about him undercutting me with the boys, either. That's why he's got to go."

"What's that going to do to your plans for trailing the herd we're going to collect? Or getting it together, for that matter?"

"Depends on whether Strang and Bynum throw in with Lance when I hand him his walking papers."

"Do you really think it's going to be that easy, Kid?" Corinne asked. "Lance will force a showdown. He's out to take over from you."

"Sure. I can see that now. I just wish I'd seen it a long time back." In a brighter voice, Manders went on, "But I don't want you worrying about any showdown between me and Lance. Most of the boys will stick with me."

"There isn't any way of handling Lance without facing him down, is there?" Corinne asked thoughtfully.

"No way I can see. But you stop worrying, Reen. Lance won't be the first man I've faced down, and I'm still on my feet walking around. I aim to be after me and him meet, too."

"I still don't like it."

"Neither do I. But I can hold the bunch together, all right. What happened outside on the trail didn't do Lance a damn bit of good. There was a lot of the boys laughing at him and Strang and Bynum when they come straggling in."

"I still think it was that U.S. marshal, the one I saw in Hanksville, who bushwhacked them," Corinne said.

"Might be. Might be there's somebody around who's just working off an old grudge against Lance, too."

"Why didn't you tell all the men about that marshal before I let it slip out, when I mentioned it last night?" she asked.

"Because I knew it'd get 'em all worked up. I didn't even tell you this before, Reen, but I know who that son of a bitch is. I knew the minute you said his name was Long."

"You mean he's somebody special?"

"Depends on how you look at it. They call him Longarm, and he's hard as old bootleather and rough as a cob. I never did tangle with him before, but I know some who have."

"Him being around doesn't worry you?" Corinne said.

"Oh, sure it does, a little bit. But after you said he'd dropped out of sight the last time you came back from Hanksville, I figure he's moved on."

"Suppose he hasn't?"

"Then we'll just have to see who's smarter, him or me," Manders said. "Now that's all the palaver I feel like tonight. Let's roll into bed, girl."

Longarm hadn't been at all displeased by the description Kid Manders had given of him. He'd grinned to himself in the darkness outside the cabin, resolving then and there that when he'd finished tonight's work,

181

Manders would have the answer to at least part of the question of which of them was smarter. He settled down to wait for the pair in the cabin to get interested in each other, as they had the night before, or to go to sleep. He didn't want them to see him or hear him when he went to carry out his own plans.

Tonight there was the same rustling of clothing being removed that whispered from the cabin into the still night air, but the bed creaked only once. It creaked again, and Longarm heard Manders's voice.

"Reen? What's the matter? Why're you just setting there in the dark?"

"I'm just thinking," the girl replied.

"Don't fret, Reen," Manders said. "Everything'll settle down tomorrow, after I get rid of Lance."

"I'm not going to Hanksville tomorrow, Kid." Corinne's voice was firm. "I never have refused to do what you asked me to do before. This time I am."

"Oh, hell, Reen! Be reasonable! We'll talk about it tomorrow, you'll see I'm right. Now stop mooning and come to bed."

Longarm decided that he'd be wasting time waiting any longer. With the sentry on top of the butte removed, he didn't have to worry about being spotted when he changed positions. He'd gotten only two paces from the blind corner of the dark cabin, though, when he saw the shadowy figures of three men moving in his direction. Quickly he dodged back against the cabin wall. He stayed at the end of the little shack, where there were no windows, while the footsteps of the approaching figures grew louder. Then, out of the darkness, Lance's voice rang loudly.

"I've got you covered, Kid! Don't try to go for a gun!"

"Lance?" This was Manders's voice. "What the hell are you trying to pull off?"

"If you ain't guessed yet, you'll know soon enough," Lance retorted. "Strang, you or Bynum strike a light!"

A match flared inside the cabin. Longarm judged that those inside would be too engrossed in themselves to notice him. He edged up to the window and looked in.

Kid Manders was sitting up in bed, his torso bare, the covers bunched around his waist. Lance stood beside him, a pistol in his hand, the muzzle pressed to the Kid's head. One of the outlaws—Longarm didn't know whether it was Strang or Bynum—stood blocking the door. His revolver was drawn too. The third man stood beside the table, a pistol in one hand, a smoking match in the other. Corinne stood against the wall at the end of the cabin. She held her blouse in her hand, but was still wearing a shift and skirt and boots.

Manders repeated, "What in hell are you trying to pull off, Lance?"

"That ought to be as plain as the nose on your face, Kid. After you and Reen left, I asked the boys if they was satisfied with the way you been handling things. They wasn't. I asked 'em if they wanted me to take over, and they said they did. So that's what I'm doing. You're not the boss anymore, Manders!"

Chapter 16

"You've gone out of your head, Lance!" Manders exclaimed. "Put that gun away now, and quit acting loco!"

Lance made no move to obey. He kept the revolver's muzzle pressed against Manders's temple. He said, "You're the loco one, Kid. If you didn't have shit where your brains ought to be, you'd see you're finished."

"I'm a hell of a long way from being finished!" Manders retorted.

"Ask Strang. Ask Bynum," Lance invited.

Now Longarm got his first clue to the identities of the two men who were backing Lance's play to push Kid Manders aside. Until now, he hadn't known which was Strang and which was Bynum, but Manders was looking at the man standing by the table.

"How about it, Strang?" Manders asked. "After I've got this job all set up, are you turning your back on me?"

Stolidly, without showing any emotion in his face or voice, Strang nodded. "Lance is boss now, Kid."

Lance said, "You ought to've listened when I told you we was tired of setting on our asses, Kid. But I'll get things moving!"

"You start moving too fast, before everything's set up right, and you'll all be sitting on your asses in jail," Manders shot back. He turned to the others. "You ever think about that, Strang? Or you, Bynum?"

It was Bynum who answered. "Sure, we thought about it, Kid. But you just ain't been getting us noplace, is the trouble."

Corinne spoke for the first time. "You'd better stop acting too big for your boots, Lance. Listen to what the Kid's trying to tell you. He's got more brains than all the rest of you put together."

Longarm saw that Corinne was not afraid. Her resistance might give a spur to the Kid, he thought, and a wrangle over leadership that would split the gang would make his own job easier.

Lance turned his head to look at Corinne, but kept his pistol at Manders's head. He said jeeringly, "Well, look who's trying to boss things now! But you'll get over that, Reen. Maybe you can wrap the Kid around your little finger, but you're going to find out I'm different."

"I don't want to find out anything more about you than I already know, Lance," Corinne replied coldly.

"Nobody's asking you what you want anymore," Lance told her. "From here on out, you'll do what I want you to."

Longarm saw Manders's eyes turning toward his gun. The Kid's gunbelt was hanging on a peg driven into the wall above the foot of the narrow bed. He felt like telling Manders that there wasn't a chance he could reach the weapon, but he had no intention of being anything except a silent, unseen spectator at the drama unfolding in the cabin.

Corinne said to Lance, "If you've got it in your mind that I'm going to have anything to do with you, Lance, you're wrong. I'll stick with the Kid, wherever he goes when he leaves here."

Lance laughed, and managed to combine a snarl with a sneer in his low-pitched chuckling. "The Kid ain't going anyplace, Reen. Or you, either. I'd be real soft-headed for sure, if I let him or you get away from the Roost before the job's finished up."

"If you think I'm going to help you wind up the job, you *are* soft-headed, Lance," Kid Manders said. "Or if you think Reen's going to help, either. Ain't that right, Reen?"

"You're damned right it is!" she agreed. "Whatever

185

Lance has got in mind for you is good enough for me too."

Lance laughed again. "You two do beat all! God-damnit, get it into your heads that what you want ain't what you're going to get! You'll change your mind about helping, Kid. I'll put Lopez to work on you. By the time he's carved you up a little bit with that knife he's so handy with, you'll be begging to help us. Or maybe I'll let him carve on Reen first."

Manders started to say something, but before he could speak, a new voice intruded. Longarm heard the voice a few seconds after the hard, cold muzzle of a rifle barrel was pressed into the base of his skull and the man holding the gun commanded him, "You move a finger and I'll blow you to hell!" Then, louder, he called, "Lance! Get out here! I caught somebody sneaking around!"

Lance whirled to face the window, but kept his gun at Manders's head. "Chesty?" he called.

"Yeah," replied the man holding the rifle on Long-arm. "I don't know who it is, but he was spying in through the window."

"Bring him in here!" Lance ordered.

"You heard what the boss said," Chesty told Long-arm. "Keep your hands still and march!"

Swearing at himself for letting his attention become absorbed by the events in the cabin, Longarm had no choice but to obey. He walked in front of Chesty to the door, and Bynum stood aside to let them enter. The little cabin was crowded when Longarm and his captor got inside.

Lance gazed at Longarm, his jaw jutting angrily. He asked, "Who in hell are you? And how'd you get in here?"

Longarm said nothing.

Lance looked to Chesty. "How'd you catch him?"

"Easy as sliding in fresh owlshit," Chesty replied. "I was going up to the rim to relieve Breed, and I seen him spying in the window there. He was so busy watch-ing inside, he didn't hear a thing when I sneaked up in back of him."

186

"Take his guns, Strang," Lance ordered. "Then we'll see what he's got on him."

Longarm made no resistance when Strang lifted the Winchester off his shoulder and laid it on the table, or when the outlaw took his Colt from its holster. Before the search could be continued, though, he said quietly, "I'll tell you who I am. My name's Long, and I'm a deputy U.S. marshal. I'm putting all of you under arrest."

Lance began to laugh, almost maniacally. So did Strang, who was still standing in front of Longarm. Bynum's eyes were goggling out. Longarm couldn't see Chesty's face. Kid Manders and Corinne were staring at the scene with eyes and mouths wide open.

Suddenly, Lance's crazed laugh cut off abruptly. He stared at Longarm. "Did you say your name's Long?"

"Yes."

"I'll be damned! You're the one they call Longarm! The one that's supposed to be top dog! And here I got you right where it hurts! Now wouldn't that put a shine on a cow turd!"

"You won't have me long," Longarm said quietly.

"We'll just have to see about that!" Lance shot back. He said to Chesty, "You better get on up to the rim. Breed's going to be wondering what's going on down here. There's enough of us to handle this marshal bastard." As Chesty went out the door, Lance told Strang, "You keep your gun on him, Strang. From what I've heard, he's a slippery son of a bitch that's hard to keep ahold of."

Strang laid Longarm's Colt on the table beside the Winchester and drew his own gun, which he'd holstered while relieving Longarm of his weapons. He moved to Longarm's side and shoved the muzzle of his revolver into Longarm's ribs.

"You just stand quiet and don't give me no trouble," Strang growled, adding menacingly, "if you want to keep alive."

There was a moment of silence in the cabin. Longarm could see that Lance was trying to make some kind of decision, any kind of decision, to give himself the

187

authority he'd taken and suddenly found crowding his ability to handle. Lance's eyes kept darting from Kid Manders to Corinne to Longarm. ◆

Finally, Lance said, "All right, Kid. You ought to see by now you ain't got no choice but to go along with me."

"I don't see anything of the kind," Manders replied. "Hell, Lance, you don't know all the ins and outs of my scheme. Sure, you know I got some men in Hanksville working for me, but that ain't saying they'll work along with you. They don't know you from a mule's hind tit."

"They can learn real quick," Lance replied. "And I guess Reen knows all there is to know about how you got things set up."

"You leave Reen out of this!" Manders grated.

"Get wised up, Kid. I'm taking over from you. That means I'm taking Reen, too."

"Now I've got something to say about that!" Corinne broke in. "And I've told you before, Lance, I don't want any part of you. You make me want to puke every time I look at you!"

"Mind your tongue, Reen, or you'll be sorry!" Lance threatened.

"You don't scare me, Lance," she said scornfully. "You're just a little man trying to step into a big man's boots. And it looks to me like you're finding out they don't fit you."

"Maybe you better let up on her, Lance," Strang suggested. "We still need her or the Kid to tell us the whole setup."

"When I want to hear from you, Strang, I'll let you know!" Lance snapped. "You just go on watching that Longarm close, and leave this little bitch for me to take care of!"

"Keep your damn dirty hands off Reen, Lance," Manders warned. "You've already got enough to answer to me for!"

"Answer to you, shit!" Lance retorted. "I'm answering to nobody for nothing anymore, Kid! I'm calling the shots, remember!"

Lance stepped over to Corinne and grabbed her by the wrist. He pulled her out roughly into the center of the crowded little cabin. "You're acting too damned high and mighty to suit me," he snarled. "You need a good lesson to show you where you fit in here, now that the Kid's not in charge!"

Corinne glared at Lance, but said nothing.

"You're going to be my woman now," Lance went on. "And my women hop when I say jump! You get me, Reen?"

"I don't want you, Lance. I never did," she said with an icy chill in her voice.

Longarm, listening closely, could detect no trace of fear in Corinne's tones.

"I don't give a fuck what you want!" Lance was almost shouting. His face was reddened with anger under its dark tan. "You'll do what I want! And I'm going to prove that to you!"

Holstering his pistol, Lance bent Corinne's arm back and down until he'd forced the girl to her knees. He fumbled the buttons of his fly open.

"Now take out my cock and suck it!" he commanded.

Corinne ignored him. She turned her head slightly to one side and stared, stony-eyed, into space.

"Do what I tell you!" Lance ordered.

Still, Corinne paid no attention to his words. When Lance increased the pressure on her wrist and bent it until her body was forced forward, Longarm saw a grimace of pain flicker across her face, but she composed herself quickly and set her features again into an impassive mold.

"Goddamnit!" Lance grated. "I'm going to show you I'm boss! Get out my prick and put it in your mouth!"

From the bed, Kid Manders called, "Don't do that to her, Lance! I'll kill you if you do!"

"Shut up, Kid!" Lance snarled. To Bynum he said, "Keep him covered and kill him if he moves!"

Bynum shifted his position in the doorway, and swung his revolver to cover Manders.

Lance told Corinne, "Get out my cock, damn you!

189

I'm going to show you in front of everybody who's boss here now!" When Corinne still made no motion to obey, Lance reached into his open fly and liberated his flaccid penis himself. He increased the pressure he was applying to Corinne's wrist, and with his free hand, he grabbed her hair. He pulled her head around.

Longarm saw the muscles in Corinne's jaw tighten stubbornly. He glanced at Bynum, and saw that the outlaw had taken his eyes off Kid Manders to watch Lance and Corinne. Out of the corner of his eye, Longarm saw that Strang, too, was watching the two in the center of the room. Only the continued pressure of Strang's gun in his ribs kept Longarm motionless.

Lance pushed his hips forward and at the same time pulled Corinne's hair to force her face into his crotch. He gritted, "Go on, damn you, bitch! Start sucking!"

Flicking his eyes at Corinne, Longarm saw the muscles in her jaw working as she clenched her teeth. He looked past Lance and the girl at Manders. The Kid was sitting upright in the bed, staring in angry fascination at Corinne and Lance.

Lance released Corinne's wrist. Her arm fell numbly to her side. Lance grabbed her jaw with the hand that had held her wrist, and with his thumb gouging into her cheek, he tried to force Corinne's mouth open. The two were swaying back and forth in the center of the floor. Lance still had not succeeded in his effort to open Corinne's mouth. Suddenly, she brought up her free hand, grabbed his crotch hard, and twisted.

Lance began to scream. "Let go of my balls, damn it! You're twisting 'em off!"

Dancing with pain, Lance was trying to pull away from Corinne now. His arms were flailing the air. He regained control for a brief moment, long enough to backhand Corinne and knock her to the floor.

As Corinne fell, Kid Manders moved. He sprang from the bed, trying to reach his gunbelt. Bynum had taken a step forward when Corinne fell, forgetting that his job was to keep Manders covered.

Lance saw Manders rising from the bed. He forgot his pain and drew. His first shot missed. Manders almost had his hands on the gunbelt when Lance's second shot took him low in the back. The impact of the heavy .45 slug threw Manders into the wall. He hung against the rough stone surface for a moment, as though suspended there, then crumpled slowly to the bed.

Strang instinctively took his gun out of Longarm's ribs and started swinging it to cover Manders. Longarm snaked the derringer from his vest pocket and shoved it into Strang's gullet. The slug that he triggered went upward through Strang's head and took off the top of the outlaw's skull along with his hat.

Lance was swinging his revolver wildly from side to side, looking for a target. Corinne lunged forward when she saw Lance's pistol moving toward Longarm, and tripped Lance. He fell backward. His head thudded on the end wall of the cabin, and when he dropped to the floor, he lay still.

Bynum was still off-balance. Longarm used the second barrel of his derringer to put a bullet through the outlaw's chest. Bynum tried to stand up, but failed. His body folded and he collapsed in a heap on the floor.

Corinne was on her feet now, going to the bed where Manders had fallen. She tugged at the Kid's inert body and finally got it turned over. Manders's eyelids twitched and his eyes opened. He looked up glassily at Corinne.

"Kid!" she cried. "Are you all right?"

Longarm was moving to the table, a short step. As he scooped up his Colt, he heard Kid Manders whisper weakly, "No, Reen. I ain't all right. That son of a bitch Lance has killed me."

"No!" she exclaimed. "I'll take care of you, Kid! I won't let you die!"

Longarm glanced around the room. He knew there were very few minutes left for him to act. The outlaws in the caves, the sentry at the passageway, and the second sentry on the canyon rim must all have heard the shots.

He called to Corinne, "We got to get out of here in a hurry!"

"Go ahead." She flung the words over her shoulder. "I'm going to stay here with the Kid. Unless we can take him with us."

"There's not any way we can do that," Longarm said urgently. "If we don't leave this place right now, we never will!"

"Then go by yourself! I won't leave him!"

Weakly, Manders whispered, "Go on, Reen. Go with Longarm. I'm done for. You can't fix me up. I'm going to cash in."

"No!" she sobbed. "You'll get well!"

"I seen too many men shot." Manders's voice was a ghostly thread, wavering in the sudden stillness of the cabin. "I know when I'm finished. Go on! Hurry!"

Distantly, Longarm heard voices from the canyon floor. They were far off now, but he knew they'd get closer fast.

"You got to come right now," he said to Corinne. "I can't leave you here with a roomful of dead men!"

"They're not all dead! The Kid's still alive!" she insisted.

"Not . . . for long . . . " Manders's voice trailed off to silence. His body went limp in Corinne's arms.

With disbelief in her voice, she whispered, "He's dead."

He started around the table to the bed. His eye caught Kid Manders's gunbelt hanging on the peg. He pulled the belt from the peg. It was heavy in his hand, the cartridge-loops filled with shells.

He took Corinne's arm and pulled her to her feet. She stood staring at the Kid's body. Manders's jaw had dropped open and his eyes were taking on the death-glaze.

Longarm slapped Corinne on one cheek, then on the other, not too gently. She shook her head, but her eyes lost their wild, fixed stare and focused on the room.

"You can't help the Kid," Longarm said. "He's dead." He thrust the gunbelt into her hands. "Here, take this. We're going to need it."

She accepted the gunbelt unthinkingly, and stood looking down at it, a frown forming on her face.

Longarm said to her, as he holstered his Colt and slung his Winchester over his shoulder by its improvised sling, "We got about half a minute to get out of here. Now move!"

Corinne was turning slowly away from the bed where Manders's body lay. Her eyes fell on Lance. He had begun to regain consciousness, and was starting to sit up. Corinne took Manders's gun out of its holster and shot Lance in the head. He fell back lifeless on the floor.

Longarm grabbed Corinne's arm.

She hung back, saying, "My blouse. Or a coat!"

"No time for that," Longarm snapped. "Come on just the way you are!"

Outside, the voices were closer, louder. Longarm bent over the table and blew out the lamp. He blinked to adjust his eyes more quickly to the darkness. He was still holding Corinne's arm. The oblong of the door began to appear to him, a dark frame around the lesser darkness outside the cabin.

Longarm dragged Corinne to the door and out of the cabin. She followed without resisting. She still had the Kid's revolver in one hand, the gunbelt in the other. Longarm guided her along the cabin wall to its end, where the little shack would be between them and the approaching outlaws. The fire had died and the moon had not yet risen. A glow above the box canyon's back rim showed that moonrise was close, though. In the distance, Longarm saw the bobbing glow of a lantern, carried by one of the outlaws approaching from the caves.

"Move faster!" he urged Corinne. "We got to make it away from here before they think about lighting more damn lanterns!"

"Where are we going?" she asked listlessly.

"Don't worry about it. Just keep your feet moving as fast as you can!"

Longarm was leading the girl toward the canyon wall, still keeping the cabin between them and the outlaws. They were out of range of the lantern when its bearer brought it up. He went into the cabin with the light, giving Longarm and Corinne time to get to the vertical wall of the box canyon. Longarm tugged at Corinne's arm, leading her in the direction of the passageway. She kept trying to look back at the cabin.

"Forget what's back there," he told her roughly. "There ain't anything in that shack but dead men." Then, bluntly, he added, "And that includes the Kid. Remember, you saw him die. He's dead, Corinne. He can't help you, you can't help him. Now walk faster!"

Longarm's harsh words brought Corinne back to reality. She started sobbing, but she also began to try to keep up with Longarm. Relieved of the need to pull her after him, Longarm moved more quickly too.

They were creeping along close to the canyon wall. Just ahead of them lay the entrance to the narrow passageway that led out to Goblin Valley. Longarm's eyes had adjusted to the dark by now, and he saw the sentry standing in the cleft in time to stop. He pushed Corinne against the canyon wall and hugged it himself.

Their movement caught the lookout's eye. He called, "Who in hell are you, there? What's wrong at the cabin?"

Longarm answered the outlaw's questions with a shot. The angle was bad and the range too great, for he missed. The sentry fired back, but his rifle slug plowed into the hard earth of the canyon wall where it curved beyond the spot where Longarm and Corinne stood.

Longarm's second shot was closer. He saw the lookout back into the passageway. He pulled Corinne's arm. "Come on," he commanded her. "Hug the wall as close as you can."

Halfway to the entrance, the sentry poked his head out of the passage. Longarm had expected the move. He sent another shot at the lookout. The slug took the man's hat off, but missed his head. Longarm saw him pull back into the cleft.

"You stay a step in back of me," he told Corinne.

"Don't shoot, no matter what. You might hit me. You got that?"

"Yes. I can handle a gun. Don't worry."

Keeping his head and ass down, Longarm ran in a narrow zigzag to the passageway. He saw a vague movement against the black slit and let off a shot. There was no gunfire in reply. Longarm reached the passage, stopping short of the opening. He took his hat off and showed it in silhouette against the rim of the opening. Two quick shots came from the cleft. Both missed the hat.

Longarm dropped to the ground and holstered his Colt. He'd used two of its five rounds, and might need the three that remained. He freed the Winchester and belly-crawled to the passageway. Pushing the muzzle inside the cleft, he loosed three shots as fast as he could work the lever. He heard the slugs singing as they ricocheted off the stone walls. Then the lookout's feet clattered as the man retreated around the first bend in the winding passage.

Over his shoulder, Longarm called to Corinne, "Come on. We can get inside that crack now. And once we're there, there's not a way in the world they can get at us! Now hurry!"

Her footsteps told him she was running. He let her go by him, into the passage, and followed her. For the moment, at least, he could breathe more freely.

Chapter 17

Even a yard or two inside the passageway, the darkness was intense. In front of Longarm and Corinne, the fissure was quiet. Evidently the lookout was being very cautious in returning the fire that Longarm had loosed from his rifle. A faint gleam began to outline the canyon end of the passage. Above, the night sky showed more stars than seemed real, between the wavy lines that defined the top of the passage.

Corinne said, in a subdued voice, "Well. We're here, I guess. But what good does it do us, Marshal? There's one of the men between us and the outside."

"Sure. And a dozen more keeping us from going the other way, even if we wanted to," Longarm replied. "Thing is, Corinne, this cut's so narrow and twists around so much that the two of us can keep anybody from getting at us from either end."

"As long as our ammunition holds out," she reminded him.

"Well, it's going to be up to us to see that we don't waste our shots," Longarm answered. "And that ought to be easy."

"We won't have to do much shooting to make them keep their distance," Corinne agreed. "You know, that's one of the things about the Roost that used to worry the Kid. He kept wondering what would happen if he and the rest of the boys got bottled up in the box—how they'd manage to break out. That's why he had them make that trail up the cut on the other side. He thought that if somebody did manage to seal this entrance, they could handle the situation by getting up on the rim and driving them off."

Longarm was immediately interested. "Did Manders talk to the others about that plan of his?"

"Oh sure. They had to know what to do if the squeeze came."

"Then we can look for somebody to start sniping at us from up above there." Longarm indicated the slit of sky above their heads.

"I hadn't thought about that." She frowned thoughtfully. "But you're right, of course. As soon as one of them thinks about it, they'll go up the back trail and try to get at us from the top."

Longarm studied the overhead opening for a moment, then said, "I wouldn't worry too much about that, Corinne. They'd sure have to lean out if they do any aiming, and that'd make them easy targets."

She looked up and examined the slit. "I hope I'm good enough, if the time comes."

"You said you could handle a gun," he reminded her.

"I can. But I've never shot anybody." She stopped short, shook her head, and added, "Except Lance, tonight. Do you think I killed him, Marshal?"

"You killed him, all right. The thing that occurs to me now is, who's going to take over with both him and the Kid dead?"

"That's hard to say," Corinne replied, after a moment's thought. "Red might. Or Bowers. If Lopez wasn't a Mexican, he'd be a good bet, but the boys wouldn't follow him. I'm glad too, because Lopez is the toughest and smartest, next to Lance and the Kid."

"In other words, the job of being boss is up for the toughest of the gang to grab it."

"That's about it."

"You think they'll have a wrangle over who to pick?"

"Maybe. The Kid would've been able to tell you better than I can. I didn't have all that much to do with the men."

"I don't guess it matters much," Longarm told her.

"I figure we've got an hour or so before they get everything sorted out and start bothering us."

"I'd say you're right." Corinne sat down on the floor of the fissure and leaned back against the wall. "All at once, I'm tired out. Things were happening so fast, back there at the house . . ." Her words trailed off into silence.

"Hey, Cotton! You in there?" a voice called from the canyon floor outside the passageway.

Longarm moved up to the opening, motioning for Corinne to stay back. He peered out. Two of the Roost's gang stood outside, a few yards from the entrance.

"Cotton!" one of them called again.

Beyond the point where Longarm and Corinne had stopped, a voice answered, "Stay clear out there, Bowers! There's two of 'em just inside the pass! I tried to keep 'em out, but they drove me back! It looked to me like one was the Kid's woman!"

Longarm fired just as the two men outside hit the ground rolling. He wasn't sure he'd winged the one he'd chosen as a target, but thought he'd missed, for there was no shout of pain after his shot.

His question was soon answered. To the right of the entry a voice called, "You get hit, Red?"

"No," came the reply from the left. "I felt the breeze, though."

Now the first man raised his voice. "Cotton!"

From behind Longarm, Cotton answered, "Yeah, Bowers!"

"You block them bastards from where you are! Don't let 'em get out, you hear? Me or Red will go get some help!"

"All right," Cotton responded. "I'll do the best I can!"

Longarm said in a half-whisper to Corinne, "We can sit down and rest a spell. It'll take them a while to pull something together."

Corinne had gotten to her feet with the first shout, and now she sat down again. Longarm sat down opposite her. The cleft was so narrow that their feet

198

almost touched. He said nothing. *Give it time*, he thought. *Once she sorts out what's happened to her, she'll see what she's got to do.*

After a long period of silence, Corinne raised her head. Both she and Longarm had full night-vision now. He could make out her features across the short distance that separated them, and knew that she could see him as clearly as he saw her.

She said, "I hope that canteen you've got is full, Marshal."

"It is," he replied. "If we're careful, there's enough water to keep us from getting thirsty for two or three days, if we don't take too many baths." Longarm slipped the canteen's carrying-strap over his head and passed it across to her. He lighted a cheroot while she drank. Now that the gang knew where they were, there was no further point in trying to hide a cigar's glow.

When Corinne had recapped the canteen and laid it on the ground beside her, she said, "You came pretty well prepared, didn't you? I'm just beginning to see that you knew what you were taking on. You led me right here to the passage from the house. I hadn't realized until now that you knew exactly where to go."

"Well, I had a pretty good idea, after I scouted the place."

"You mean you've been in here before?" Her tone showed her incredulity. Then she gasped. "That was you last night!"

"Guess it must've been."

"How'd you locate the place? The Kid swore nobody knew about this box canyon. It's not on any maps."

"Oh, I just followed the Kid and Lance back when they left Verda Blankenship's."

Corinne shook her head. "The Kid told me a few stories he'd heard about you. That was after I'd mentioned your name to him, after I ran into you in Hanksville. I didn't believe his stories then, but I do now. It was you, not Ed Crowder, who tied up Matt last night."

"It was me. Who's Ed Crowder?"

"He was the Kid's segundo before he got crossways of Lance. I guess Crowder got a raw deal," she went on thoughtfully. "I can see, now, that Lance had his mind set on taking over from the very beginning." She paused and said dispassionately, "I'm glad I killed the son of a bitch."

"Oh, he had it coming, all right," Longarm said. "But you never answered my question about this Crowder fellow."

"We thought it was him, coming back to snoop, who tied Matt up last night. Lance started that. He jumped up and began blaming it on Crowder, and everybody just took it for granted that's who it was. He knew the layout, you see. Knew the lookouts by name, everything." She cocked her head curiously and asked, "How did you get in tonight, Marshal? Not past Cotton, surely?"

"I didn't come through the cut here. I went up the outside of the butte and came down the path."

"You climbed that butte? My God! All of us thought that was impossible! But how did you get by Breed?"

"He was the lookout on the rim?" When Corinne nodded, Longarm said unemotionally, "I had to kill him."

Corinne fell silent. Longarm let her think, as he had done before. He'd done what he had in mind, he was sure. By now, the girl must realize that, from the day he'd arrived in Hanksville, he'd been a step ahead of Kid Manders and his gang.

A scrabbling of feet on hard earth reached Longarm's ears. He said quickly, "They're going to try to bust in! Cotton might hit us from behind when they do. You look out for him. I'll handle the front end."

Corinne was on her feet before Longarm finished speaking. She picked up Kid Manders's gunbelt and pulled the revolver out of its holster.

"I'll do my best," she promised grimly.

"Sure you will. Just flatten out on the floor and shoot when you hear a noise from the outside."

Longarm crawled to the entrance. A single shot rang

out from the canyon. He pushed his rifle up at the ready. Behind him, he heard the clatter of footsteps and the echoing boom of guns. The moon had come up, and in its bright light he saw the half-dozen men in front of the passageway, coming on the run, bending double. Longarm picked off the one in the center. The others hesitated for a moment, then came ahead. They were pouring lead into the passage, but their slugs were flattening against the walls above Longarm's head. He dropped another of the attackers. The rest turned and ran, scattering on both sides, to get quickly out of Longarm's limited field of fire.

In the passage, the shooting had stopped after a half-dozen rounds. Longarm decided it was safe to leave the opening into the canyon unguarded for a minute or so. He scrabbled back to where Corinne crouched, pistol in hand.

"I drove him back," she said triumphantly. "I don't think I hit him, though. I was just shooting blind."

"That's all it takes," he assured her. Then he added, "I think we can rest a minute or so. They won't try rushing us that way again soon. I knocked over two out of the six that was trying to get in from the canyon."

"It sounded like there was only one gun firing behind us," she told him. "But I don't think it'd have made any difference if there'd been a dozen."

"No. I look for them to try to get us from above, next. The moon's up now. Looking up, we can see them better than they can see us."

"It'll take a while for them to get in place, if that's what they do have in mind," Corinne said thoughtfully. "They'll have to climb up the path, and then, if they intend to attack us from both sides up there, it'll take the ones going the long way a good half-hour to circle back here and get in place."

Longarm nodded. "That's about what I figured." He studied Corinne's face and decided it was time to make sure which way she was going when the final chips were pushed in the pot. He said, "I better tell

201

you, Corinne. As far's the law's concerned you're my prisoner right now."

Corinne stared at him through the darkness for a moment, and began giggling. When she could speak, she said, "That's the funniest thing I've ever heard, Marshal! You pull me out of a bad hole, we fight off the boys together, we're trapped with no way out, and here you make sure I know I'm under arrest!"

"I was just reminding you," Longarm replied.

"Does it make any real difference? We're still in the same boat together, whether I'm free or your prisoner."

"It makes a difference, Corinne," Longarm assured her. "If I know I can count on you to stick by me until this thing is over, and stand up in court as a federal witness later on, even if it means going against them fellows you been on the same side with until now, I can take off my arrest notice."

"Marshal, I've got no more friends left out there in the Roost, now that the Kid's dead. He was the only one I gave a damn about. I couldn't care less what happens to the others."

"Well, that answers me halfway," Longarm said.

"I'll go the rest of the way, don't worry, even if I don't see why a few words about me being under arrest or not being under arrest matters very much. Yes, I'll stick with you. Damn it, you haven't given me any choice at all! What Lance was trying to do to me, back in the cabin, that wasn't even a hint of what the rest of the bunch would do. They'd make me take them on three at a time. I've heard them talk about doing women that way!"

"I ain't figuring on turning you over to them, of course," Longarm assured the girl. "But you're wrong about those few words not making a difference."

"Maybe you'd better explain."

"If I can say you volunteered of your own free will to help me, and then to be a federal witness, you can walk out of all this scot-free."

Corinne didn't reply at once; Longarm could see that she was trying to find some hidden meaning in his offer. At last she said, "I didn't understand you were offering to get me off, Marshal. I still don't see how lifting your arrest will help, but I'll take your word that it will. And I'll keep my word to you."

"If I hadn't been real sure you would, I wouldn't have offered. And you'll see, it will make a difference later on."

Corinne didn't bother to beat around the bush or disguise her curiosity. "Why are you so damned sure there's going to be a 'later on'? I've got a feeling you know something you still haven't told me. If you do, I'd like to hear what it is."

"If the plan I've got started works out right, we won't have to worry much after about noon tomorrow."

She looked at him, her face twisted in a frown that came close to being a smile. "You mean because we'll both be dead?"

"No. Because there ought to be a posse here from Hanksville by then. I can't guarantee it, but I'm pretty sure it'll get here."

Corinne's mouth dropped open. "You've fixed it up for a posse to come to the Roost? How? You must've been here most of the night. You couldn't have ridden to Hanksville and back."

"If things work out, you'll see how I done it."

"Why didn't you just wait and come with the posse?"

"I wanted to be here in case something out of the way happened with the gang. I got a hint it might, from the way you and the Kid was talking about Lance last night."

Corinne sighed. "And it did blow up, didn't it? I just remembered, I haven't even thanked you for getting me out of that cabin, Marshal. You know I'm grateful to you, I suppose."

"I didn't do it to get any thanks from you, Corinne. I was—" Longarm stopped. A half-dozen pebbles pelted down at their feet.

"It looks like they're up above us," Corinne said.

"They'll hit us from the front and back and above all at the same time, if they're smart," Longarm told her. "We'll split up, like we did before. Just remember, keep close to the wall. If you can find an overhang, get under it."

Corinne nodded. She inched toward the outer end of the fissure. Longarm slid along the wall toward the opening that led to the canyon.

Their wait was very short. Longarm had barely reached the spot where he could see the fissure's opening, bright now with the light of the moon bathing the canyon floor, and the flames of a fire built in the usual place, near the center of the enclosure. He did not wait for the outlaws to start shooting. He leaped out, spun to the right, and spent three of the Colt's slugs on the group that waited on that side of the canyon. Then he dropped and rolled back into the cleft, shooting at the bunch on the left. For a full minute after he'd gotten inside the opening, bullets sent up dust clouds in the area directly in front of the fissure.

Longarm had left his Winchester on the floor of the passage. He reached for it. Deeper in the passageway, he heard pistolfire. A man's head and shoulders appeared in silhouette in the moonlight-defined gap at the top of the passage. Longarm's rifle cracked. The outlaw's body plummeted silently through the darkness, and crashed onto the floor of the passage. His gun bounced out of his dead hand. Longarm felt the man's waist for a gunbelt, discovered one, fingered along it, and found the shell-loops filled. Keeping an eye trained above him, and listening for footsteps from the canyon opening, he unstrapped the outlaw's belt and hung it over one shoulder. Then he turned back toward the opening.

A glance outside showed him that the attackers had regrouped. Now they were all on one side of the cleft. All six chambers of the dead outlaw's gun were loaded. Longarm emptied it at the group, and the outlaws scattered.

Gunfire was still echoing from the far end of the passage when Longarm got back inside. He ran along the narrow, twisting path, reloading the dead outlaw's revolver as he moved. Corinne was backing up toward

204

him. Longarm stepped to one side of her and peppered the darkness ahead. The firing stopped and retreating footsteps sounded, fading to silence.

Corinne was panting. "There's somebody else with Cotton at the outside opening now! They didn't give me time to reload!"

"I figured they'd get another man or two at the outside end of the passage," Longarm said. "If I climbed up that butte outside, one or two of them could sure get down. Or maybe they just let one man down on a couple of joined lariats."

"They'll be coming at us from both sides, then!"

"They were already doing that, as long as they had just one man out there," he reminded her. "But how many they've got don't count. There's only room for two at a time to get to us." He handed her the dead outlaw's gun and belt. "Here. That'll even up the odds, next time they hit us."

"You think they'll try again?"

"They're sure to. They can't move till they're rid of us."

"How long do you think we have?" Corinne asked.

"Hard to figure. Might be they'll wait until daylight, figuring they'll have more chance to hit us then. They ain't tumbled to it yet, but they make bigger targets than we do."

"How long is it until daybreak?"

Longarm looked up. The moon was invisible, but the brightness of the sky told him it was still shining. He lifted out his watch, and took out a cheroot. He lighted the cigar and read the time by the light of the same match.

"Four o'clock, a few minutes after."

"Dawn won't come for another hour, then," she reflected. "Full daylight in two hours."

"About that." Longarm read the fatigue in her voice. "You better catch some shut-eye. I'll stand watch."

"You probably need sleep worse than I do. You must have been up all night last night and tonight, too."

"I'll get along. Stretch out and rest now."

"As soon as I reload."

Longarm nodded. He didn't mention that he'd reloaded the instant the shooting stopped. He watched her insert shells in the chambers of the two pistols, then lower herself wearily to the ground. She rolled close to the wall, and almost at once was asleep.

Longarm sat down, his back to the side of the passage. He was tired, but knew he'd be good for the rest of the night. He rested his head against the rough sandstone, but his hatbrim was in his way. He pulled the hat down over his face and closed his eyes to rest them for a moment. The next thing he knew, Corinne was shaking him by the shoulder.

"Marshal! Marshal Long! Wake up! I think they're getting ready to hit us again!"

Chapter 18

Longarm rolled to his feet, pushing his hat back on his head as he rose. To his surprise, it was daylight. He snapped, "Damn it, Corinne! Why didn't you rouse me when you saw I'd dropped off?"

"Because I know you have to sleep sometime, just like other men," she snapped back. Longarm grinned; she hadn't lost her spirit. She added, "There's no hurry. As soon as I woke up, I went to look in the canyon, and they were all down by the fire, some of them lying down. They were either hurt or asleep."

"You said they're moving on us, though."

"They are. But they've just started."

Longarm went to look for himself. There were eight or ten of the outlaws heading in a straggling line for the entrance to the passage. He could see others, still lying in front of the fire, and knew those at the outside opening must be making preparations to move; perhaps they were already moving. Those advancing across the canyon floor all carried burning branches.

"They're going to try to smoke us out," he told Corinne.

"Damn! How do we handle that?"

"I don't know," he admitted. He brought up his rifle. "This is the only way I can see."

Aiming carefully, Longarm dropped the man in the center of the advancing line. The men on either side let their torches fall and hurried to help the one who'd fallen. His shot was not meant to kill, but to cripple; it occurred to him that the outlaws would let a dead man lie and keep advancing, but two of them would be needed to answer the plea of a wounded companion and carry him back to a safe place.

His idea proved correct. Two of the outlaws picked up the man whose thighbone Longarm's rifle slug had shattered, and started back to the fire with him. The others, seeing their strength reduced by a third, let their torches fall and began pouring rifle fire into the cleft. By then, Longarm and Corinne were around the first bend in the tortuous passage, where only an occasional spent bullet came ricocheting off the wall and dropped harmlessly to the ground.

Longarm thought of the fissure's outside opening. Motioning to Corinne to follow him, he ran for the outside entrance as fast as the weaving, winding passage would permit.

Three-quarters of the way there, Longarm smelled smoke. He called back to Corinne, "Drop, fast!" Then he hit the dirt himself.

Torchlight flickered in the dusky passage. Longarm wondered what a ricochet would do at close range. He aimed at the curving stone wall, at waist level, and triggered the Winchester. The slug screamed off the rock, and an instant later, a man's hoarse yell of pain echoed through the cleft.

Longarm fired again, without results. "Lucky shot," he muttered. "Never do it again in a million years."

Shifting his rifle to his left hand, he started ahead, bending low, zigzagging from side to side, drawing his Colt as he ran. He saw a flaring torch ahead, and aimed by reckoning, firing first to one side of the blazing limb, then to the other. The torch dropped, to be smothered by a man's body falling on it. The odor of burning flesh drifted nauseatingly through the fissure. Retreating footsteps reached Longarm's ears.

"Let's get back," he said to Corinne. "I'd guess there were only two or three of them coming from the outside. We can handle them without too much trouble. It's the ones in the canyon that bother me."

They retreated to the canyon end of the passage and peered out cautiously. Except for one man who sat on the ground facing the fissure, a long rifle shot from the canyon wall, the outlaws had retreated to the fire. There were no signs that they were preparing another attack. Instead, they seemed to be busy cooking. A few yards away from the group around the fire, there were several blanket-covered bodies.

Longarm said with grim satisfaction, "I'd say we've cut 'em down to size."

"Do you think they've given up?" she asked.

"Not by a long shot. Hell, girl, they can't afford to. They got us bottled up, but we got them in the same fix."

"What's going to happen, then?"

"Oh, they'll come up with some new way to try to get at us." A phrase he'd forgotten sprang into Longarm's mind. It was a term he'd heard his grandmother use, when he was a boy in West Virginia, and it hadn't meant anything to him until he'd grown up and was riding a Union Pacific diner from Omaha to Denver. He'd seen the chef preparing a seafood spread, and the words of his grandmother suddenly made sense. He said to Corinne, "Those fellows have found out that getting us out of here's about like opening a clamshell with a toothpick."

Corinne smiled. "I'd like to have a dozen cherrystone clams right now, Marshal. Or anything else that I could eat. I'm starving."

"I could stand to put away a good meal myself. I didn't figure on all this hullabaloo busting out. Too bad. If I had, I'd have put some jerky in my pocket before I left my horse."

"We could be a lot worse off, of course," she said. "If anybody had told me yesterday that I'd be holed up here with a U.S. marshal, fighting off the Kid's men, I'd have told them they were crazy."

"Sometimes the whole world gets crazy. But if we can hang on for another three or four hours, we ought to be all right."

Corinne's smile faded. "We'll hang on. There's not much left for them to try, is there?"

"Not unless they've got some dynamite."

"Don't worry. The Kid didn't plan to blow up anything. There's no blasting powder or dynamite or anything like that in the Roost."

"I didn't figure there was, or they'd have used it last night." Longarm started back along the passageway. Corinne followed him.

"What are we going to do now?" she asked.

"We better take a look at the other end of this thing, and see what we're up against there."

Around the spot where the body of the torch-bearing outlaw Longarm had dropped still lay, the odor of charred flesh was still strong. Corinne gagged as they stepped around the corpse, but said nothing. As the end of the passage came in sight, a brilliant slit against the dusky walls of the fissure, they flattened themselves against the rough sandstone and sidled along to where they could look out. Far enough away from the opening, and close to the vertical wall of the butte, two of the gang stood watch. There was no way to get a shot at them except by going outside the passage.

Longarm shook his head. "It's a Mexican standoff. We can't get to them, but they can't get to us, either, as long as we stay in here. So we'll just let them play their cards, and see if we can't pull out a few trumps when they throw down."

"There's not much more they can try, is there?" She frowned. "We've stopped them when they tried to shoot us out and burn us out. What's left?"

"I don't rightly know. But they're scheming something, I'd bet on that."

"I guess we'll wait, then."

"Yep. Wait and rest. It's about all we can do. And I'd say the best place to do our waiting is back at the other end. Those two outside of this end don't seem about to start anything."

Back at the opening that led to the canyon, they found that little had changed around the outlaws' fire. The gang was eating, sitting on the ground around the blaze in a loose circle, with plates on their knees. Both Corinne and Longarm felt their mouths begin to water at the sight of food, but neither complained of the hunger they felt. Settling down at the mouth of the passage where they could watch without being seen from outside, they prepared to wait.

Leaning back against the wall, Corinne closed her strange, topaz-colored eyes. Longarm hadn't had an opportunity to look at her closely since the day they'd met in the courthouse at Hanksville. Even then, he'd seen her for only a few minutes, while his mind was occupied with other matters.

She was wearing the corduroy riding-skirt that she'd had on when he first saw her, or its twin, and luckily hadn't taken off her boots the night before, when they'd had to run from the cabin. Above the skirt, her once-white shift was streaked and stained with dirt. The shift Corinne wore was sleeveless, gathered at its top with a drawstring and held up by thin shoulder straps. One of the straps had broken during the night's frantic activity, leaving her shoulder bare. The light suntan that gave a golden hue to the skin of her face stopped below her chin. Her shoulders were a translucent white, marred now by black specks of powder-smoke and the dirt they'd picked up when she'd dropped to the ground to avoid gunfire.

With her head leaning back against the wall, her slightly-too-long jawline was foreshortened, and the dimple in her square chin thrust into prominence. At the angle from which Longarm viewed her, Corinne's full lower lip hid her short, thin upper lip, and made her nose look shorter, her entire face less aquiline. Her hair disarranged from much running and dodging during the night, wisped around her head in stray locks that had escaped from the barette that held it in a straight, gathered fall down her back.

Longarm felt his own eyes growing heavy. The short nap he'd had in the morning was no substitute for a night's sleep, and last night had been his second sleepless one in a row. He stood up, moving quietly, and walked a few steps into the passage, to the place where they'd cached the canteen. A scanty swallow of water refreshed him, and he wasted a few drops by moistening his palm and passing it over his dustgrimed face. Wide awake now, he went back and resumed his vigil.

Midmorning came before the outlaws made a move. Two of them, one carrying a scrap of white cloth, left the fire and started a slow walk toward the passage. Both men wore gunbelts, but neither carried a rifle. They walked with their hands well away from their holsters, palms down.

Longarm called, "Corinne!" She stirred and opened her eyes. "Best you wake up. There's a couple of the gang coming. I got a hunch they want to parley."

Corinne stood up and moved to Longarm's side. She nodded when she saw the men. "That one on the right is Red Garrity. The other one is Lopez. I don't know too much about either one of them, though. The Kid didn't like for me to be too friendly with the men. He was always a little bit jealous."

"I can see why. You're a good-looking woman, Corinne."

Unexpectedly, Corinne blushed. The flush of pink spread from her face down her neck, and suffused her bare, dirt-streaked shoulders. Almost bashfully, she said, "Well! That's the last thing I ever expected to hear you say to me, Marshal Long."

"Look here, we been through enough now so we can be sort of like friends. My friends mostly call me Longarm."

"All right, Longarm. My friends call me Reen. But I guess you noticed that while you were watching and listening. You must've seen—"

Longarm interrupted her. "I can forget as easy as I can remember, when I want to. Now we better stop those fellows before they get too close." He raised his voice. "That's far enough, you two! If you've come to give up, we'll see what we can work out."

"Give up, shit!" Red Garrity replied. "There's no call for us to do that. We got you outgunned about five or six to one, and we got plenty of grub and water. How about you throwing in your cards?"

"We're not hurting for anything," Longarm replied confidently.

"*Por Dios*, why do you tell us the lie?" Lopez asked. "We all know you do not have water and food. Is it that you are so tired of living, you and the *señorita*, so you wait for us to kill you?"

"We been doing more killing than you have, Lopez," Longarm said flatly. "All you got to do is turn around and start counting. And if you ain't got something more interesting to say, you can start walking back to where you come from."

"Now hold on—" Red began.

"You ain't said a thing we're interested in hearing," Longarm broke in. "So there's no need to keep on chattering. Go on, now! Git!"

For a moment, the two outlaws stared unbelievingly at Longarm and Corinne. Then, with a liquid shrug, Lopez turned away and started back to the fire. After a moment's hesitation, Garrity followed him.

Corinne waited until the two were out of earshot before she said, "You didn't give them much room, did you?"

"There wasn't much need to," Longarm replied. "They had their best chance last night, and they knew it. Oh, I guess they'll make another stab at getting us, but all we've got to do is be careful."

"Careful!" Corinne exclaimed.

"Sure. There ain't a thing changed, except that it was dark last night, and now it's daylight. They can see to shoot better, but so can we. And inside here, good shooting ain't all that important. Give us another few hours, and it's all going to be settled our way."

"I hope you're right," Corinne said, but her voice reflected her doubts.

Garrity and Lopez had reached the other outlaws by now. The shrunken gang gathered into a compact huddle, and although what they were saying was in-audible, there were many angry gestures and an oc-casional shove exchanged, telling Longarm and Corinne that the discussion was heated. The group broke up at last, and the rustlers strung themselves out in a higgledy-pigglegy line as they moved to the far side of the canyon. One man with a rifle stayed to guard the passage.

"What's back there that'd pull all of them in the same direction?" Longarm asked.

"Nothing. Nothing except the corral. And I don't see what good horses would do them," she frowned.

"They got something in mind, that's for sure. Might be they're going to try to ride over us." Longarm shook his head. "Couldn't be that. They know damn well that a horse is easier to hit than a man."

"We'll know soon enough, I suppose." Corinne rubbed her hands over her face and grimaced. "Longarm, have we got enough water so that I can sponge off my face? I don't think so well when I'm grimy and dirty."

"Sure. Just take it easy."

"I will." She walked back to the niche in which the canteen had been cached.

Longarm turned his full attention to the canyon floor. The angle at which the corral lay in relation to the passage's opening made it impossible for him to see what was going on. He could only get a glimpse of a corner of the pole enclosure, and an occasional flicker of movement. To have seen the corral clearly would have required Longarm to leave the passage, and he had no intention of being a sitting duck for the watching rifleman between the passage and the fire that still burned in the canyon's center.

Corinne returned. "What are they doing?" she asked.

"I can't tell yet. They've got some scheme worked up with the horses, though. All of 'em are up by the corral except that one out there they left to keep an eye on us."

"I'm ready for it, whatever it is, now that I'm clean."

Longarm looked at her. The grimy streaks were gone from her face and arms and shoulders, and her hair was arranged neatly. Except for the thin shift, which made only a pretense of hiding her jutting breasts and dark aureoles, Corinne could have been any young-old miss, ready to attend an afternoon tea party.

"You look real nice," he told her.

Before she could thank him, hooves drummed across the floor of the box canyon. Sweeping around the inner edge, skirting the mouths of the caves, four mounted outlaws were driving a half-dozen horses. The driven horses were not saddled. At the same time, three more of the gang came running up, carrying rifles, to join the lone sentry.

"They're going to drive those horses in here!" Longarm exclaimed.

"But why?"

"You ever been kicked by a spooked horse? Or had one come down on you with his front hooves after he'd reared up?"

"Good God! No!"

"I've seen men killed that way," he told the girl soberly. "Now you hyper back in the passage a ways. I need elbowroom."

"Isn't there something I can do to help?"

"Not up here, there's not. You go back a ways, and see that nobody comes at us from that direction."

Corinne nodded and started away, down the floor of the fissure. After six or eight steps, the first bend in the passageway hid her from sight. Longarm took a final glance at the galloping horses, to judge their speed, and stepped back to the bend. He saw the tactics the gang had chosen. If they could drive even two of the half-dozen unsaddled mustangs into the passage, with its narrow sections and many curves, there was a better than even chance that Longarm and Corinne would be unable to escape getting knocked down and trampled by the shod hooves of the panicked animals.

Those bastards know damn well a wounded horse is a hell of a lot wilder and harder to kill than a calm one, he thought.

To the accompaniment of wild yells from the riders driving them, and the cracking of pistols as the mounted men laid down a barrage of shots to drive Longarm back from the opening, the horses swept by.

215

Longarm hadn't been expecting that; he'd been poised to fire. He'd looked for the gang to drive the animals in on their first sweep. Now he saw the plan better. The outlaws would drive the mustangs around the interior wall twice, perhaps even three or four times, to get up speed and to instill into the driven beasts the excitement that a gallop creates in all horses. Then, when Longarm didn't expect it, the riders would head the beasts into the fissure.

Although he was confident that he could drop one or more of the unsaddled horses as they swept by, Longarm held his position at the beginning of the fissure's curve. The rifle-carrying outlaws on foot were standing ready, in line with the entry. They could see into the passageway in daylight; all they needed to make their shots count was for Longarm to show himself.

Outside, the thudding of hooves announced the second approach of the horses. Again, Longarm held his rifle at the ready. He knew he had only three or four seconds to make his shot, and knew, too, that an excited horse will plunge ahead a dozen yards under its momentum, even as it is dying. His first shot must kill, and kill cleanly.

Louder and louder, the hoofbeats echoed on the resounding walls of the narrow passage. Rifle shots cracked from the outlaw snipers. In a moment, the pistols of the riders added to the din. Only a few of the slugs entered the passageway. The snipers with rifles were forced to shoot blind. In a position where they could look in and see Longarm, they'd have been exposing themselves to his return fire.

This time, the riders turned the unsaddled mustangs. Longarm got a bare glimpse of wild eyes showing white below pulled-back ears and a flowing mane, then he fired. The heavy slug from the Winchester went through the four-inch area in the animal's chest that led to its pounding heart. The mustang's momentum carried it forward into the mouth of the passage. Longarm saw the animal rear high, its ironshod hooves flailing in the air above him. He stepped back just in time. The horse came down on its forelegs just as it died. The forelegs crumpled. The animal's head hit the floor and there was the sharp crack of its neck vertebrae snapping. Then blood gushed from the animal's mouth and it lay still.

Behind it, a second horse was following too close to stop. It saw the body of the dead animal in time to rear up, and Longarm put a slug through its raised chest, into its heart. The second horse almost lunged over the first in its dying throes, but ended on top of the first one that fell. The carcasses of the two animals effectively blocked the entrance of the passageway. Longarm heard the meaty thump of pistol slugs in the bodies of the fallen animals.

He felt like shouting, but contented himself with thinking, *You sons of bitches sure outsmarted yourselves that time! You gave us a stopper we can't get over easy, but neither can you. All that fancy trick did was to make it easier to stand you off the next time you try to rush us!*

Chapter 19

Although the shooting had ended outside, and the hoofbeats had died away, Longarm held his position. For all he knew, the outlaws might have planned another assault on foot in the moments immediately following the horse-drive. The longer he waited, the more certain he became that, after a look at the plugged entrance, the rustlers had called off any plans they might have had to attack, and were palavering again, trying to think up a new scheme. He decided it would be safe to go to the outside entrance and see what Corinne had discovered.

"Nothing," she said, when he asked her, after making his way through the fissure. "The same two are still keeping watch out there, but all they seem to be doing is sitting."

"If that's the case, we might as well sit too." Longarm let himself down, with the wall at his back.

"How about the other opening? Isn't it dangerous to leave it unguarded?"

"Not for a little while." Briefly, he told her about plugging the opening to the canyon. "So I don't look for them to try climbing up over those two horses," he concluded. "They fit tighter than a cork in a fresh bottle of whiskey."

Corinne sat down across from him. "How about the posse? It should be getting here soon, shouldn't it?"

"Depends on how long it took them to get organized and set out." He looked at the fissure's opening above their heads. "The sun's just about at noon. Give 'em another two hours, maybe three."

"What if no posse comes?"

"Then we'll just have to find a way to sneak out of here tonight. I got a horse around on the side of the butte. We can ride double into Hanksville. Of course, the gang would all be gone by the time I could get a few men to come back with me. I'd hate to see that, when we got them penned up in the box canyon, just waiting for me to take all of them in one scoop-up."

"What happens after you arrest them?"

"Unless there's a federal charge against them, they'll go to Salt Lake City for trial."

"Where will you go, after that?"

"To headquarters. Denver."

"Longarm? Could you take me to Denver with you? You said you weren't holding me under arrest."

"You'd have to come back here to give evidence."

"No. I want to go on East."

"To where?"

"Illinois, I suppose."

"That's home?"

"It was. I came West to teach school up in Wyoming Territory; that's where I ran into the Kid. That was over a year ago. I thought I was being really brave, going off with an outlaw. But now the Kid's dead, and all I want is to get out of this kind of life."

"You're ready to go home, then?"

"I think I was ready quite a while ago. But I wasn't going to walk out on the Kid; he was depending on me."

"Tell you what, Reen. I don't say no, and I don't say yes. We'll see what happens when all this is wound up, and talk about it then."

"As long as you don't forget."

"I won't." Longarm stood up. "I guess you might as well stay here for now. I'll go see what's happening in the canyon."

At the plugged exit, Longarm climbed up the slick, soft bodies of the dead horses and looked out into the canyon. At first, he thought it was deserted except for the four unsaddled mustangs. They were wandering aimlessly around, looking for graze and finding none. Longarm picked his way down the slippery rump of the topmost horse and stepped out of the passageway. A bullet plowed into the earth at his feet, as a rifle cracked from the cabin. He ducked back into the fissure and surveyed the floor of the box canyon. Unless the outlaws had all taken to the caves, which he didn't consider likely, there was no one in the canyon but himself and the rifleman.

Taking off his hat, Longarm went as close to the edge of the passage as he dared, and risked peering around it for a second look. He still saw no one on the canyon floor, and was pulling his head back, when a blur of motion caught his eye against the canyon's rim. He looked again, and saw the silhouettes of three men standing at the top of the crevice through which ran the path to the top. Knowing that the rifleman in the cabin was waiting for him to show himself again, Longarm drew back his head and sat down on the rump of the dead mustang.

They've cooked up some new scheme, old son, he mused. *And it sure looks like they aim to come at us from the outside opening.*

There would be enough lariats among the outlaw gang to string together into a rope that would reach from the top of the butte to the ground. Going down the wall would be easy, with a rope to hold onto.

When he explained his reasoning to Corinne, she agreed with him. "I've never had to climb over a dead horse, to say nothing of two. But I can see how it'd be a slow job."

"Slow ain't the word. My bootsoles were skittering off every whichaway when I tried it. Took me a good five minutes."

"So we know they'll be coming from the outside. I suppose we'll just handle it the same way we did before?"

"Looks like. We'll walk back a ways before they get here, and pick out the best bend to stand 'em off at."

Both Longarm and Corinne had walked the length of the passage so often that they remembered each curve it made, what lay ahead of them, and what was

220

behind. They were approaching a wide spot in the fissure when Longarm began, "Now, right up ahead—"

At the same time, Corinne was saying, "Just a few feet further—"

They stopped, grinned at one another, and moved on to the curve each of them had started to suggest. Coming out of the wide portion—wide enough for three men to walk abreast with shoulders touching—the sandstone walls narrowed abruptly and jogged into a S-curve. In the daylight, the floor of the fissure was no darker than the shaded area under a wide-spreading tree. The S-bend gave a defender three stages of retreat, if retreat became necessary, and reduced the risk of being surprised from behind, or of being struck by ricocheting slugs.

After they'd walked through the S in each direction, Longarm said, "I guess it's about the best place. The best I remember, anyhow."

"Yes. We should be able to hold them off here until your posse gets here," Corinne agreed, then added, "if it's going to get here at all."

"It'll get here, I'm pretty sure. It's still early. Give them time."

"It's afternoon," Corinne pointed out.

"It's a long way to Hanksville, too," Longarm replied. He lifted the canteen strap over his head and put the almost-empty canteen against the wall in the center bend of the S-curve. "Now we better quit worrying about the posse and rest while we got the chance."

They sat down silently and waited. There was a patch of sunlight near the top of the passage wall. Longarm watched it as it crept slowly along the surface of the stratified sandstone. The snail-like progress of the bright patch had a hypnotic effect. He got so interested in observing the little splotch of light that Corinne had to call his name a second time.

He jerked his head down. "What is it, Reen?"

"I thought I heard something."

Longarm stood up and walked to the end of the S-curve nearest the outside opening of the passage.

In a moment, he heard a noise too, a muffled scraping or grating sound.

"Guess it's time we made ready," he told the girl.

Corinne came to join him. The scraping noise grew louder. A bend in the fissure, twenty yards from the tip of the S where they stood, kept them from seeing what was causing the noise. Over the occasional grating sounds, they could hear footsteps and low voices.

A strange object inched into sight around the bend they were watching, and it took them several moments to realize what it was.

"It's the table out of the cabin!" Corinne exclaimed.

"And that'd be the mattress off the bed that they got tied over the front of it," Longarm added.

As the lash-up improvised by the outlaws rounded the gentle bend, they could see it clearly for the first time. It moved slowly, the men behind it carrying the upended table by its legs. Small as the table was, it spanned most of the width of the passage. The mattress that covered the tabletop—which formed the front of the shield—was not very thick, but Longarm knew it would slow down a pistol slug enough to keep the bullet from penetrating the boards of the tabletop. All that could be seen of the advancing outlaws was an occasional glimpse of a moving foot in the few inches of space between the bottom edge of the mattress and the floor of the passage.

He told Corinne, "Don't waste your shells. Just keep behind the curve. I'll see what I can do with the rifle."

Longarm sent two fast shots from the Winchester into the shield. The mattress swallowed the slugs. All that he could hear was a small thudding sound as the lead hit the wood behind the mattress. A yell of triumph went up from the outlaws.

The shield inched along the passage. Its progress was slow, for the men carrying the table could not see where they were going without exposing themselves. They'd had enough experience with Longarm's deadly accuracy to take any risk of letting him see an arm or leg or shoulder. Scraping the sides of the wall as it

222

moved, the tabletop continued its advance. Longarm and Corinne watched it helplessly.

"Now what?" Corinne asked.

"Back up. We got no choice."

"We'll run out of backing-up room pretty quick."

"I know it. There ain't any other way to go, though."

They began backing slowly. The shield came on relentlessly. It got to the narrow S-bend and stuck; the men carrying it could not maneuver the table-legs through the sharp curve. Longarm watched closely. The outlaws began to tilt the table, seeking an angle that would let the legs clear the curve. One of them exposed a leg. Longarm sent a bullet plowing into it. A screech of pain cut the air as the wounded outlaw staggered back behind the table.

For a moment the attackers kept seesawing their shield, but it was jammed hopelessly. There was not room for them to work without exposing themselves—a risk they were obviously reluctant to take.

Longarm fired through the triangular gap between the bottom corner of the table and the passage wall. One of the outlaws raised his pistol above the top edge of the table and returned Longarm's fire. The man was shooting blind, his head still below the shield, the wrist of his gunhand twisted awkwardly. His slugs wasted themselves on the wall at the back of the S-curve.

Longarm stopped to reload his Colt. He told Corinne, "Keep on peppering them. Try for that gap, maybe you'll get lucky like I did."

She started shooting, spacing her rounds as she'd watched Longarm do. The tabletop was no longer moving. Another revolver appeared over the top of the shield, but the man firing it had no more success than had the one who'd tried the same thing earlier.

"We got 'em stalled," Longarm told Corinne. "We'll keep them here as long as we can. There's other narrow places further back; maybe we can—"

He broke off. Shots and shouts were coming from the outlaws' side of the shield. They waned, then increased.

"That'd be the posse," Longarm announced calmly. "All we've got to do is just hold on right where we are, Reen."

"I was just thinking I'd heard all the gunfire I wanted to," Corinne said. She was smiling. "But those are shots I'm really glad to hear!"

Longarm took his Winchester and went up to the shield. He pushed the muzzle into the gap between the wall and the edge of the table, then bent down to sight quickly and fire. There were no targets in his sights; the outlaws had all flocked to the outside exit.

Firing continued from the direction of the outside opening. Longarm braced his foot in the crack between the wall and the table, and lifted himself up. The top edge of the table came just above his waistline. He leveled the rifle and waited.

Almost as soon as he'd placed himself, the first outlaw came running along the passage toward him. It was Lopez. He saw Longarm's leveled Winchester, dropped his pistol, and raised his hands. The next man was right on Lopez's heels. He saw Lopez in the attitude of surrender, then saw Longarm. Without being told, he too let his revolver fall and hoisted his hands high.

Along the passageway, the gunfire died away. Three more of the gang came pelting into sight. One of them was Garrity. He skidded to a stop behind Lopez and the other man, and opened his hand to let his weapon fall. Slowly he held his arms up. The others lost no time in following Garrity's example.

Sheriff Franklin came puffing down the passageway. He stopped so suddenly that he almost fell, and stood there panting, looking at the tableau.

"Glad to see you, Sheriff," Longarm said casually. He might have been greeting Franklin across the breakfast table. Which, in a way, he was. "Figured it was about time for you to get here."

Waving his pistol at the outlaws, the sheriff said, "Verda told me there's fifteen or sixteen of these crooks here. Where are the rest of them?"

"There's one or two bottled up in the canyon. All the others are either dead or nursing gunshot wounds."

"You did that by yourself?" the sheriff asked incredulously.

"No. I had some help." He said to the outlaws, "You men make yourselves useful. Get this table out of the way."

Without the need to dodge bullets, the outlaws got the table free in short order. Longarm said, "Here's the young lady that helped me."

"Corinne?" Franklin stammered. "How the devil did you get into this with the marshal?"

"That's a story that'll have to wait," Longarm told him. "Now the canyon opening further on is blocked too, but your prisoners can get it open for you."

"What's blocking it?" the sheriff asked. "Another table?"

"No. Just some dead mustangs. They were all I had back there."

Shaking his head, Sheriff Franklin herded the desperadoes down the passage in front of him. "Maybe you better go along and back him up," Longarm told Corinne in a low voice. "He don't look to me like he's fit to herd sheep any more, let alone a bunch that's got Garrity and Lopez in it. You don't mind, do you?"

"Not if it'll help." Corinne turned and followed the sheriff.

Longarm went to the outside opening. Verda Blankenship was standing beside a wagon. Judge Walton's wheelchair was lashed to the wagonbed, and Mudo and Sody were untying the ropes. The judge held a shotgun in his lap. At one side of the cleft, two men, strangers to Longarm, held rifles on three of the outlaws. Two of them had been wounded during the fighting in the passageway. One had a bloodstained bandanna wrapped around his head, and the other had ripped the sleeve from his shirt to tie around his crippled leg. Beyond the wounded men, a body lay.

Verda saw Longarm come from the fissure. "Long!" she called. "If you're not a sight for sore eyes!"

"You look pretty good to me too, Verda."

"She looks better to me, Marshal," Judge Walton said. "But I'll talk to you about that, and some other

225

matters, later on." He gestured toward Mudo and Sody, who had freed the wheelchair of its lashings and were getting ready to lift it off the wagonbed. When the chair had been deposited safely on the ground, Walton went on, "After Verda told me how it was here, it took me a little while to get Jess Franklin moving, but once he started, he did the best he could, considering it was midnight and men were hard to find. Jess's deputy wasn't around to help him, either. Did we get here in time?"

"Plenty of time, Judge. And I'm sure glad you decided to come along too."

"Hell! I wouldn't have missed it for the world!" the judge replied. "This is the best medicine I've had since I was crippled!"

Longarm turned to Sody. "There's enough of us here to see that those prisoners get to where they ought to be. If you'd do me a favor . . ."

"Name it," the barkeep said promptly.

"My horse is tethered over by the northeast wall of the butte. I'd be right grateful if you'd ride over and lead him back."

"You won't need a horse tonight, Long," Verda said. "It's too late to go back. We've got grub in the wagon for supper and breakfast."

"It ain't the horse," Longarm told her, "It's my bedroll that's on it. I ain't had a comfortable sleep for quite a while, and I figure I got one due me tonight."

Judge Walton called to the Hanksville men, "Ed! Tom! You might as well start those prisoners to the canyon, they can all walk. Just follow that rockfault—" he indicated the passageway— "and we'll be right behind you."

Mudo pushed the judge, in his chair, through the passage. Longarm and Verda walked behind.

They reached the canyon opening, and the Hanksville possemen prodded their captives to the area beyond the firepit, where Sheriff Franklin and Corinne were guarding the rest of the outlaws. Judge Walton signaled to Mudo to stop. His sharp eyes had seen the tarpaulin-shrouded bodies of the dead members of Kid Manders's band.

"When you set out to clean something up, Marshal, you don't do it by halves," he told Longarm. "I can't approve officially, but you've saved the courts a lot of trouble."

"I didn't choose to get rid of 'em, Judge Walton. But when somebody starts shooting at me, I got a habit of shooting back."

Walton was looking around the canyon wall. "I'd forgotten about this place being here until Verda showed me your map. I camped here a few times, years back. But it seems to me like there were three caves over there instead of two."

"Things change, Uncle Frank," Verda said. "A slide might've covered up the third cave."

"Yes. I suppose so. I'll have a closer look, later."

When the Hanksville possemen joined Sheriff Franklin, he'd dismissed Corinne. Longarm had seen her start toward him, and now, as she came closer, he said, "I want to talk to you about that girl, Judge. She's helped me straighten out this mess a whole lot."

Corinne reached them and said, "Longarm, the sheriff's going to have the prisoners bury the bodies before supper. I'm going over to the cabin and get some clothes."

"Why don't you go with her, Verda?" Longarm suggested. "Maybe she'd like some help."

"I can manage by myself, thanks," Corinne said.

Verda broke in, "Maybe you'd prefer the marshal to help you."

"I told you, I can manage."

"Let's see," Verda said sweetly. "You'd be the Kid's woman, I guess. Reen, they call you."

"And you're Verda. I've heard a lot about you."

"It's mostly true, too, honey," Verda snapped. To the judge, she said, "I'll go get supper started, Uncle Frank. Sody'll be back soon, and I'll ask him to help me." She flounced off in the direction of the firepit.

Corinne looked after her a moment, then looked at

227

Longarm, her eyebrows raised, and headed for the cabin.

"There doesn't seem to be anything for us to do," the judge said to Longarm. "Let's go look at those caves; my curiosity's all stirred up. And you said you wanted to talk about that girl Corinne."

"She's going to need some help from the law," Longarm told Walton as they made their way to the caves. "With Kid Manders dead, she'll be about the only witness the prosecutor can count on. You think that's worth helping to get her off for?"

"I'd say it is." The judge nodded thoughtfully. "And I've kept this to myself so far, but since I understand that our prosecutor might have been mixed up with Manders, I'm asking the governor to appoint me as a special prosecutor. I'll do everything I can, Marshal."

"Thanks."

"I owe you that for sending Verda back to me. I've worried about her a lot."

"I don't earn any credit for doing that, Judge. Me sending her to you was a pure accident."

"Whatever it was, it was a good thing, and I won't forget it."

They were near the wall in which the black mouths of the caves yawned. The two openings were more than a hundred yards apart, and their shapes indicated that they must have been formed in the distant past by an underground stream or river.

Judge Walton signaled to Mudo to stop. He scanned the canyon wall between the caverns and frowned, pointing. "The third cave was right there, where that slab of rock is. It wasn't very deep, and the mouth was small. I recall having to crawl on all fours to go into it." He pointed to the rock slab. "Mudo. Go see what you can find there."

Mudo began prodding with his knife along the top of the stone that leaned against the canyon wall. He found a fingerhold and heaved. The slab toppled out, away from the wall, and revealed a low, narrow opening.

The judge nodded. "Damn it, I knew I was right! Somebody must have covered it up."

Longarm could see shapes in the cave. He went in to investigate. Kneeling, he struck a match and held it inside the opening. He didn't need the stenciled markings on the long, narrow wooden cases—U.S. ARMORY. SPRINGFIELD, MASS.—to tell him that he'd found the missing rifles he'd been sent to Utah Territory to track down.

"You just done me another favor, Judge," he called. He studied the stone slab that had hidden the cave mouth. "If it's all the same to you, I'd like for you to keep mum about this. Mudo, let's you and me put that rock back where it was."

They replaced the slab and trickled earth around its edges. Longarm explained to Judge Walton, "Somebody's going to come after those rifles one of these days. I got to find out who it is. I need to arrest the ones that stole those guns before I can close my case. And that's something I aim to do, if I have to stay here the rest of the year!"

Chapter 20

Supper, in the gathering dusk, was a quiet affair. The outlaws ate apart from the others. They were a subdued group. The freshly covered graves between the firepit and the corral had a very sobering effect on what remained of Kid Manders's gang.

Bobby Mason rode into the canyon when they were halfway through the meal. The beefy deputy reined in a short distance from the fire, and swaggered over to stand in front of Sheriff Franklin. He complained, "Damn it, Jess, you ought to've waited for me! It took me a while to find out what was happening after I got back to town from Torrey, and then I had to follow your tracks to find this place!"

"We managed without you pretty well, Bobby," the sheriff replied. "As it turned out, Marshal Long had things pretty much in hand by the time we got here. All we had to do was the cleaning up."

Bobby looked around, and saw Longarm sitting on the other side of the fire, between Verda and Corinne. He stared hard at Corinne, and Longarm saw her body tense. Bobby said nothing to Longarm, but his lips compressed and his jaw muscles bunched angrily. Then he looked over the prisoners and counted them, and turned back to the sheriff.

"Hell, Jess, from what I was told in town, there was a gang of fifteen or more out here. Looks to me like Long let half of 'em get away!"

"Look again, Bobby," Judge Walton said. He pointed at the graves—rectangular mounds of fresh earth, dark against the unbroken soil around them. "There's the rest of the gang."

Bobby stared and gulped. He opened his mouth, found nothing to say, and closed it again.

"We're glad to have your help, Bobby," the sheriff said. "It's a long ride back to town; you can help us a lot on the way in."

"I'll do better than that, Jess," Bobby said. "I'll stand guard tonight. You and Ed and Tom and Sody's had a hard day, I guess."

Franklin nodded. "That'll be fine with me. We'll have a good rest and start out fresh in the morning for Hanksville."

Judge Walton said, "And that means we'd better turn in pretty quick. I'm ready, I know, and I suppose the rest of us are, also. The ladies can sleep in the cabin, and—"

"No, Judge!" Corinne broke in. "I don't want to sleep in that place! I'd have a nightmare if I tried to!"

"One of the caves, then," the judge suggested. "We'll put the prisoners in the other, so it'll be easy for Bobby to watch them. The rest of us can make do right here by the fire."

"Suits me," Longarm said. He stood up, stretched, and yawned. "It'll take a harder bed than the ground to keep me awake tonight."

Everyone in the box canyon, prisoners and captors alike, was suffering the letdown that follows a long period of frenzied activity. No time was wasted in getting settled. The Hanksville possemen gave Bobby a hand in herding the outlaws to one of the caves, then they returned to bed down around the fire while the deputy sheriff sat where he could watch the cave-mouth. Verda and Corinne walked slowly and silently to the other cave, and disappeared inside. Mudo prepared Judge Walton's bed and helped him into it, then curled up at the judge's feet. Jess Franklin spread a blanket near the possemen, and Sody followed suit. Longarm fixed his own bedroll and lay down. The ground was hard, but he was used to hard beds by now.

A variety of snores soon rippled through the dark, still night. The moon had not yet risen. Longarm propped himself up on an elbow. The gloom was too thick for him to see the canyon wall. He rose noiselessly, and was strapping on his gunbelt, when he became aware of Mudo's obsidian eyes watching him. He laid a finger across his lips and shook his head. Mudo nodded, and stayed motionless.

There was no cover to hide his movement over the canyon floor, but once he'd gotten out of the fading glow of the dying fire, Longarm knew the darkness would hide his movements as he angled to the canyon wall and followed it around to the caves. He slid into the mouth of the one occupied by Verda and Corinne, and stopped just inside the opening. He could hear the rhythmic breathing of the two sleeping women, but his silent movements hadn't roused them. Crouched in the mouth of the cave, he could just make out Bobby's shadowy bulk in front of the other cave.

A faint glow, the promise of moonrise, was lighting the sky above the canyon rim before Longarm saw what he'd anticipated. His eyes caught movement. A shadow glided from the cave where the outlaws had been placed and stopped beside Bobby. In a moment, Longarm saw two shadows, those of Bobby and another man, walking silently toward the canyon wall.

A whisper reached Longarm's ears. It was Bobby's rough voice, caught in mid-sentence. ". . . and they damn well better still be there, or you won't get out of this place alive."

"I tell you, the guns are safe!" Longarm recognized the accent; it was Lopez speaking. The outlaw went on, "I have tell no one, as we agree. You and me, we are the only ones who know."

"We better keep it that way too," Bobby replied. "I want to get something out of all this to pay me for my trouble."

Now the sounds of hands scratching in earth came to Longarm's straining ears. He waited until he heard the muffled thump of the stone slab as it fell to the ground, then rose to his feet and came out of the cave.

Close at hand, he could see the two men who were kneeling in front of the third cave. He edged noise-

232

lessly along the canyon wall. He heard Bobby say, "I guess they're all right. I can tell by feeling of them cases that they ain't been opened."

"So I have try to tell you, *amigo*," Lopez said. "Now you must arrange for me to escape, no? Without me, you will never find the Apaches who will pay us *mucho dinero* for new rifles."

"I'll see that you get out of the Hanksville jail," Bobby replied. "The sheriff's a doddering old fool. I can get away with just about anything I want to."

Longarm judged that he was close enough to act. He stepped out of the darker shadows that clung to the canyon wall and said in a mild, conversational tone, "Don't count on getting away with anything anymore, Bobby. You're going to be in a cell yourself. I'm arresting you for theft of U.S. Government property."

"God damn you, Long!" Bobby grated. He jumped to his feet, his hand dropping to his gun butt.

Longarm had his Colt out first. Its report cracked through the night's silence before the deputy could draw. Bobby sat down heavily, his body slumping as it folded, his beefy hands clutching spasmodically at his gut. He fell slowly to one side, and lay still.

Lopez raised his hands high. "I have no gun, *Señor* Marshal! Do not kill me too!"

"I ain't about to, Lopez. I want to keep you alive. You got some talking and explaining to do."

Men were running toward the caves by now, and Verda and Corinne were coming from the one they occupied. Longarm waved away all questions until everyone had gathered around him. Then he addressed the sheriff and Judge Walton.

"There wasn't but one way those rifles could've been hid in that cave," Longarm told them. "It had to be one of the men with Kid Manders."

Corinne interrupted, "The Kid didn't know anything about the guns, Longarm. I'd have known too, if he'd had any idea they were hidden there. All of us thought there were only two caves here in the canyon."

"I sort of figured that's how it had to be," Longarm

233

said. "Of course, I didn't know who it was, and I wasn't sure Bobby had anything to do with them, but I saw how close he looked over who was left out of Manders's bunch, when he rode in tonight." He turned to Lopez. "The judge might go easier on you, if you tell us the whole thing now."

Lopez shrugged. "*Por seguro.* It is only a little you have not guess. It is with Strang I steal the rifles, when Bobby tell him where they will be. We hide them here to wait while the army give up looking for them, so it is safe to take them south to Arizona, to sell to the Apaches. But while we wait, Strang is meet with Lance. He is know Lance, from before. And Lance is bring the Kid, who has the plan to steal *los ganados*. So, we join with the Kid while we wait."

Sheriff Franklin asked incredulously, "You mean Bobby was in this thing all along?"

"It is like I tell you," Lopez replied. "I tell you true, Sheriff. Why now should I lie?"

"I think you can believe him, Jess," Judge Walton said. "You just gave Bobby too much rein, and didn't watch him close enough."

"Seems like what I need is somebody to watch *me*," the sheriff snorted. "I guess it's time I quit, Frank. When I get so old and forgetful—"

"We'll talk about that later," the judge told him. "Right now, we'd better get back to bed." He turned to the Hanksville possemen. "Ed, I guess you and Tom can lay Bobby away where the others are buried. This fellow—" the judge jerked his head at Lopez— "won't mind digging the grave." He gestured to Mudo, who took the handles at the back of the judge's wheelchair and turned it around.

Longarm felt a hand on his arm. It was Verda's. "I was hoping we'd—"

"So was I. Too many things happened. But I'll be staying in Hanksville a few days. There'll be time, don't fret about it."

"Just so I'm sure you won't be riding off tomorrow, I guess I can wait. But don't make me wait too long." Verda kissed him quickly and started back to the cave.

Longarm watched her go, and shook his head, smiling. He lighted a cheroot as he went back to his own bed. It was one of the few nights he remembered when he was ready to go to sleep before finishing his bedtime smoke.

"Hanksville's a slow town to wake up," Longarm remarked to Corinne as they came out of Mrs. Holcomb's boardinghouse. "Here it is, the morning half gone, and nobody seems to be stirring."

"I'm sorry, I'm to blame for getting us started so late," she said. "But you'll have to admit that we haven't had much of a chance to talk about our plans. Verda's managed to take up most of your time."

"Now that's neither here nor there," Longarm replied. He'd watched the barely concealed tug-of-war between the two women, but hadn't interfered. He'd be leaving Verda, while between Hanksville and Denver, he and Corinne would certainly have plenty of time to get to know one another better. She'd needed time too, for whatever regrets she had to evaporate.

"I can't travel all the way to Denver with just the clothes I have on," she continued. "But being in court testifying hasn't left me much time to shop. And you know I didn't want to carry anything from the cabin at Robber's Roost that'd remind me of the place."

"You take whatever time you need to shop," Longarm told her as they stopped in front of the general store. "An hour or so won't matter, and you might as well travel feeling comfortable."

"I won't be long," Corinne promised. "I just need a blouse or two, and some underthings. Then we'll go right on to the livery stable and get the horses and ride out."

"I guess I won't come in with you, then."

Corinne smiled. "You're no braver than any other man when it comes to being with a woman while she's buying underthings, I see. Go ahead, I'll meet you at the livery stable."

"I got a better idea. I'll stop and say goodbye to Sody. I'll keep my eye on the street, and when you pass by the saloon, I'll be ready to step out and join you."

Longarm walked down the street to the saloon. Sody took the almost-empty bottle of rye from the backbar and set it in front of him.

"You timed your drinks pretty well," the barkeep said with a smile. "I hope you packed the rest of your case so that none of the bottles will get broken on the trail."

"Don't worry, I took care of that." Longarm filled his glass. "You better join me and finish this bottle, Sody, seeing as it's sort of a special occasion."

"Thanks, I'll stick to my regular. But I'm tempted, this time. You did a fine job of cleaning out Robber's Roost for us folks here in Hanksville."

Longarm swallowed his first sip of whiskey before answering, "No credit due me, Sody. Just did what my job called for." He took another sip. "One thing bothers me, though. That big box canyon's a natural place for robbers and rustlers to use. After you pin on your sheriff's badge next month, you might keep an eye on it pretty careful."

"I will. And if I'm going to have a goodbye drink with you, I'd better get me a bottle." Sody was fishing in the barrel for the sarsaparilla, when the door was shadowed. He and Longarm turned to see who'd come in. The newcomer was a youth—a boy, really, peach-fuzz-faced and trail-dusty. Sody asked, "You looking for somebody, son?"

"Nope. I just stepped in for a shot of red-eye to start my day off right," the youth said. His voice wavered between the high pitch of boyhood and the deeper one of maturity. He leaned an elbow on the bar and eyed Sody. When the barkeep made no move to serve him, the boy asked, "Well?"

"I can't pour a drink of whiskey for a kid as young as you are," Sody said. "You're big and husky enough, but you and I both know damned well you're not old enough. Now why don't you just run along and come back in a couple of years."

"You listen to me, barkeep—" the youth began angrily.

Longarm cut him short. "Sody's right, young fellow. Don't start hard liquor till you're older. Now if you're real dry, I'll buy you a bottle of sarsaparilla—"

Eyes slitted, the boy looked Longarm over. "I don't take advice or favors from nobody, mister!"

"You'd better listen to him, son," Sody said. "This man's a U.S. marshal, and he's just put away a real bad outlaw gang."

"That so?" The boy stared at Longarm. "What's your name, Marshal?"

"Long," the tall federal man replied.

"His friends call him Longarm," Sody put in.

"Well." The boy's voice wavered. He extended his hand. "I guess I'm pleased to know you, Marshal Longarm. I'll drink a sarsaparilla with you."

While Sody fished out another bottle of pop and opened it, Longarm asked the youth, "You got a name too, I guess?"

"Sure," the boy replied. He took the bottle from Sody and drained it, then put the empty bottle down. "My name's Cassidy. But my friends call me Butch. I'll see you around, Marshal."

Touching the brim of his dusty hat with a forefinger, the youth swaggered out of the saloon.

SPECIAL PREVIEW

Here are the opening scenes
from

LONGARM AND THE SHEEPHERDERS

twenty-first in the bold
LONGARM series from Jove

Chapter 1

Marshal Billy Vail was leaning over his clerk's new-fangled writing machine, watching the pale young man go at it, when Longarm entered. Vail turned quickly at Longarm's entrance, his eyebrows lifting in surprise.

"On time for a change! I can't believe it," the chief marshal cried happily. He straightened up and almost rubbed his hands together in glee. It was obvious at once to Longarm that his boss had an assignment for him and was looking forward to sending him off. He never liked to see dust settling on Longarm's Stetson.

"What have you got for me?" Longarm inquired, stopping in front of the marshal. His chief wasn't all that much to look at, and that was the truth. The man was running to lard, trapped as he was behind a desk. In his own time, Marshal Billy Vail had shot it out with a passel of borderland desperadoes and a considerable number of Comanches, north *and* south of the border. But all that was in the past. Though Billy Vail wasn't more than fifteen years older than Longarm, it was a sobering experience for the tall lawman to see what could happen to a man in that short span. It was one very good reason why Longarm did not mind that Billy Vail kept him on the trail.

"Get in here, and I'll tell you," Vail answered, marching ahead of Longarm into his office and moving around behind his desk.

Longarm followed in after him and closed the door. Slumping into the red leather chair in front of Vail's desk, he glanced at the banjo clock on the oak-paneled wall. Longarm was startled. He was indeed early. Ten minutes early. He hadn't realized he was that anxious to get into action.

Longarm took out a cheroot and lit up as he watched Vail poke doggedly through the pile of paperwork that just kept settling on the poor man's desk—a blizzard from Washington, D.C., was what it was, and there was no end to it that Longarm or Billy Vail would ever get to see.

"Here it is," Vail said exultantly, pulling out a folder and opening it. He read a few paragraphs silently, then glanced up at Longarm. "Ever hear of Ruby Wells, Nevada?"

Longarm shook his head. "Can't say as I have. Should I have heard of it?"

"No reason in the world," Vail said. "It's in the middle of the Ruby Mountains. You know that territory. That's why I'm sending you back there."

Longarm nodded. He remembered, all right. He had passed the Rubies on his way to the headwaters of the Humboldt and into the Great Basin, where a ruthless logging combine had been bent on stripping the mountainsides of every tree and shrub.

"I remember the country, Billy, but not Ruby Wells. What's the trouble? More loggers?"

"Train robbers."

"I'm listening," Longarm said, leaning his head back and puffing contentedly on his cheroot. The skinny cigars were a weakness he occasionally chided himself for, usually when he wasn't on a case, and his confinement in the overly civilized—to his point of view—city of Denver began to get on his nerves.

"Outlaws boarded a train in California, waited until they were in the middle of nowhere, then forced their way into the mail car."

"By 'nowhere,' I take it you mean Nevada Territory."

"That's right. Once they were inside the mail car, they gunned down the postal clerk in cold blood. They had no provocation; the man wasn't even armed. Then they looted the safe of gold coins being shipped from the U.S. Mint in San Francisco. After that, they pulled the brake cord. There were riders waiting at trackside with spare mounts, and the outlaws disappeared into the Rubies."

"And you think they're holed up in Ruby Wells?"

"I've looked at the map," Vail said, leaning back in his chair and watching Longarm carefully. "The Rubies would make a fine place to hide out until the heat dies down some. But when it does, they'll have to board a train at Ruby Wells to get out of there. They sure as hell couldn't ride out. Water holes are miles apart, and they don't have mules, they have horses. You got any idea how heavy that gold is?"

"Okay. So you want me to go to Ruby Wells and nose around, see if I can get a line on where those jaspers might be hiding out."

"That's the ticket. Keep an eye on the occasional trains that pass through. We'll have other deputy marshals at other widely spaced stops. This is one case where almost every federal office west of the Mississippi is sending men. That murder of a federal employee has the Post Office and Washington screaming for action. Since you know the area, we're sending you to the town where they're likeliest to show up, so keep a lookout for any suspicious strangers you see riding into town."

Longarm took the cheroot out of his mouth. "Since when do you have to tell me my business, Billy?"

"Hell, I'm just repeating what I was told. The heat's on for this one, Longarm. Washington wants action."

Longarm stood up. "Just don't tell me my business, Chief. I don't care what those lard-assed bureaucrats write on those reports. I know what to look for, and I know how to stake out a town. I'll watch the trains and I'll keep my eyes peeled for strangers, and I'll keep my ass down and my mouth shut. If those buzzards are in the Rubies, I'll sniff them out."

As he stood there with his cheroot clamped in his mouth, Deputy U.S. Marshal Custis Long was an imposing sight. His lean frame stretched to well over six feet tall, and looked as tough as saddle leather. His John L. Sullivan mustache, his hair, and his Stetson were brown, along with his tweed vest and suit. His shirt was blue-gray, and he wore it with a black shoe-string tie knotted at the neck—the tie he wore only as a grudging concession to Justice Department regulations, which required such neckwear to be worn by all field personnel. He tended to discard it as soon as he was out of sight of Denver. His boots, of cordovan leather, were low-heeled army issue. His Stetson he wore with the crown telescoped flat on top, tilted slightly forward, cavalry-style, above his dark-browed, gunmetal blue eyes.

Vail sighed. "I know you'll do your job, Longarm. No need to get your bowels in an uproar. Take the train from Fort Douglas, Utah, and bring a horse with you. I figure that's the best and quickest way to get there. Now get your vouchers and rail pass from that clerk of mine, and get out of here. And I'll be remembering what you just said—if those buzzards are in the Rubies, you'll sniff them out."

Longarm snugged the snuff-brown Stetson down securely onto his head and left Vail's small office, wondering if just maybe he hadn't bitten off a little bit more than he could chew. But then again, he didn't chew tobacco, he smoked it. And all he had told the chief was that *if* those murdering sons of bitches were in the Rubies, he would flush them good and proper. And he would. *If* they were there.

Longarm arrived in Ruby Wells four days later, supervised the unloading of his horse, and then went to find a livery. His impressions of Ruby Wells were not at all encouraging. He had come to the place in search of unsavory characters—riders who looked and acted suspiciously. The difficulty was, that description fit nearly every citizen of Ruby Wells. It looked to Longarm as if the town of Ruby Wells was where old and unwashed gunslicks and desperadoes came to die—more than likely in a flash of gunfire and amid the tinkle of exploding glass.

As soon as Longarm had found a hotel and a barber shop with a bathtub, in that order, he searched out the town marshal and found him on the porch in front of his small frame jailhouse, sitting on a wooden chair with his legs crossed in front of him on a hitch rail. A toothpick was sticking out of one corner of his mouth. Like Longarm, the marshal sported a John L. Sullivan mustache, but there the resemblance ended. The marshal looked like bread dough on the rise, with his clothing exerting a frantic but futile effort to keep him in some rough semblance of human shape.

As Longarm paused beside him, the fellow made a truly herculean effort, managing to uncross his legs and get to his feet. By the time he was standing in front of Longarm, he was perspiring freely and his grimy face was beet-red.

"Name's Custis Long," Longarm introduced himself. "You should have had a wire that I was coming."

"Sure, I got the wire," the fellow replied, almost as if Longarm had just suggested he couldn't read. "You're here about that train robbery."

"That's right, Marshal. What can you tell me?"

"You want to go inside my office? Cooler in there, and I got a bottle."

Longarm shrugged and followed the man into the small office-jail. The place stank of slop jars that were not kept clean, and stale vomit. The marshal, of course, noticed nothing. He reached into a drawer as soon as he was sitting behind his desk, and brought out a somewhat depleted bottle of rye whiskey. The two glasses he brought out after it were full-sized.

"Say when," the marshal said as he poured Longarm's drink.

"When."

The marshal pushed Longarm's drink across the desk to him, and Longarm sat down on a wooden chair beside the desk. As Longarm took the drink, the town marshal said, "My name's Wills Toady, but I s'pect you knew that." Wills had poured himself half a tumblerful of the whiskey. He threw it down as if it were fresh spring water, made a quick face, and then looked cheerfully at Longarm.

"And all I can tell you about that train robbery is that I don't know a damn thing. I been sittin' out there keepin' my eye peeled for any mean-lookin' strangers. Trouble is, they're all mean-lookin', what with this damn range war heatin' up."

"Range war?"

"Sheepmen comin' in—or trying to." Wills wrinkled his fleshy nose in distaste. "This here's cattle country. Ain't no room in it for them grass-killin' sheep."

"How many were in that train robbery for sure? I'd like to know that, Wills."

"Six. Four on the train, two more with the horses along the right-of-way. They're up there in the Rubies, I'm thinkin', just bidin' their time, waitin' for all this federal heat to let up some. With all that gold, they got good reason to hole up and wait a bit."

"Unless they get anxious to spend a little of the loot," Longarm reminded the man.

Wills Toady looked at Longarm carefully, through watery eyes. "I suppose they might get a trifle anxious, at that. But, like I said, this town's fillin' up with undesirables, so it's harder'n hell to figure out who's a train robber and who's in here to cut up them sheepherders."

Longarm thought he ought to try to get the range war straight in his head—find out who was who and what was up—but he didn't like talking to this fat lawman any longer than he had to, and he was in this country to find those train robbers. Killing an unarmed postal clerk was not only a federal offense, it was an outrage that Longarm was anxious to avenge. Longarm finished his drink and stood up.

"You figure those robbers are still up in the Rubies, eh?" he asked.

Wills Toady tilted his head so he could peer up at the tall lawman. "Maybe they is, and maybe they ain't. I figure the best way to find out would be to go up there and take a look-see." The man's broad face broke into a yellow grin. Then he reached for the bottle to pour himself a second libation.

Longarm thanked the man and left the little office. *Trouble is, what that tub of lard suggested is right on the money,* he thought. *The only way to find out where those varmints are holing up is to hightail up there to those Rubies and start sniffing around.*

Longarm was already more than anxious to get the smell of this mean-looking town behind him. On the single main street, running at right angles from the train station, he counted eleven saloons. His hotel was at the end of that street, with a sheer bluff scrubbing its back. If the saloons stayed open through the early hours of the morning, Longarm was going to have some difficulty in getting to sleep. For a moment he considered the possibility of riding out that evening, then thought better of it. He would get what sleep he could. That train ride had been no pleasure.

Longarm sat bolt upright, his double-action Colt .44 swinging out from under his pillow, the muzzle searching the darkness of his room. And then the woman screamed again. It came from the next room and had that shrill, cutting quality to it that always made the hair on the back of his neck rise straight up. Swiftly, Longarm swung back his covers and padded on bare feet across the floor, kicking aside the pieces of crumpled paper he had scattered there earlier as a safeguard. Pulling open the door, he stepped out into the dim hallway. A single wall lamp cast a yellow glow over the dank passageway; there was enough light to show Longarm the open door next to his room.

Even as he started down the hallway to the door, a third scream issued from the open doorway and Longarm heard a low, guttural laugh, punctuated by a sharp, stinging slap. He heard the woman's gasp of pain.

"Go ahead," the man's voice said to the woman. "Let out another scream if you've a mind to. They ain't no one goin' to hear you in this town!"

"That so?" Longarm asked, stepping into the room. He had not bothered to climb into his britches, and now stood in the doorway in his longjohns, his sixgun gleaming blue in the light from the single kerosene lamp on the dresser.

The man and woman were on the bed, neither of them wearing very much. The girl had a profusion of long dark hair, setting off a pale, almost alabaster complexion. Both of her full breasts were exposed, the nipples erect from the excitement of her battle with the lean, blade-faced individual who was atop her.

"What the hell do you want, mister?" the fellow snarled.

"Sleep," Longarm replied. "I want to get some sleep. Get off that lady and out of this room."

The man was furious. His long blade of a nose seemed to get even sharper as he pushed himself back off the woman to stare fully at the tall intruder. His lidded eyes were cruel, and the line of his lean mouth contemptuous. He fairly bristled with an unashamed, perverse energy. Had Longarm found him in the act of murdering a neighbor with a dripping ax, the fellow would have been no more outraged at Longarm's interruption. He was a man who did what he wanted, *when* he wanted, and brooked no interference from anyone.

"Well, damn your eyes!" the fellow snarled. "If you want sleep, get back into your room and get to sleep, then. And leave us be! Now git!"

Longarm was almost amused at the man's truculence. He seemed to pay no heed at all to the pistol in Longarm's right fist. Longarm looked at the girl. "You want this jasper out of here?"

She seemed confused. The man had already slapped her around, and there was no way she could tell how effective Longarm was going to be in dealing with her assailant. She did not know on which side to place her chips. Longarm realized her dilemma instantly, and made her choice for her.

He strode into the room, grabbed the back of the fellow's nightshirt, and flung him off the bed. The man landed on his back, the rear of his skull banging harshly against the wall. For a moment the man lay stunned. Longarm heard the girl's gasp of dismay.

When the fellow's confusion cleared up and he was able to gaze up at Longarm, the lawman said quietly, menacingly, "I'll tell you this once more. Get your things and get out of this room. Leave this girl be. I suggest next time you pick a girl who's partial to a man of your talents."

For just a moment, the fellow regarded Longarm with his cold, lidded eyes; then he struck. Like an uncoiling rattler, he flung himself from the floor and, fastening both arms around Longarm's waist, he burrowed his head into the lawman's midsection and bore him relentlessly back. Longarm felt the breath explode from his lungs as the wall slammed him with stunning force, cracking his head smartly. The Colt dropped from his fingers as he sagged, his senses on the brink of unconsciousness.

His opponent stepped back swiftly and brought his right fist around with sledging force, catching the meaty part of Longarm's jaw. Lights exploded deep within Longarm's skull, and he glimpsed the face of the girl, her dark eyes wide in her pale face, as he slipped sideways to the floor. The man proceeded to kick at Longarm's body then, with vicious, meticulous care. Longarm covered up his head while the blows rained on him, his head clearing slowly, his rage at this treatment building to an exultant fury as he contemplated what he would do to this vicious bastard. Abruptly, his hand snaked out and caught the man's foot, almost upending him.

The fellow pulled free of Longarm's grip, snatched up the lawman's dropped Colt, and regarded the still-prone Longarm with his lidded eyes. "You gettin' much sleep now, mister?" he inquired. His narrow face creased into a humorless grin. He raised the revolver and leveled it at Longarm. "Think maybe you'll be takin' that sleep right now!"

It was then that the girl decided on which side to pitch her penny. She flung herself off the bed and onto her attacker's back, one pale arm circling his neck and pulling him abruptly back. The fellow's gunhand went up as he fired. The bullet smashed a hole in the wall just over Longarm's head. Longarm hurled himself up off the floor and caught the man with a murderous, chopping blow to his midsection, just below the breastbone. He reeled backward, the girl still clinging to him

248

frantically, his knees buckling under their combined weight. The girl flung herself away, and before the fellow sagged to the floor, Longarm brought up a stiff left to the man's face, swinging his head around sharply, then finished him off with a roundhouse right to the point of his chin. When Longarm completed his follow-through, his back was to the man.

The fellow went back with such force that his head slammed through the room's thin wall, and when he came to rest finally, his scraggly hair was gray with plaster. Longarm looked down at the slim, unconscious man with something bordering on admiration. His figure was slight, there was little heft to him. Yet he had proved to be a fierce opponent, whose malice gave him a kind of supercharged energy.

In his arrogance, however, he had tried to shoot Longarm down in cold blood. He had the heart and the soul of a killer, and no matter how admirable his fury might seem, it was a force that Longarm realized he could not allow to range freely—for his own and for other's safety. He reached down, grabbed the man's nightshirt, and hauled him upright, grunting only slightly with the exertion; then he turned, faced the window, and hurled the man out through it. The explosion of shattering glass was followed by the sound of cries from the street below.

Longarm went to the window and looked down. The girl's assailant had landed on the porch roof just under the window, then rolled off. The still-unconscious man appeared to have landed on two men passing by. Longarm could not be certain of this. All he could see in the dimly lit street were three sprawled bodies, two of whom were shouting angrily and twisting about on the ground. A crowd quickly gathered about them. The two men were hauled to their feet, then all eyes were directed upward at Longarm, standing with his upper torso leaning out through the broken window.

Longarm paid no attention to their shouts, and when he saw the man he had just hurled from a second-story window stir and get groggily to his feet, then slink off through the gathering crowd, he ducked back inside the room and turned to the girl.

"Who was that?"

"That bad man, oh yes!" the girl cried.

"I know that, ma'am. But I would like to know his name."

"Cal Wyatt," she told him.

Heavy footsteps sounded in the hallway outside the door, followed by an impatient pounding. "Open up in there!" demanded the town marshal.

Longarm pulled open the door as the girl hastily covered her nakedness with a blanket. "What kept you, Toady?" the weary lawman demanded.

Startled to see Longarm facing him, the red-faced marshal pulled up abruptly. There was a sixgun in his right hand. He hastily dropped it back into his holster. "Marshal Long!" he cried. "What are you doing in here?" And then his eyes caught the figure of the girl, reclining now on the bed, the bedsheets held up about her neck. He looked with alarm at Longarm, then. "That's Carmen! Carmen Montalban!"

"Is that who she is? Thank you, Wills. A little while ago, she was rassling with that piece of human garbage I tossed out the window. Her screams were not being noticed worth mention by you or anyone else in this town. And I was trying to sleep next door. Now why don't you just go back to your office and let me get back to sleep?"

The man swallowed, then nodded quickly. He backed up a step, turned, and hastened down the corridor. Longarm closed the door and turned to the girl.

"Why was the marshal so upset to see you, Carmen?"

"My father is Pablo Montalban, and it is known what he would do to any man who molested me."

"I see. And what would he do?"

"He would kill him."

"Do you think he will kill Cal Wyatt?"

"He will try, if he learns what that man tried to do tonight."

"Pardon this question, ma'am—but what were you

250

doing in here with Wyatt? Did you come up here to discuss the weather?"

The girl's face darkened. "You are right," she admitted. "I was a fool. I should never have trusted Cal Wyatt. But he promised to tell me what had happened to Manuel."

"And who is he?"

"He is my intended. But for too long now, he has been missing in the mountains. I am certain that Cal's boss, Slade Barnstable, is responsible. I just know he is. He will do anything to stop those of us who herd sheep. Cal said he knew what had happened to Manuel. He said he would tell me." She looked up at Longarm then, and he saw the tears streaming down her cheeks. "I had to know. We were soon to be married, at the next shearing." She looked away from Longarm then, her thick, luxuriant hair cascading down over her face as she lowered her head. Longarm thought he heard a sob.

"What did he tell you, Carmen?" Longarm asked softly.

Her voice was muffled as she thrust the knuckles of her right hand up to her mouth. "He said Manuel is dead. He said all the sheep are gone too. The entire flock, all of it, was rimrocked!" She looked up at Longarm then, and flung her hair back, her eyes wide. "And then, the pig, he laughed at me and tried to take me!"

"That's when you started screaming?"

"Yes."

Longarm went to the window and looked down at the street. A small crowd was still milling about in front of the hotel, and every once in a while, one of the crowd would turn and look up at the shattered window. Cal Wyatt's recent exit from the hotel was still the hottest topic in town. Longarm turned from the window and looked at Carmen.

"Is this your room?"

She nodded.

"You came into town alone and checked into this room?"

Again she nodded.

"You must love Manuel very much."

She bowed her head. "But Carmen is such a fool!" she said heatedly. "My father . . . he will say I am spoiled now. Even if Manuel is alive, I will not be allowed to marry him!" This last came out as a despairing wail.

Longarm went over to her and placed his hand gently on her shoulder. "I'll go with you to your father's camp tomorrow, and try to explain. Maybe I'll be able to lie some, as well."

Carmen looked up at him. *"Señor!"* she cried. "How can I thank you?"

"By going into my room and sleeping there. I'll sleep here, just in case Mr. Wyatt returns. Tomorrow you'll ride with me into the Rubies. Maybe we'll find that Manuel is alive and well—and I'll get a line on six men I'm looking for."

"Six men?"

"I'll explain that to you later, ma'am. Now why don't you go on into my room? I think we can both use the sleep. It's going to be a long day tomorrow."

She nodded and got up from the bed, her ripped dress held in place by one hand. Before she darted past him and out the door, she reached up quickly and kissed him on the side of his face.

Longarm saw her safely into his room, took his own clothing and gear into her room, and then closed the door. He was still thinking of the warmth of that peck on his cheek when he fell asleep for the second time, the sound of the crowd in the street below his window reminding him of the roar of a distant beast.

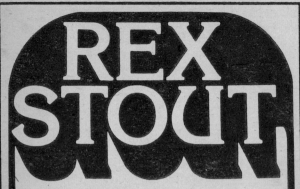